PLYAN

KRUNG THEP BOOK 1

MARIA KUHN

ISBN: 978-1-8384303-1-3

To the Land of Smiles

PLYAN (เปลี่ยนแปลง)
SWITCH/CHANGE

verb:

1. make (someone or something) different;
alter or modify.
2. replace (something) with something else, especially something of the same kind that is newer or better; substitute one thing for (another).

noun:

an act or process through which something becomes different.

"One moment can change a day, one day can change a life and one life can change the world."

Buddha

CHARACTERS

Taylor Family
Luna – 16 year old American expat
Luke – Luna's 12 year old brother
Mark – Luna's dad/Khun Mark
Susan – Luna's mom/Khun Susan

Khun Pak – driver
Khun Bo – helper/cook
Mom Luang Teerawat – Khun Mark's boss
Thanpuying Wassana – his wife
Channon – Veterinary Assistant
Khun Kannika – Channon's mom

Apichart Family
Nui (Benjawan) – 16 year old Thai
Duen/Duenswang – Nui's sister 13 years old
Krit – Nui's older brother
Tum – Nui's younger brother
Khun Yaa – Nui's grandmother
Khun Bpoo –Nui's grandfather

Khun Varaporn – Nui's aunt
Khun Karl – Varaporn's husband
Eve and Jenny – their daughters, Nui's cousins (six and four
years old)

Pi'Ohm – street food stall owner
Toey, Dearn and Apple – Nui's friends

LUNA

BANGKOK, SEPTEMBER

"THAT'S IT! I'M NOT GOING. YOU CAN'T MAKE ME."

I plopped down at the breakfast table with a determined huff, daring Mom to contradict me. Unfortunately, my scowl turned into a squint as the sun beamed directly into my eyes. Irritated, I dragged myself up again to lower the blinds.

Mom called my bluff easily. "Oh, really?" Her lips twitched slightly, as she struggled to remain stern. "You know you are going. It's non-negotiable."

I hate it when she gets like that. Deflated, I took a sip of coffee and tried another track. "But it's not fair. Why do I have to waste my Sunday on this stupid buddy programme?"

Mom sighed into her cup. "Seriously? Not again. How many times do we have to have this discussion?"

"As often as it takes. Until you listen to me."

"Luna, that's enough! You've been complaining about this for two months now. I'm tired of your whining. What else were you planning to do? Just go and have fun with Nui. It's the perfect day to be out."

I hated to admit it, but it did look nice outside. After days of torrential rain, the sun had finally come out and the sky was crystal clear, but I wasn't ready to concede defeat yet.

"Well, why don't you go then? I don't want to hang out with Nui just because she's my official tour guide." I insisted.

"Why are you so stubborn?" Mom threw up her hands, clearly annoyed now. I was getting to her. "Every time we move, you make this big fuss about not wanting to do this or that. Can't you, for once, give it a try? This is a great chance for you to see Bangkok like a local."

"For you, everything is great, beautiful and exciting!" I countered. "You say the same thing every time, but you never ask what I want."

"And you are very ungrateful. Do you know how many kids would love to have the opportunities we have given you? Not everyone gets to live around the world like you do. What is your problem?" I could tell, she was close to losing it, but I didn't feel like giving in.

"Oh yeah? Well, feel free to take all those kids! Or even better, take Nui, she's dead set on traveling anyway. I never asked for this, and just because you and Dad like being expats, doesn't mean I want to be a chameleon and change every two years. How many more moves do we have to make before you finally decide it's enough?" I knew I was being obnoxious, but I couldn't help myself.

Mom turned away and swallowed hard. Or maybe she was counting to ten. But then she wiped her eyes and smoothed back her hair, a sure sign that she was really upset. Shit. Guilt trip.

"Oh, come on, Mom! I know you and Dad mean well, but why can't you understand how difficult this is for me. You had your friends growing up, but I've never had a best friend or—God forbid—a boyfriend, and I'm sixteen! I'm just tired of this. We never stay anywhere long enough to make real friends. Nui is only around because the school threw us together but I want to pick my own friends."

Mom blew her nose and regrouped. "Nui will be here soon. You better get ready. We can discuss this later. Do you have enough money? You are paying for her lunch, taxis and any fees I hope?"

"Yeah, but Nui always haggles anyway. She's so cheap."

"Luna! Be nice. She's really making an effort for you." Mom admonished me. "And don't forget to put on some sunscreen. Dad's home for dinner tonight. Make sure you're back by six, ok?"

"Whatever! I better get ready for my 'baddy'!" I mocked Nui's accent without much enthusiasm. Great. First a fight with Mom, and now I had to face The Pest. There goes the weekend.

NUI

"I'M OFF, KHUN YAA," I CALLED OUT TO GRANDMA, AND bent down to scratch Joey's head. He wagged his short, stubby tail running towards the front door, clearly hoping to go for a walk. "Sorry, Joey. Not now. I'll see you later."

"Where are you going, Nui?" Grandma walked out of the kitchen wiping her hands on a towel. "Aren't you supposed to be helping your parents at the shop?"

"I can't, Grandma, I promised to take Luna to Koh Kret this morning."

"Did you check with your mom that it was ok? You've been spending a lot of time with your new friend lately, Nui. Don't forget that you have family obligations too. And why haven't we met her yet? You've been to her house a few times." Grandma normally had the sweetest smile, but now she was frowning at me. "Who's paying for all those trips?

And when was the last time you were at the temple? You should come with Grandpa and me today."

"But, Grandma, you know that the school asked us to show the newcomers the city. I'm only doing my job. And Luna is paying for everything, anyway. I really have to go now. I'll see you later."

"Not so fast, Nui! We don't accept charity from anyone; you know better than that. If you need money, you ask your parents."

"It's not charity, Grandma, I'm doing her a favour. She would never get to see anything in Bangkok if she was on her own. I think she's kind of scared and lonely."

"In that case, bring her here for lunch today so we can all meet her. Don't be late." Her tone was final. No point in arguing when she was in this mood.

"Ok, fine. I'll see you later." I put my palms together in front of my chest to wai to Grandma one last time in deference but rolled my eyes as I turned to leave. The last thing I wanted to do was introduce Luna to my family. With her attitude she'd consider it slumming. I wasn't sure why I'd told Grandma that Luna was lonely; with me she was just plain arrogant. *Serves you right Nui. Now deal with it.*

GETTING ON THE SKYTRAIN, I WAS STILL ANNOYED WITH myself. Arguing with Grandma was a big no-no. As the matriarch of the family, her word was law, but equally she was the most caring woman in the world and deserved my respect. But bringing Luna home was bound to be a disaster. She basically lived on another planet. With her attitude, I was convinced that I had the worst buddy in the whole school. She was totally passive with zero interest in anything. Despite that, I had my own reasons for sticking close to Luna, even if that meant I had to swallow my pride occasionally. Today, she would just have to step outside her cushy world long enough to get a glimpse of how the other half lives. This could be either very interesting or very painful. *Ok, deep breath and smile! Let's see what mood she is in today.*

I pressed the doorbell.

LUNA

I FELT LIKE SLAMMING THE BEDROOM DOOR BEHIND ME, BUT knew from experience it wouldn't make a difference. I sat down on my bed feeling sorry for myself. Was it too much to ask, to be able to make my own decisions just once? Why did adults always think they know best? I sighed in frustration.

The doorbell rang and I could hear Khun Bo, our helper, walk to the front door. Shit! Nui's here already. I decided to make her wait. I slipped out of my bathrobe and nightshirt, and jumped into the shower. For a second I even thought about washing my hair, which would have added more time, but I figured I shouldn't push it too far.

Irritated, I put on shorts, a tee-shirt and sandals, and dumped my backpack on the bed, while I tried to decide what to take.

Sunscreen—check.
Money—check.
BTS pass—check.
Sunglasses—check.
Baseball hat—check.

PULLING MY HAIR BACK, I THREADED THE PONYTAIL THROUGH the cap. All the while, I was muttering to myself, "Why do I have to do this stupid programme? She always makes me do things I don't want to do. I'm so sick of this. I bet if Dad was here I wouldn't have to go. Why is she being so mean?" The more I grumbled, the more annoyed I became.

And Nui was such a pain. Always so cheerful. I decided to just ignore her. Maybe she'd finally figure out that I didn't want to become her friend, that she should just leave me alone. Why did she have to take the stupid buddy programme so seriously?

I had talked myself into a really crappy mood and I was determined to not enjoy a single minute of the day. I slipped on my sunglasses, swung my backpack over my shoulder and turned off the lights. On my way to the living room, I banged on my brother's door, to share some of my irritation.

NUI

KHUN BO SENT ME TO THE LIVING ROOM TO WAIT. I LOOKED around. Gosh, what would I give for all this space? Our own house would have fit twice into this apartment.

"Oh, hello Nui! Nice to see you. I hear you have something special planned for today." Mrs Taylor looked so chic in her floaty blue summer dress, with her Jackie O' sunglasses perched on shiny blond hair. "I'm just on my way out. I can't wait for Luna to take us to all the secret spots you've shown her." She smiled and even returned my wai elegantly.

As if! Luna probably doesn't remember a single place.

"Oh, I'm sure she'd love to." I lied. "If not, I can take you kha." It would probably be more fun anyway to take Mr and Mrs Taylor, than to have to put up with Luna.

"Have fun. Just be back by six, ok?" Mrs Taylor waved as she walked out.

. . .

HER HIGHNESS FINALLY DEIGNED TO SHOW UP. SUNGLASSES
and a baseball cap hid her eyes and she barely acknowledged
me. *What is it with her? Would it kill her to at least pretend
and smile?* I deliberately exhaled loudly before I accidentally
made some harsh comment. *Let her be, Nui. If she wants to
be miserable, so be it.* I wasn't going to let her ruin my day.

"Hi Luna, ready?" I faked a smile. "I thought we should
go to Koh Kret this morning while it's not so hot, and then
my family wants to meet you for lunch. You ok with that?"

"Whatever! I just have to be home by four."

Seriously? What a stupid lie! You're pathetic Luna!
Again, I decided to let it go. *Maybe it's best anyway that we
don't spend more time together.*

Taking the skytrain to the end of the Sukhumvit line, then
a three-wheeled tuk-tuk and finally a longtail boat to the
island, didn't take too long by Bangkok standards. We rented
bicycles and pedalled leisurely along the small pathways,
winding through tropical forests and gardens. Luna bought
coconut ice cream and we sat down in the shade of a large
lime tree. Eternally optimistic, I thought I'd make another
effort.

"So, how do you like Koh Kret?"

"Hmm, it's nice! I had no idea there's an island in the
middle of Bangkok. So peaceful." Luna admitted.

OMG, what just happened? She actually likes something?
I couldn't help feeling smug. *Gotcha!*

"Chai laew kha. Only locals come here so it never gets
too crowded. I like to pretend that I've left Bangkok for a
while." I chuckled at my own foolishness. "I'm sure you had
secret spots like this in your other cities too, chai mai kha?"

"Hmm, not really. But I hardly looked, anyway." Luna
sounded wistful while licking her ice-cream.

"How come? You didn't explore the places where you

lived?" I couldn't keep a touch of criticism out. "I would have!"

She stared across the river and replied dismissively. "When you have moved as much as I have, it all becomes same-same after a while."

"Really? How many places have you lived? America? Bangkok? And..."

"Ha! See? That's what I mean. I have an American pass-port but I've never even lived there. We've moved eight times already! It's crazy." Luna threw her arms up in irritation to make her point. She sounded more frustrated than angry, but I was stunned. This was the first time I'd actually seen her agitated about anything. It must be a sore subject.

"Oh, lucky you! It sounds so much more interesting than being stuck in one place where nothing ever changes, don't you think?" I wasn't sure if I wanted to rile her up even more or make her see how fortunate she was compared to my boring life.

Luna wasn't having any of it. "You think? Do you have any idea how difficult it is to start all over again and leave your friends behind? And even worse, you're forgetting that I'm always the outsider, no matter where I go. You at least know where you come from and where you belong. And you can still travel later if you want to. Sometimes, I feel like a boat without oars, just floating around without an anchor or steering."

Wow, what's gotten into her?

"Well, I'd switch with you in a heartbeat. You at least have the chance to experience different places and then make a decision later where you want to live. And besides, if you're a boat without anchor then I'm like a plane that's hooked to the ground and can't take off. Not sure what's worse?!"

Luna stared at me as if she'd seen me for the first time,

and her lips started twitching. We burst into giggles at the same time.

"Oh my God, this is so pathetic. We're a bunch of losers." Luna wiped tears from her eyes.

"Yeah, but hey, we do have something in common after all." I winked at her, then glanced at my watch and jumped up. "Oops, it's time for lunch at the Apichart mansion! Ready to meet my family?"

5

LUNA

We were both quiet on the skytrain back to Nui's house, lost in our own thoughts. In hindsight, I was surprised that Nui hadn't given up on me earlier, considering my crappy attitude. I cringed at the thought of how standoffish I had behaved. Perhaps it was the fight with Mom, or maybe I was just tired of pointlessly pushing against things and not getting what I wanted, but I'd finally had enough and admitted defeat. Strangely, I felt relieved.

The past three months had been frantic, as I'd tried to settle into a new routine. Technically, by now I should have been used to adjusting to unfamiliar people, places and norms, but it never became easier. As a family, we had done a few exploratory trips to Thailand before the move, but with Nui as a guide, Bangkok came alive in ways that a normal tourist would rarely get to experience. Surprising myself, I was keen to explore further.

Bangkok was by far the craziest and most confusing place I've ever been to, and that was saying something after Shanghai, Hong Kong and Delhi. We had arrived during the rainy season. The hot, sticky and humid weather was on par with other tropical cities, but the lightning storms were on a different level altogether. The thunder practically vibrated in your bones, and the rain was like an ocean wave trying to drown you. Streets flooded frequently because the drains couldn't cope. It was disgusting to have to wade through the filthy mess. Sidewalks were double height to offer some buffer, but even when it wasn't raining, they were so undermined by standing water that you got splashed anyway just by stepping on a paving stone. My bare legs always looked like I had run through a mud field. Nui suggested I simply wear flip-flops and carry a pair of shoes or sandals if needed.

To compensate for the heat outside, the Thais must have decided it should be freezing indoors. Imagine taking a sauna followed by an ice bath and you get the idea. Instead of turning up the air conditioning to make it more comfortable, they offered blankets in the movie theatres! Totally absurd. Same as with the flip-flops, I learned to always carry a shawl in my backpack.

Everything in Bangkok was yin and yang; super high-end condo buildings right next to shanty towns. Ultra-luxurious hotels like my dad's next to backpacker places without aircon or other amenities. Ferraris and Lamborghinis next to scooters that carried a family of five plus a basket, or three, of necessities. Open-sided tuk-tuks next to a fleet of neon pink, yellow and green taxis that might, or might not, take you where you want to go, depending on the driver's mood. And in between, an army of motorbikes and moto-taxis angling for pole position at the stoplights. Trying to cross a street turned into a game of chicken most of the time.

Temples and shrines were everywhere and not just for show. All Thais wai'ed in passing towards the bigger ones, and at six o'clock in the evening, everyone, including us foreigners—farangs—stopped to listen to the King's anthem blasted over loudspeakers in public spaces.

Perhaps it was my imagination, but I always thought Bangkok had a distinct smell like no other city. Most likely it was the combo of street food stalls next to heavy traffic, and the incense from the shrines.

Cruising above it all was the skytrain, possibly the best invention ever for Bangkok, which gave a birds-eye view of the whole mishmash while whisking you across town in—naturally—freezing conditions.

The strangest thing about Bangkok was that somehow it all worked. People generally were relaxed and polite. Welcome to the Land of Smiles!

NUI

I was amazed at what a difference our little trip to the island had made. I sort of understood Luna's point about feeling unsettled, and her frustration about the frequent moves, even if my life was the complete opposite and I hated being stuck.

"Take your shoes off and don't forget to wai to my grandparents and parents, ok?" I instructed Luna. We were late walking into the kitchen. Grandma was by the stove and whatever was cooking smelled delicious, as always. She had been a cook at a local restaurant when she moved to Bangkok from Chiang Rai, and food is still king in our home.

My grandfather, parents and younger sister and brother were already eating and chatting at volume. Only my older brother, Krit, was missing. He was finishing up his military training. Just a normal lunch. Joey rushed over to greet us. I didn't know if Luna was afraid of dogs, or simply overwhelmed by the noise level, but she hung back shyly. I quickly introduced her and she dutifully but rather clumsily wai'ed to everyone, even Duen and Tum who grinned at the obvious mistake. As younger kids, they were expected to greet her first.

Grandma motioned for us to sit down and started piling rice and green curry on Luna's plate. Wide-eyed Luna gave me a pleading look and I had to explain that she was mostly vegetarian but occasionally ate fish. The conversation went back and forth as Grandma pretended to be deeply insulted by someone refusing *her* chicken curry. But, in her typically accommodating way, she quickly whipped up some extra stir-fried vegetables. I think Luna instantly became Grandma's new groupie, even if she didn't know what she was missing by not eating the curry

I was waiting for some show of attitude from Luna but was surprised by how easily she relaxed into the meal given that she didn't understand a thing. It must have been Grandma's magic touch! Not at all what I had expected. I had to wonder whether I might have a chip on my shoulder, myself.

After that first visit, Luna's attitude changed so dramatically, I was tempted to mark the day in the calendar.

LUNA

I LOVED GOING TO NUI'S HOME. HER GRANDMA WAS SO sweet and she treated me like one of her own grandchildren. It was all so unpretentious, and while I felt self-conscious at the beginning, that quickly changed. Everyone talked over each other, teased each other and they all laughed a lot. I only understood half of what was going on, even with Nui's translation, but everyone seemed so relaxed and happy. *So, this is what a normal family looks like. I want that.* In the following weeks I more or less invited myself over, even though Nui would have rather been at our house, which was usually as quiet as a tomb. I invited her to Dad's hotel a few times to make up for the luncheons since I knew she couldn't normally afford the meals there. Our friendship took off, mostly because I gave up pretending I didn't care.

I was fascinated by Nui's traditional customs. We released fish into the river, supposedly for good luck. It seemed pretty illogical since they had to have been caught first, but who was I to argue, and who doesn't want some good luck? My banana leaf raft for Loy Krathong, November's water festival, looked more like a shipwreck, but as it floated down the Chao Praya with thousands and thousands of other rafts lit with candles it was a magical moment, and I became teary-eyed. And again, it was all for 'good luck'.

She also explained this 'Khun' title to me. When we had first moved, dad's hotel had organized a 'cultural immersion lesson' for the family to learn the do's and don't's of Thai customs. Basically, it's the equivalent of Mr or Mrs, but here everyone is addressed with 'Khun' and their first name. So, Mom is Khun Susan, Dad is Khun Mark and so on. There are a few other titles, especially for kids (nong) and elders (Pi'), but Khun normally works for everyone except royalty.

"But why do you address your own grandma as Khun Yaa? I thought you don't use Khun with family members." I asked Nui.

"You do if you are polite and Khun Yaa is pretty old-fashioned that way." Nui explained.

"Is Yaa her first name then?"

Nui laughed, "No it means Grandma. Don't worry, you get used to it. My parents don't insist on formalities so I can call my mom Khun Mae or sometimes just Mae or even Mom."

"You guys are so complicated." I shrugged.

"I know it's weird but the good thing is that you can address them the same way I do."

"What? You mean I can call your grandma Khun Yaa too? Really?" I liked the idea of that.

Nui nodded. "Yes, it's totally acceptable here. Makes things easier for sure."

The one thing I never got the hang of was bargaining.

Longtail boats were the worst. Nui made me try it a few times. I kept glancing at her to see if the price was alright but she shook her head before finally taking over; other people were waiting in the boat and getting impatient.

"Ok, so how do I know how far to go?" I was curious, despite myself.

"Easy." Nui looked around the boat and counted the people. "The more people already on board, the lower you can go, because he will make enough money anyway."

"Oh, bloody hell! How was I supposed to know that?" I threw up my arms in frustration.

Nui laughed out loud. "See, that's why you need your *baddy*, chai mai kha?" She purposely exaggerated the mispronunciation. Oops! Nui's English was generally very good, even if she sounded like a movie actor sometimes. She had learned most of it watching American films and TV shows, as Thai schools did not practice much conversational English.

Bangkok International School was pretty much the same as all the others—mostly expat kids and a cast of international teachers and Thai support staff. Thankfully, it wasn't too far from our apartment on Sukhumvit, Soi twenty-one. 'Suk' was the main artery running through Bangkok, with stop-and-go traffic, day and night.

All major streets had minor numbered 'Sois' or streets on either side—even on one side and odd on the other. Corresponding numbers were never directly opposite though, so people really have to know where they are going. A warren of sub-Sois turned the whole layout into an anthill rather than a grid system. Our apartment was on the seventh floor of a newly built condo complex with a good-sized swimming pool and terrace on the second floor, a gym, and a twenty-four-hour doorman. My brother Luke and I had our own en-suite bedrooms, and my parents' bedroom was big enough to tango in. The last bedroom was supposed to be for a maid, but Mom didn't want any live-in help, so it had become a small office instead. Mom hired a driver, Khun Pak, but Luke and I used the school van most of the time.

My favourite thing in Thailand was the food. Our helper, Khun Bo, came from Mae Sot, a tiny village on the border to Myanmar, and she often cooked for us. She had worked for another expat family before us and spoke a bit of English. Though If I had to compare her food to Khun Yaa's I'd have to say: plain vanilla vs double chocolate fudge? No contest!

NUI

VISUALLY, LUNA AND I ARE POLAR OPPOSITES. LUNA LOOKS like her mom and the Hollywood version of 'American girl next door', wavy, blond shoulder-length hair, big blue eyes and curvy. In the US, she probably is a perfectly normal size 'M' but in Bangkok lazy shop assistants often just waved her off. 'You too big!' She joked about it, but I could tell it was grating on her. In all fairness, compared to me she IS big. Sometimes I had to laugh when I saw our reflection in shop windows or mirrors – day/night, tall/short, blonde/black, white/brown skin - reversed blueprints.

The three month buddy programme was coming to an end but I'd become used to hanging out with Luna. I even enjoyed the bitching sessions our conversations usually became.

Luna was frustrated with her parents' attitude that their lifestyle choice was the ultimate way of living, forgetting that they themselves had had a 'normal' childhood. According to Luna, being a 'global citizen' was just a marketing gimmick if you had no other choice.

"You know they give us this fancy label, 'Third Culture Kids', and claim it's a huge advantage, but I'm always the outsider, no matter where I am. Just once, I'd like to fit in as a local. You know, actually belong."

My own gripe was about my limited options and the expectation I should do my family's bidding while putting my own preferences on hold.

"Everyone makes such a big deal about how we should respect our elders, and that they know best. I think they just want to control us and not let us have our own ideas. I feel like such a fraud sometimes. At school we're supposed to question everything, but at home I'm just supposed to say yes."

Our lives were miles apart. I had to get up earlier to help around the house or in the shop, go to the temple, participate in all family and religious events, and look after my young cousins. Luna had zero responsibilities. In her house, no one bothered her. Khun Susan was often out with her women's groups and Luna's dad was working all the time. Not sure what Luke was doing besides his football training and matches.

My younger sister Duen and I shared a bedroom and bath-room with the boys too. Luna always had money to spend, and she often paid for movies or drinks, as I had usually run out of my weekly allowance. It made me feel uncomfortable, but Luna always downplayed it. It was easy to be generous when you had money. Hers was the latest iPhone while mine was a hand-me-down from Krit, my older brother. But what I most envied was that she had seen so much of the world already, while I was stuck in a sub-Soi.

LUNA

DECEMBER 5TH WAS THE LATE KING'S BIRTHDAY AND officially Father's Day, a public holiday in Thailand. Nui came over after lunch. Normally, she would have had to go to the temple with her family, but she used some upcoming tests as an excuse to get out of it. Luke was at a friend's house and Mom was meeting with one of her expat groups. We were taking a short break from studying. Nui seemed subdued somehow.

"What's wrong Nui? You're so quiet today." I asked her.

"You know I was thinking, wouldn't it be great if we could just swap our lives sometimes to see what it's really like?" Nui asked.

"What do you mean? What what is like?" I was distracted by Khun Bo dropping off some lychees and water.

"Well, you know. If you could be me and I could be you and we could both see what it's really like to live each other's lives. You keep saying you want to have a home base, and I want more freedom."

"Yeah, that would be fun, but it's just wishful thinking."

I sighed.

"Hmmm, maybe not," Her eyes were unfocused, as if she was mulling over one of her political issues. "Have you ever heard of people having 'out-of-body experiences'?" She asked.

"Sounds a bit woo-woo," I laughed. "Anyway, what has that got to do with experiencing each other's lives?"

"Ok, this may sound crazy, but did I tell you how my friend Apple is really into meditation and spirituality?"

"Yeah, so what? Is she a shapeshifter?" I rolled my eyes.

"Hear me out before making fun of it, ok mai?!" Nui replied. "She was telling me about this monk who teaches some kind of transcendental meditation, and apparently he and some of his students are so advanced that they have had out-of-body experiences. I'm not saying they switch bodies, but they get into a trance through some kind of… oh, I don't know, maybe self-hypnosis, and I'm wondering that if you can leave your own body, could you then also get into someone else's body or mind? I would be able to pick you and you could pick me. Wouldn't that be cool?"

"You're kidding me, right? There is no way you can morph into another person just by sitting and ohm'ing for a while."

"Ja bah ror! Now you're just being stupid! I'm not saying you physically switch bodies, but perhaps it means you could feel like you're walking in someone else's shoes but still know who you are. You would get a completely different perspective. And what if you could request or direct your mind to connect to a particular person? Do you think that's possible?"

"How would *I* know? Have *you* ever meditated?" I asked.

"I tried it once. Grandma does, but that's just to unwind, I think. But what if it's possible to take it further?"

I stared at her. "Are you serious? You've watched too many movies, Nui! This is real life and things like that don't happen in real life!"

"Well, it could be worth a try, no? At the very least we'd have a good time and relax," Nui said.

"And where is this monk and why would he teach us? And how would we explain to him what we want to do? I'm pretty sure meditation is not supposed to be used like that."

"But why shouldn't we try?" Nui insisted. "There's no harm in it, and I am curious to see your life from your perspective. Aren't you keen to see mine?"

"Yeah, but you already know how we live, and I know how you live, so what's the difference?"

"Don't be so ngo! Oh what's the English word?" Nui was waving her hands in frustration. "Dense! Right now we're just visitors, not members of the family. I thought you wanted to know how it feels to live like me. So you can compare it to your own life and decide what you like better."

"You know, this is not a competition, and it doesn't make sense anyway," I said. "I can't be you and you can't be me. End of story."

"Fine! So, you were all just talk, and you're actually ok where you are. Guess you already have it made. I better leave." Nui shuffled her papers together and stood up.

"Stop being so annoying!" Now, I was irritated too. "You know perfectly well we can't switch, so what's the point?"

"The point is to try something different, and if it doesn't work, it doesn't work. We've got nothing to lose but we won't know unless we try. Why are you always so negative? Now you don't even want to give it a go, so stop bitching about your life already." Nui was red in the face with anger. I had never seen her that way. *What's gotten into her?* Normally, she was persistent but always easy-going with a ready smile.

"Ok, ok, chill! Sit down and let's think this through. How would you even convince this monk to teach us?" I asked. "And how would I explain to my parents this newfound interest in meditation?"

"Don't worry, we can work all that out." Nui replied, practical as ever. Perhaps she sensed I was ready to compromise after all. "We could tell our parents and the monk that we are doing a social study project for school . Maybe to see if meditation affects us differently because of our backgrounds and cultures or something like that."

"That's pretty far-fetched and silly, but it might be just enough BS to actually work," I grinned, warming to the idea.

"Ok, why don't we see if we can convince our families and the temple, and we'll just see where it leads. Deal?" Nui asked.

"Ok, deal!" I laughed. "In that case, we should probably start right away so we can use the holidays for this."

"Oh, you're not going away for Christmas?" Nui asked, surprised.

"Nah, Dad has to work, and since we've only been here for a few months, Mom wanted to stay here. Maybe we'll just go to Vietnam or Bali or somewhere for a few days after New Year's. I suppose Christmas is not much of a holiday here, anyway."

"Ha! Just wait and see," Nui grinned. "We take decorating to a whole new level."

. . .

WE MAPPED OUT A GAME PLAN. FIRST, WE DID SOME research to pick up a few arguments for our proposal. Strangely enough, our social studies teacher, Mr Campbell, jumped at the idea, and with his approval it was easy to convince our parents as well.

Mom was a bit sceptical at first, as I had never before shown interest in anything spiritual, but she was happy that Nui and I had bonded over a mutual interest.

Nui's parents apparently were pleased that I (*seriously?!*) had convinced Nui to get into meditation and distracted her from political crusades. I wondered why none of them thought it odd for two sixteen-year olds to want to visit the temple instead of going shopping or to the movies during their holidays. We must have been pretty convincing, and despite myself I was becoming excited and a bit nervous. I honestly can't remember what we'd been thinking, but once we got started it snowballed very quickly. I don't believe Nui nor I were taking it very seriously; we were only eager for something different and venturing 'out of body' sounded just crazy enough for us.

Nui talked to her friend Apple to get us enrolled at Wat Pathum. Class size was limited, but with her endorsement we were allowed to join. The temple was sandwiched between two mega shopping malls in the centre of Bangkok. By now, I had given up finding anything odd about this side-by-side arrangement.

Apple was really only her nickname. Everyone in Thailand has one, as most Thai names were super long and impossible to pronounce, at least for us foreigners. Nui's name was really Benjawan. I was glad her nickname wasn't a fruit. I wouldn't have been able to keep a straight face calling her Plum or Grape.

"I'll meet you outside Paragon tomorrow morning at

eight," Nui reminded me the night before we were due to start. "Apple will be at the temple at eight thirty. And remember, wear comfortable clothes; we're going to be sitting for a while. Shoulders and knees need to be covered."

"Yeah, yeah, I've got it! You've only told me about a thousand times."

"Sorry, but I want to make sure we get this right." Nui was starting to make me nervous.

It was the first day of our winter break and I wasn't really crazy about the early morning start but figured one day at least wouldn't hurt.

NUI

I was waiting in front of Paragon, the mega shopping mall next to the temple. It was pleasantly cool. Winter had arrived.

"Morning Nui. Ready?" Luna tapped me on the shoulder.

"Morning Luna. Are you nervous?"

"Yeah, a bit," she admitted.

"Me too. Let's just see how it goes and if we don't like it, we'll just leave, ok?"

Entering Wat Pathum was like stepping into a parallel universe. The street noise was magically absorbed by the tropical gardens inside. I even turned around once to confirm that morning rush hour was still in full swing outside. The temple itself was set back from the street in what had once been royal gardens.

"Wow, this is so pretty." Luna was impressed.

"Isn't it? This used to be much bigger, but they sold parts of it to build the malls. I wish they had kept it like it was."

I had seen the Wat many times from the skytrain but had never been inside. Different-sized buildings were clustered around a white stupa in the centre of the square. Except for the golden dome of the chedi, all had multi-tiered red-orange roofs that were only allowed for temples, palaces or other important buildings.

"What are those figures on the roofs?" Luna asked.

"Garudas. They represent birth and Heaven."

Apple was waiting for us near the main structure, a big open sala with bamboo shades that could be lowered during the rains. Just off to the left was a small gated area with a beautiful spirit house where a handful of people were praying and offering incense. Temples were generally open to the public for prayers, but early in the morning it was almost empty.

"It's so quiet. Where is everyone?" Luna asked, turning in circles.

"The monks must be still on their alms rounds."

"What do you mean?" Luna looked puzzled.

Apple explained in halting English. "Monks cannot earn money; they rely on us to cover whatever they need for food and clothing and the temple. We have to donate a bit of money for our class too, you know?"

"Yes, Nui told me. I brought some." Luna confirmed.

"See, you're already gaining merit for yourself." Apple nodded approvingly.

We were early enough to offer our own prayers and Apple had brought incense sticks and loops of yellow marigold flowers as gifts. I showed Luna how to hold the lit incense between her palms, bow her head and offer a prayer. She was pretty clumsy and dropped a few sticks before she could place them in the sand filled urns. *Was she nervous*? Maybe she was self-conscious as the only farang there, but no-one really cared.

Fifteen minutes later we heard the slaps of bare feet on stone. A long line of orange-robed monks and lay helpers walked back into the grounds with their alms bowls full of food. Lunch had to be eaten before noon, followed by fasting until the next day.

"Come on, we go to class." Apple hurried us along.

She led us towards a small sala to the left of the main temple. Slipping out of our flip flops we entered, looking up towards a beautiful golden seated Buddha statue smiling down on us from the other end of the hall. His palms faced upwards from his lap, but I had forgotten the special meaning of that gesture.

In front of the statue was a small altar with candles, flowers and food offerings. A monk, eyes closed in prayer, sat on a raised bench in perfect lotus position facing a small group of students on carpets and mats in front of him. We were the youngest by far.

LUNA

OH NO! I CAN'T SIT LIKE THAT.

Apple must have read my mind and whispered, "No worry, you can sit other way but feet go away from Buddha and Ajaarn Anurak."

Crap! It wouldn't be easy to sit still for so long on the hard floor, but I didn't really have time to think about it.

Apple, Nui and I approached on our knees, wai'ed to the Buddha and sat behind the other students. The monk cleared his throat. He seemed pretty young to be teaching a class in a major temple like Wat Pathum, but I have never been good at guessing ages. For all I knew, his meditation kept him young.

Nui and Apple sat comfortably in the lotus fold while I tried to arrange my legs into a somewhat bearable cross-legged position. I wasn't sure how long I could sit that way but I had no other choice.

"Sawasdee khrup." the monk began. Oh shit! I realized I

had a much bigger problem. What the heck had I expected? It hadn't even occurred to me the lesson would be taught in Thai.

"We have some new students today and so I will give a few instructions in English before continuing in Thai."

My eyes popped open and I stared at Ajaarn Anurak. He didn't look at me, but his lips turned briefly upward. He knew he had surprised me. His English was impeccable.

Nui nudged me and urgently whispered, "Don't look at him. It's rude."

He went on, explaining. "We frequently have students from different parts of the world, so many temples now have a few English-speaking brothers. Let us get started. Some of you may have meditated previously, but most of you are new to this particular temple and class, so we will start at the very beginning."

I knew I was breaking a rule, but I couldn't help peering through half-closed eyes at our teacher. Despite his shaven head, I thought he was very handsome and his excellent English was an added bonus. *Earth to Luna... Pay attention.*

"As you know, the basic teachings of Buddhism aim to end suffering in all beings. Most of the suffering is caused by our own thoughts, and meditating is meant to calm your mind so you can become mentally and emotionally clear. It allows you to connect with your inner source energy. I will guide you through the steps and then you can continue to meditate on your own. If you feel your thoughts starting to wander, don't fight them, just bring your attention back to your breath. It sometimes helps to repeat the words 'here and now' to yourself, and then feel your breath flow in and out. For now, close your eyes and follow my voice." He repeated the introduction in Thai.

"INHALE TO A COUNT OF FOUR, HOLD FOR FOUR AND SLOWLY exhale to a count of eight."

He alternated between English and Thai and I could hear the deep inhale and exhale of Apple and Nui next to me.

"As we relax our bodies, our minds come to rest too. Feel your eyelids relax, let this feeling move down to your face, your throat, your neck, your shoulders, your arms into your fingertips, your chest, your abdomen, your hips, your thighs, your knees, your calves and all the way down to your toes. Feel your breath flow through your body in one continuous cycle as you inhale and exhale."

His voice was deep and soothing, and I stopped listening too closely. Instead, I started to worry I might embarrass myself and fall asleep. *Not happening. Your sore butt will keep you awake,* I thought irreverently and almost giggled at the thought. *Keep it together Luna. You can't blow this. Nui will never forgive you. Inhale, hold, exhale.*

Just then the monk's voice changed. I couldn't quite tell how he did it as the pace didn't noticeably vary, but for some reason it felt almost hypnotic and I completely forgot about my butt. I was pleasantly relaxed and drifting in my head.

"Imagine a ball of pure, warm light, of love and compassion, just inside your chest. The light is pulsing in time with your heartbeat. Inhale and feel the light expanding, covering your whole body in a white bubble. Now, include the person next to you. Feel it expand even further to cover this building, the temple, the city, the country, and now you can see the entire planet covered in this warm light radiating out from you. Feel your connection with every person, creature and animal on this planet. Be at peace."

I honestly had no idea how he'd done it, but I could see, or rather *feel* the light inside me projecting outwards. It didn't even occur to me to question the logic of it; somehow it just felt right.

His voice drifted off and I didn't know how long we'd been sitting like that, but I had forgotten all about my discomfort.

"We are now coming out of this meditation. I will count from one to five and at the count of five you will open your eyes and feel refreshed and calm. One, two, three, four, five. Take a deep breath and release. Open your eyes."

I was smiling when I opened my eyes. Glancing at Nui and Apple, I saw the same expression on their faces.

"I hope you enjoyed our practice this morning. I encourage all of you to go through the same process again later today. The more you practice, the easier it will be to relax and absorb the energy of the universe. I will see you all again tomorrow at the same time."

"Come on," Apple urged us forward. "Ajaarn knows you have question for school. He talk for a few minutes."

NUI

THE OTHER STUDENTS WAI'ED AND SHUFFLED BACKWARDS OUT of the sala. Luna looked dazed, so I decided to start.

"Khob khun maak kha Ajaarn Anurak for letting us join the sessions. We are very grateful." I wai'ed and elbowed Luna who followed suit.

"As I said, we welcome all seekers. I understand that you had a particular reason for being here?" Ajaarn Anurak replied in English.

"Yes, we have a few questions for you. Luna here and I have become friends since she arrived in Bangkok, and we were talking about how different our lives are— our background and culture—and we were wondering if meditation would affect us differently because of that."

"Why would meditation affect you differently because of such mundane things? Meditation is very personal, and it's aim is to bring mental clarity. Your personal experiences might be slightly different, but the result of the meditation would be the same. I believe you will come to understand this as we deepen our lessons. Keep your mind and heart open and we will talk again after a few sessions to see what you have learned. Practice the breathing exercise on your own or together as it will help you progress more quickly."

With this, he gracefully rose from his lotus position and walked off towards the main temple.

Luna and I looked at each other. "Wow!" She said. "That was pretty cool. I didn't expect to like it, but it was so peaceful. I'm really glad he speaks English too. He's got a fab voice."

"Come on, let's get tea and talk more," Apple suggested.

Paragon had just opened and the food court in the basement offered 'street food deluxe'. There were also around thirty full-service restaurants in the building, but I liked the food court best, as you could pick and choose different things from different vendors, Thai or international.

Apple and I ordered Thai iced tea, a supercharged black tea mixed with sweetened condense milk, poured over ice. Luna hated it and treated herself to a regular latte. We sat at a communal table.

"So, what you think of first lesson?" Apple probed.

"To be honest, I had no idea what to expect but I thought it was pretty cool. I felt great when we finished, and I even forgot about my sore butt," Luna joked.

"Ah yes, you need use more cross leg," Apple smiled. "So, keep going?"

"Oh, definitely," Luna and I responded in unison.

"Ok, see you tomorrow, same time. Bring incense and flowers for prayers!" Apple slurped the last of her tea and waved as she moved off.

LUNA

"Do you think it's going to work?" Nui asked. She was fiddling with her straw, as usual unable to keep her energy contained.

"You know, Nui,' I grinned, "meditation must be good for you! I think this was the first time I've seen you sit still for more than five minutes."

She looked up surprised, clearly unaware of how fidgety she was.

"Really? Hmm, ok, but anyway, so what do you think?

"You mean, will we have an out-of-body experience? Who knows? But at least we're in it now and we should keep going to see how far we can take it. We still have to write the essay anyway," I reminded her.

"So, when and where do we practice?"

"We can go to my place," I suggested. "It's quiet there."

"I need to pick up some things in Siam Square for Mom now. But I'll text you later, ok? Maybe this afternoon?"

"Sure. See you later! This is going to be fun." For some reason, I felt a little shiver down my back, or perhaps it was just that icy air conditioning.

———

THAT AFTERNOON, NUI AND I SAT CROSS-LEGGED ON THE floor in my bedroom trying to muddle through the breathing exercise. At first, we couldn't decide who would do the counting, but since Nui had meditated previously I figured it should be her. She tried, but her voice just didn't carry the same weight as Ajaarn Anurak's and I felt my mind wander this way and that. 'Here and now' didn't help either.

"You know what? I'm going to record the session tomorrow, so we know what we're doing. You think that's ok?" I thought out loud.

"I'm not sure if it's allowed, but I guess it can't hurt to ask."

"Well, it's not like he needs to know. I have my phone in my pocket anyway and can just set it to record."

"We should at least ask. Seems wrong to just tape it." Nui was apprehensive. I didn't have those scruples.

"Ok, fine. I'll see you tomorrow at the temple, ok? I can pick up some flowers and incense on the way. I have to go past Erawan shrine anyway."

"Great, thanks. See you tomorrow."

———

"HOW WAS THE MEDITATION THIS MORNING?" MOM ASKED over dinner.

"Did you ohm and chant?" Luke smirked.

"No, we didn't! What would you know about meditation anyway pea-brain? It was actually quite nice and relaxing, but it was only our first session, so we'll see."

"Language, Luna!" Mom scolded half-heartedly. "I'm glad you enjoyed it. Next thing we know you'll be coming to yoga with me."

"As if. Luna can barely touch her toes," Luke laughed.

I ignored him. He was just a brat.

"Guys! Can we please enjoy our dinner without a fight?" Mom stepped in.

The rest of the evening was peaceful. Luke played video games in his room while Mom and I watched 'Moonlight'.

I SLEPT UNUSUALLY WELL AND WOKE UP EARLY WITH PLENTY of time to pick up the flowers before class.

This morning, I felt a bit more comfortable walking into the temple. We started again with the breathing exercise and then onto the white bubble thing. I still didn't really know what to make of it, but it felt pretty good to sit there and not think about anything else. The class went by quickly and I didn't get a chance to ask Ajaarn Anurak about recording his lesson.

Our own practice was a repeat of the previous day.

"I think we're missing the point," Nui complained. "Meditation is not supposed to be dependent on someone's voice but on what your mind is doing! I don't know why this is not working."

"Ok promise me that you won't get mad," I said sheepishly.

"Why would I get mad?" Nui was suspicious.

"Just promise," I insisted.

"Ok fine."

I picked up my iPhone. "I know we said we were going to ask but there was no time, so I just recorded the session," I admitted.

"Arai wah! You did not! I thought we'd agreed that you can't record someone without permission. We have laws against that." Nui instantly blew up. I had forgotten that she was such a straight shooter.

"I know, I know but you promised not to get angry," I pleaded. "I will ask him tomorrow, ok? And if he says no, I'll delete the recording. You can watch me. Can we just try and see how it goes with his instructions?"

Nui wasn't so easily placated. "You definitely have to ask him tomorrow. Just don't tell him you already have a recording. That's probably enough to get us kicked out right away. I can't believe you did that."

"Fine, but can we just try it now?"

"We might as well." While still angry, Nui was curious enough to see if the voice made any difference.

Sure enough, as soon as we heard the monk's voice it became much easier to settle in and relax. The sound was almost hypnotic.

"Nui, do you think he's hypnotizing us?" I asked, after the last countdown. "I definitely feel different when he speaks than when I try to have my brain tell me the same things."

"I don't think so," Nui considered. "But yah, his voice is definitely more powerful. I guess he's had years and years of practice. Maybe we can ask him if there is something special he does."

14

NUI

THE NEXT MORNING WE WERE THE FIRST STUDENTS IN THE sala. Luna was nervous as she asked Ajaarn Anurak about the recording, but I figured as a farang she would more easily be forgiven any breach of etiquette.

To my surprise, he just nodded. "If it helps you with your own practice, then by all means go ahead and record it. We are not in the eighteenth century anymore, see?" Out of some deep pocket in the folds of his robe he extracted his own iPhone.

Luna wai'ed to him. "Khob khun maak kha."

I shrugged, but naturally she had to rub it in, "See! You just have to ask. No big deal!"

We developed a tight pattern over the next two weeks. Luna's family was going to Bali for a short trip after New Year's and we still had to write that essay.

Each morning we went to the temple for the hour-long

class and each afternoon we repeated the session at home. I think our parents were amazed by our enthusiasm but neither set commented much on it. They were all just happy that we took it so seriously. They might have thought differently if they knew our real objective.

Both Luna and I were becoming much better at focusing and releasing any thoughts. Each day, the monk added another component to the session. Sometimes it was a word to reflect on, sometimes an image, sometimes sounds or a mantra, and each day we were able to better visualize the white light and ourselves as being connected to every creature on the planet.

15

LUNA

IT HAPPENED IN THE MIDDLE OF THE SECOND WEEK. I WAS focusing on the word we'd been given, 'sky', and all of a sudden, I felt as if I was hovering above the group looking down at myself. Shocked, I involuntarily gasped and the vision immediately faded. I opened my eyes and saw Ajaarn looking at me intensely as if he knew what had happened.

What the heck was that? I always thought out-of-body was just a phrase that people used when something weird happened to them, but I had actually seen myself sitting cross-legged at the back of the class. I was stunned. The last thing I had been consciously aware of was a stream of energy gaining momentum moving up and down my body. The 'lift' felt almost natural.

I couldn't wait for class to be over so I could talk to Nui.

We went for tea and coffee. Apple hadn't been able to join us that day.

"You look so excited," Nui said, after we sat down. "What happened?"

"Did you notice anything different today?" I was cautious as I still didn't quite trust the experience.

"I felt a lot lighter when he was repeating the sky mantra, but I suppose that was because I was thinking of flying. Why, what was different for you?"

"Don't laugh, but I was actually flying. I mean not physically but I saw myself suspended above our heads and looking down on us. It was so weird. I don't really know how to describe it."

Nui stopped slurping and stared at me, "You had an actual out-of-body experience? Oh! My! God! Are you serious? How did you do it?"

"I'm not sure I did anything, it just happened. It was pretty neat. I want to see if I can do it again and hold it for longer."

"Oh, wow!" Nui was excited. "I didn't expect this to happen so soon. Now I really want to see if I can do it too. Same time this afternoon?"

"Sure. What do you think, should we double our sessions? We don't have much more time before school starts again."

"Let me talk to my mom to see what time she needs me, but I'm pretty sure it'll be ok."

"Great, see you this afternoon."

———

NUI CAME OVER AT THREE O'CLOCK AND I TOLD KHUN BO that we needed to study and could not be disturbed. We were halfway into our first session when I felt that surge again and suddenly saw myself from above. This time I managed to hold the picture a bit longer. Nui was staring at me when we finished the count.

"You did it, right?" she asked.

"Yeah, the same thing as before but I was there a bit longer. How could you tell?" I still felt a bit dazed.

"It's odd, but the air felt like it does just before a thunderstorm, you know, electric."

"Oh, ok, I didn't feel that. What about you? Any change?" I asked.

"Not really," Nui was disappointed. "Can we try again?"

"Sure, whenever you're ready."

I was a bit tired but Nui was keen to keep going so we started the recording again. I couldn't fully relax this time but I did suddenly feel a shift in the air. It felt just like Nui had said, electric.

"And?" I asked, when she opened her eyes.

"Oh my God, this is so cool! It wasn't scary at all but kind of serene. What about you?"

"Not this time, I think I'm too tired." I envied Nui but at the same time was glad we had both managed our first 'spacewalk'.

"Do you think if we keep practising, we'll be able to hold this for longer?" Nui wondered.

"I would think so. My second time was already better than the first. I guess you were right that it is doable. I just never thought we'd get there so quickly. But now what? Do we talk to Ajaarn about it? Do you think he can explain what happened?"

"I'm sure he can but we need to be careful that he doesn't become suspicious of why we're asking," Nui cautioned.

"Well, we haven't gone anywhere near switching minds, so there's nothing to worry about, is there?"

"True, but it's a bit weird that we got here so fast when other people take years and years of practice."

"It's early days yet so let's see what happens next, ok? Let's not talk to anyone about this, it'll just freak them out. We'll just have to practice more and see if we can both do it at the same time, ok?" I was exhausted and wanted to take a nap.

"Sure, that's fine. I gotta run anyway. See you tomorrow."

NUI

LUNA AND I WERE JUMPY WITH NERVOUS ANTICIPATION WHEN we arrived for class. Apple frowned at us, trying to figure out why we were so antsy. "What's wrong with you girls? Jai yen, jai yen! We're in a temple." She shook her head in disapproval.

Ajaarn's guiding voice finally relaxed me enough to pick up the breathing pattern. I distinctly felt Luna's shift just before I was looking down at myself. This time, I had been expecting it, and I found it easier to 'float' for longer.

Immediately after class, Ajaarn Anurak motioned to us to come forward. Apple wanted to stay too but the monk politely asked her to wait for us outside.

He looked at us curiously. "I think we should talk!"

Luna and I looked at each other and I decided to forge ahead.

"Yes Ajaarn kha, we were hoping that you could explain

what happened to us. Luna and I had out-of-body experiences, for lack of a better description, during our sessions yesterday and today. We don't know what that means or how it happened. Can you please explain it to us, kha?"

He paused for a moment to collect his thoughts. "How much do you know about vibrational energy?"

We both shrugged, neither one very good at physics or natural sciences.

"Ok, I will try to keep this fairly simple. As you know, we Buddhists believe that any living creature has a soul that is reborn in another lifeform after death. There are many different words for soul: spirit, source, inner being, life stream and so on. It doesn't really matter what the name is. Now, this 'soul' is, in essence, vibrational energy. You probably can pick up on this yourself when you meet someone and you instinctively like them or not, which means that you either vibrate on a similar level to that person, or you don't. So, you have a physical body and a soul—or source—and they co-exist within you. In other words, you are made up of two components, the physical and the spiritual, but most people are not aware of that. Meditation helps you connect to your source or universal energy, enabling you to enter a new level of awareness, which is what happened to you today." He looked at us to check we were following. We both nodded and he continued.

"It is wonderful to sense your essence, and if you can maintain this level of consciousness, it can guide you throughout your life. The energy of the soul is older and wiser and has the knowledge and wisdom of countless lifetimes of experiences. I am surprised that you have both been able to reach this level of awareness already. It normally takes years of focus. But, while it is wonderful to perceive the world around us from this elevated perspective, you should treat it with great respect. While it's unlikely, you don't want to risk cutting yourself off from your own energy and not being able to reconnect." He grew serious.

Luna and I recoiled, shocked. "That can actually happen?" I whispered. "What does that mean? Would you die?"

Ajaarn stroked his chin contemplating the question. "We don't know for sure. Like I said, Buddhists believe that the energy will flow into another living organism and what remains is the shell of a physical person no longer vibrating with life force. Other religions may have other explanations, and many people have devoted a lot of time and practice to finding out more, but there are no conclusive answers. So, I would encourage you to not try to push too fast and far, or you might lose control."

"Yes, definitely! We'll be careful," we nodded, definitely less enthusiastic than before.

"I don't want you to be afraid of meditation or spiritual practices. As I said before, meditation is meant to connect you to your inner being, to gain balance and guidance. Respect and appreciate that and you won't have to worry about possible consequences."

"Yes, of course. Thank you so much." I wai'ed to him.

"Good!" He replied and stood up. "And remember the words of the Buddha: 'Every experience, no matter how bad it seems, holds within it a blessing of some kind. The goal is to find it.'"

We both sat there motionless, trying to digest his advice.

"OH MY GOD, THIS FREAKS ME OUT!" LUNA HISSED, WHEN Ajaarn had left us alone. "We gotta stop."

"Let's not talk about it right now; Apple is waiting. We can figure it out this afternoon, ok? I need to think about it."

"What's there to think about it? Do you really want to risk becoming a human vegetable or dying? I definitely don't."

"Don't be so dramatic! He didn't tell us to stop so it must be quite safe, after all we learned it from him and not some voodoo place, ok? Let's talk later once we've both had time to digest it."

"Well, *I* definitely don't want to risk it," Luna maintained.

"Let's talk later, ok? We gotta go."

LUNA

THAT AFTERNOON, NUI CAME OVER AS USUAL FOR OUR meditation practice. After Ajaarn's warning, I had decided it was time to stop our quest.

"We're moving way too fast and we're nowhere near in control of what our spirit, or whatever you call it, does when it does what it does. I'm definitely not going to risk it," I insisted.

"So, you're not curious at all?" Nui shrugged as if she was indifferent about my decision, but somehow her words made it sound like I was being unreasonable.

"Of course I'm curious, but you heard what could happen. It's not worth it."

"But imagine, if we were actually able to control and direct our spirit where we wanted it to go." Nui threw out casually. "All we have to do is practice more and see if we can do that."

I couldn't quite figure out if she was playing some kind of mind game with me by pretending it wasn't a big deal either way. I had prepared myself to battle her about it and was still incredulous that she would even consider continuing.

"Did you actually listen? He said no one really knows what happens, and if those guys haven't been able to figure it out, why do you think we could?"

"He also said we shouldn't be afraid and just keep practicing, and if they are all doing it in search of answers why can't we be?" Nui challenged. "Didn't you like that feeling? It all seemed so peaceful and I wasn't afraid at all, were you?"

I had to agree that it was a nice feeling, and I *was* curious to see if it was possible to achieve it on a steadier basis.

Nui joked, "I promise that I will not try to enter your body while you're out of it."

"Very funny. NOT! You're not taking this seriously."

"Oh, I am, trust me, but didn't you also hear him say he was surprised at how quickly we'd got to this stage? So maybe we're both able to do even better. Wouldn't that be cool?"

She got me there. Ajaarn's praise had felt like some sort of validation. It made me feel special. My gut felt all twisted about the potential dangers but I was seriously tempted to continue.

"Ok, here's the deal. Let's continue and see if we can get better at this, but if I say I want to stop, we'll stop, ok?" I relented.

"Deal!" Nui's face split into a wide grin.

Over the next two days, Nui and I indeed became better at not only getting to the 'out of body' part more quickly, but also at observing more and staying there longer. We both became aware of what seemed to be translucent tendrils that connected us to other spirits like an intricate spider web. At one point I felt I could see my link to Nui. I had to admit it did feel good to separate from the plain old me for a little while.

We only had one more regular class at the temple, but we planned to continue our practice every day privately. Christmas had passed in a blur. There had been lots of functions at the hotel, so Dad had to work most of the holiday but he promised we'd have more time with him in Bali after New Year's. Nui's predictions were spot on though, the decorations on the streets and malls were gaudy and completely over the top. Candy-coloured plastic winter wonderlands with random reindeer, elves, Santa Clauses and angels thrown in. Ridiculous.

ON OUR LAST DAY, AJAARN ANURAK ASKED TO SPEAK TO US again after class.

"Now that we're at the end of our class, have you come to a conclusion about how meditation might affect people differently depending on their culture or upbringing?"

Nui nodded for me to proceed.

"I think we both have had pretty much the same progression and experience, so there's really no difference." I volunteered.

He smiled. "And what does that tell you?"

"I suppose, people are more alike than we think, at least when it comes to the soul or spirit part."

He nodded. "I'm glad you realized that. When you take your mind off mundane concerns like status, money or background, you realize that in essence we are all the same and all connected to universal energy. Unfortunately, all too often we let our minor differences get in the way and create suffering for ourselves and others. I hope you will continue meditating and that I will see you again in the new year."

We both nodded and wai'ed before he left.

"Okay, we're on our own now but at least we got all the recordings, so we can keep going, right? See you this afternoon?" Nui asked.

"Yup, same time, same place."

NUI

Officially, our assignment at the temple was over. *Now what?* I felt a bit lost, disappointed that after our promising start we hadn't been able to take it any further. I'm not sure what I had expected, but with Ajaarn's warning still fresh in our minds, Luna would probably want to call a halt to our practice soon.

I needed to find a way to convince her to keep pushing the boundaries a bit more, but I was running out of time as she was leaving for Bali the following week. Once she returned, she might not be interested in continuing.

Suspended in time and space, I had felt invincible, and didn't want to give that up too easily. Sure, I could continue on my own, but it was more fun with Luna, and we could compare notes on our experiences. I also hadn't given up on our idea of a mind swap, even if I wasn't sure anymore if it was doable.

After leaving the temple I made a detour to my favourite hideaway in Bangkok, Dasa Bookstore on Sukhumvit, which was on the way home. There, I could easily lose myself for a few hours, feeling like I was on a treasure hunt. It always lifted my mood. The second-hand books cost a fraction of those the bigger chain stores charged. I decided to treat myself to an iced tea, to help me out of my slump. Khun Yaa didn't expect me for lunch until noon and it was the last free day before I would have to resume at least some of my regular duties at home or in the store. My parents had been pretty generous in giving me the time off to focus on meditation.

Khun Dang was behind the counter as I walked in. He smiled and waved.

"Hi Khun Nui. Sabai di mai khrup?"

"Sabai di kha, Khun Dang."

"What are you looking for today?" He asked, but then got distracted by a customer so I just waggled my head ambiguously and moved on.

We had chatted a few times and I was always fascinated by how he knew exactly where every book was located in the three-story maze. I planned to browse and then enjoy my tea in the little lounge on the ground floor. As usual, I started my expedition on the top floor working my way down. Packed shelves lined the walls, with little seating areas and display tables in between. I had been here a million times but every time was an adventure; there was no rhyme or reason to the inventory since all books were just dropped off, donated or exchanged with the shop. You never knew what you would find, which was half the fun.

On a whim I started in the left hand corner near the window. Books were stacked flat with their spines facing outward instead of in the more usual upright position. One black and orange book caught my attention. *Adventures beyond the body. How to experience out-of-body travel.* I looked over my shoulder, suspicious that this might be some kind of hidden camera trick. I generally didn't believe in coincidences, but this was plain freaky. A shiver ran down my back. What are the odds of this book showing up here and now? I grabbed it and rushed downstairs. I ordering a Thai iced tea, commandeered one of the little tables and started reading. The American author, William Buhlman, had apparently written a few books on the subject and conducted a lot of research on it. Maybe I could find some pointers on how to advance our own out-of-body experiences.

My tea melted away almost untouched and an hour later I came up for breath to look at my watch. Oh shit! I was going to be late for lunch.

Khun Dang raised his eyebrows as he rang up the book, "Interesting subject, Nui. Didn't realize you're into that kind of subject."

I felt it necessary to explain, "It's just so odd that I saw this today. My friend and I are doing a school essay on exactly this subject so it will help."

Khun Dang nodded. "Enjoy. Let me know what you think when I see you next time."

I waved as I rushed out of the door and backtracked to the train station. I couldn't wait to read more about the techniques that the author promised would make astral travel possible.

LUNA

Nui arrived drenched. A freak, out of season storm was tempering off outside, occasional thunder still grumbling in the distance.

"I forgot my umbrella," she complained, shaking her hair like a dog, spraying drops all over the place, including on my face.

I laughed, raising my hands to protect myself. "Hey, stop it! An umbrella wouldn't have done much good anyway. Use my hairdryer if you want. Towels are in the bathroom."

"Mai pen rai, it's ok, I'm kind of used to it," Nui waved me off. 'Mai pen rai' is Thailand's universal expression for 'whatever', 'you're welcome', 'never mind' and everything in between. I simply rolled my eyes in reply.

Nui lowered herself to the floor. "Let's just do this, and then we have to work on our report too."

By now, we were both comfortable getting into the lotus

position. Ok, semi-lotus for me, but it was still big progress. As usual, we sat facing each other and started with the breathing exercise before continuing to the next stage, humming along to Ajaarn Anurak's recorded mantras.

It still amazed me that just by focusing on my inner body and breath I could quickly stop random thoughts and relax into a calm and carefree state of mind. Within a few minutes I felt a surge of energy and my spirit began to lift, and as always it felt as if my veins were tingling with effervescent bubbles. I knew I was smiling and I sensed Nui right next to me as if we were both untethered from our own bodies but connected by invisible threads.

THE THUNDERCLAP CAME OUT OF NOWHERE.

I jolted in surprise. The boom was so strong that I felt it in my bones. My body shook, and all the connecting tendrils trembled along with me. Any buoyancy I had felt dropped quickly as I lost control of my serene state and drifted back into my body. Somehow my head and shoulders listed sideways as if the force of the thunder had pushed me over.

"Wow, that was intense," I grunted. Then I opened my eyes and… looked at myself.

"Huh?" I blinked a few times. Even with the double-take I was still looking at myself. It didn't compute. "Nui?" I barely squeaked the name out.

"What?" My own lips moved in front of me and I forgot to breathe.

"Oh my God, oh my God, oh my God, Nui open your eyes!" I choked out.

"What? What's wrong?" I heard Nui's words, but they were coming out of my own mouth in my own voice.

"No, no, no! Holy shit! Why am I looking at myself?" I

punched Nui/me on the shoulder. "Come on, open your eyes. I must be hallucinating. This isn't real, it just can't be." I looked down at my hands. Nui's hands! Nui's T-shirt and skirt!

"What?" Nui opened her/my eyes and started to focus. "What the …?" She whispered.

"I don't know, I don't know. Do you see what I see?"

"I'm looking at myself. What the …?" She repeated. My voice sounded perplexed, but even more so, curious. Our eyes locked, neither of us daring to look away.

A heartbeat later, a lightbulb seemed to go off in Nui's head. "Oh wow. I don't believe it! We did it! We actually did it!" Now there was excitement in her, or rather my, voice.

"What do you mean, we did it?" I was too freaked out to think clearly.

"We actually swapped. Don't you see? Oh my God, it worked! This is amazing!" Nui sound entirely too thrilled for my taste.

"Amazing? Are you nuts? This is crazy!" I wanted to scream or cry. "How did this happen? What are we going to do?"

"But this is exactly what we wanted, isn't it? I just never thought we could do it." Nui was giddy with excitement, which was completely weird since it was my own mouth that was grinning from ear to ear. She tentatively patted my arms, legs and hair, as if to ascertain that what she was seeing was real.

"Eww, stop it! That's gross. We need to change back right now! This is all a mistake!" Tears finally spilled over.

"Just relax, ok?! Let me think," she shushed me. "I pretty sure if we were able to do this now, we can do it again and switch back, chai mai ja?" And then almost as an afterthought; "But think about it, now we can actually switch our lives for a little while like we said we wanted to. You don't have to freak out." Nui tried to be reasonable.

"What? You think I'll just go and live your life and you stay here and live mine? I don't want to be in your body and I definitely don't want you in mine!"

"But wasn't that the idea? At least for a little while? How did *you* think you would experience my life? Isn't this cool? I don't think anyone has ever done this before."

"I don't care and no, that wasn't the idea at all! You never said we'd be swapping bodies, you said it was a *mind* swap not a *body* swap. This is a nightmare! I can't pretend to be you. I don't even speak Thai," I was desperate, angry and scared all at once. Looking at myself was not like glancing in a mirror. My body had always been an extension of my mind. You don't normally have to think about it, but now that link was cut. I felt dizzy but managed to get up to look in the full length mirror of my wardrobe. Ok, now I was feeling really nauseous.

"Try it!" Nui suggested.

"That's not the point!" I replied in Thai, and to my surprise, I found I didn't even have to think about it, but it was horrible to see Nui's mouth move when I said the words. "Ugh! So what? Just because I speak Thai now doesn't mean we can take over each other's life. Arghh, I hate this." I swiped at the mirror as if I could erase the image.

"But why not? You look like me, sound and speak like me, so it'll be easy. All you have to do is pretend that you're in some kind of show, like we do at school. I'll give you some pointers and you do the same and once we're ready we'll switch back. No one will know the difference."

"But I'm not an actress and I want to switch back right now! This is not right. Remember that Ajaarn said how dangerous this is. I don't want to get stuck." I sat back down.

"But he also said that they don't know if and how spirits can move! And now we can prove it." Nui was trying hard to convince me. "How about we try it for just one day and see if we can pull it off, ok mai? And if it's too difficult we'll switch back. But at least then we'll know."

"There's no way in hell we can pull this off. I don't think we should do this, let's switch back right now."

"Why don't you look at it as an adventure, Luna? It'll be fun and one night is not a big deal." Nui proposed.

"But I want to be home and in my own bed," I was whining. "How can you be so cool about this?" And again, there was this sense of complete disconnect. In my head I was moaning, but my face looked more eager than anything. *I'll throw up if this continues.* I started gagging so I got up again to dash into the bathroom. Nui continued as if she hadn't noticed.

"Because this is what we wanted! So, now you're saying it was all just empty talk?" I could tell Nui was annoyed but tried not to show it. "We finally managed to do what we had planned and now you're backing out? At least let's try it for one night and then we'll switch back, ok?"

I had to admit I was curious about the whole thing but every time I faced myself, I felt queasy. What had we been thinking? I looked down at Nui's body. She was so petite. I couldn't wrap my mind around being so small. This completely defied any sense of self I had. *But isn't this kind of cool too?* A little voice in my head piped up. *Nobody has done this before. One night can't be that difficult, can it?*

"You really think so?" I whispered, hating myself for sounding like a wimp.

"Yes, I do!" Her reply didn't bear an ounce of hesitation.

I took a deep breath. "Ok, fine. One night, but tomorrow

we switch back, promise?!" Almost instantly I regretted giving in but curiosity had taken hold.

"Sure, sure! Let's tell our families that we have a final session at the temple to do some chores and we'll come here afterwards and do the switch back, ok mai?"

"I guess. But you have to promise that we'll do it tomorrow."

"I promise. It'll be so cool! Ok, so let's run through this. You know where we live, so just take the skytrain to Thong Lo. Key to the house is in my bag but somebody should be home. Don't forget to wai to Grandma and Grandpa. We eat dinner at six and everyone should be there. Duen and I share a room and my bed is on the left as you enter. Tum should be home too, but you can pretty much ignore him; he's just annoying most of the time. Oh, and Krit is still away in military training." Nui talked fast, as if she didn't want to give me the chance to object.

This was nothing like a simple overnight trip. Someone would be right here pretending to be me, and my parents wouldn't even know the difference. And what if we couldn't get back into our own bodies? Would I be stuck as Nui and she as me?

"I wish we never had come up with this crazy idea! What if we can't switch back?" I couldn't shake the feeling of dread.

"Why wouldn't we be able to switch back?" Nui sounded so reasonable and confident. "We did it once, so why wouldn't we be able to do it again?"

"You're forgetting that it wasn't completely intentional right now. I'm sure the thunder had something to do with it." I argued.

"We will know tomorrow. And if all else fails we can go

back to the temple and ask Ajaarn for help, ok? Let's just do this for tonight," Nui pleaded.

"Damn it. Ok, fine. So, what do I need to do? Do I help with anything? And what do you usually do in the evening?"

"Just play it by ear. We don't have a set schedule except dinner at six. You can always text me if there's a problem. Aiyaah, that reminds me, do we need to switch phones? We should be ok for one night, I think. But keep yours hidden as my parents know I have an older version. The only thing you need to do is walk Joey around nine tonight and around six-thirty or seven tomorrow. It's pretty easy and very standard," she added.

"Standard for whom?" I grumbled. "There are so many things that can go wrong it's not even funny."

"You worry too much! You know my family; they are easy. So, what about here? What do I need to know?" Nui was like an eager puppy.

"You don't have to do anything. Just have dinner with Mom and Luke. I doubt Dad will be here; he usually gets home around eight or nine. We eat at seven. Mom usually cooks on Thursdays, probably pasta or something easy. Oh God, this is never going to work!"

"Oh, come on, let's try to have some fun with this, ok? It really *is* an adventure, don't you think?"

"More like a nightmare," I mumbled and swallowed hard. "Fine, I better leave before I lose it." Getting up from the bed I admitted, "I'm scared."

"We'll be fine," Nui tried to sound supportive, but came across as more keen than worried.

I grabbed Nui's bag and opened the door. "We shall see."

Closing the door behind me, I ran straight into Khun Bo coming out of the kitchen carrying a tray with glasses and cut fruit. "Nong Nui, you are leaving? I have some food for you."

"Ehm, sorry Khun Bo. I need to go. Looks like the rain stopped". It felt odd to hear myself speak Thai, and even more strange that I didn't have to think about any translation; it was automatic.

"Yes, yes, you better run quickly before it starts again," Khun Bo advised.

At the door, I slipped into my flip-flops on autopilot before realizing that they were too big for my 'new' feet. Khun Bo gave me a puzzled look as I switched to Nui's sandals with an embarrassed shrug and walked out.

I had just pressed the elevator button when the doors pinged open and Luke stomped out. "Hey Nui, is LL home?"

"LL?"

"You know, Luna-Loser." He faked an exaggerated shudder.

"I am not a loser! How dare you?"

Luke's eyes widened in surprise, but he quickly recovered. "Huh? I didn't say you were a loser, Nui. Is Luna rubbing off on you already?" He smirked.

"Oh! Eh, yes, Luna is home. Sorry. Gotta go." *The nerve! Is that what he calls me behind my back? Just wait until I'm back home!* I furiously stabbed the ground floor button.

In a daze, I took the skytrain to Thong Lo, mentally replaying the last few hours and trying to prepare myself for a night with Nui's family without her. I didn't have a clue what to expect. Walking up to Soi fourteen, I had to refocus as the sidewalks were completely unstable with dirty water sloshing up from underneath broken stones. By the time I reached the house, my legs were spattered up to my knees.

Ok, here we go! Showtime!

NUI

Luna had just left when I heard Luke come in and Khun Bo asking if he wanted a snack before she left for the day. I couldn't hear his response but shortly afterwards the front door closed again, and the place became dead quiet.

Gosh, this is almost spooky. I was used to the constant background noise of people moving around our house, or at least having Joey for company. I flopped backwards onto the king-sized bed and spread my arms and legs. It was so soft and there was so much space. I laughed out loud, completely giddy thinking about our afternoon session. Unbelievable! I never thought it would actually work! It was so cool. For about fifteen minutes I just laid there grinning to myself and enjoying the peace. *Right, time to get some work done, Nui!* I picked up our social studies essay and wrote a few lines but my mind kept drifting and nothing quite stuck as a good intro.

Ok, forget about that. I'll figure it out later. Might as well enjoy the moment.

I looked around the room. Luna had two large built-in wardrobes, two chests of drawers, an overstuffed armchair, an ottoman and a desk, and there was still room to move around. From my bed at home, I could almost touch Duen's bed with my fingers. Curiosity got the better of me. I got up and locked the door. *Might as well see what she has in all these closets.* Feeling slightly nosy but quickly pushing the thought aside, I went through her dresses and threw a few that I liked on the bed to try on. *So much stuff. What does she need all this for?* I decided to do my own private fashion show. Using Luna's iPad, I played Rhianna on Spotify and stripped down to my underwear. I looked in the mirror. *Wow, she's so white and so big.* I touched her arms and belly, not quite sure if the sensation I felt was my own or hers. Hmmm, kind of nice to actually have some curves, as I was used to my flat chest and stomach. *Wonder what she thinks of my body?* I shrugged. *Doesn't really matter. It is what it is.*

Dancing around and lip-synching I tried on different outfits, feeling both silly and glamorous. I had just slipped on a fancy black cocktail dress and was experimenting with some jewellery and shoes when there was a knock on the door.

LUNA

I TRIED TO TALK MYSELF INTO OPENING THE DOOR. ON THE other side I could hear toenails clicking on the stone floor. Joey, Nui's mongrel terrier started whining and panting, eager for me to come in. I put the key in the lock and cautiously opened the door.

"Hi Joey, are you waiting for me?" I bent down to scratch his head. Joey came to a complete stop and then quickly scrambled backwards and started growling. He tilted his head looking at me as if to say, "Who are you?" *Uh oh, can he tell that I'm not Nui?* A sharp bark brought Khun Yaa out of the kitchen.

"What's going on? Why is Joey barking?" She frowned.

"I'm not sure," I stammered. "Is something wrong with him?" I pleaded ignorance, although I'd read somewhere that dogs were more perceptive than we gave them credit for. Joey continued to growl and scooted behind grandma while looking at me suspiciously.

Grandma, hands on her hips, regarded Joey with a puzzled frown, "What's gotten into that dog? Joey, stop it or you'll go into the backyard. Nui, go and wash your hands and then come set the table. We're eating in fifteen minutes." A critical glance up and down my body followed. "And wash your legs too, you look like you wrestled a crocodile."

Shaking her head, she disappeared back into the kitchen with Joey on her heels, grumbling and glancing back at me. The food smelled delicious and I knew from experience how good Grandma's food tasted. Kicking off my sandals I walked bare-foot down the hallway towards Nui's room. I tried to quickly remind myself: kitchen on the left with a dining nook off to the side. Directly opposite was the living/family room with a glass sliding door leading into a small backyard. Nui's grandparents' bedroom and bathroom. Duen and Nui's room was at the end of the hallway, and her brothers' directly opposite. Their shared bathroom was next to the boys' room. Their parents' bedroom was upstairs and had its own small bathroom too. The house was pretty spacious but it seemed cramped with so many people living here, especially compared to our own apartment.

Duen was on her bed, bobbing her head to music on her headphones. She casually waved when I walked in. By the time I came back to the kitchen Khun Yaa had already put out plates and bowls. I grabbed them without a word and started setting the table. Bowl next to plate, spoon on the right, fork on the left. I would have to remember to eat the Thai way using spoons and no knives. Joey was watching me, cautiously, while keeping his distance, emitting the occasional gruff rumble. *Can't blame you Joey, I don't know what to make of me either right now.*

"How is your friend Luna, Nui? Did you have a good time this afternoon?" Grandma asked. "You're awfully quiet."

"Luna is fine, but she and I have to go back to the temple tomorrow morning for some final instructions."

"Everything ok? Do you want to talk?" She looked at me with a sweet smile. I knew Nui was very close to her grandmother, maybe even more so than her own mom. I wasn't exactly sure how old she was, but to me Khun Yaa looked to be in her early seventies. She had a round brown face that was lined with wrinkles, and lots of laughter lines around the eyes. She was even smaller than Nui but more padded around the middle. She somehow reminded me of Moana's grandmother from the Disney movie. And just like Moana's granny, she was someone I felt shouldn't be underestimated; she could probably see right through me.

"No, it's ok, Khun Yaa. Just something I need to work out. I'll let you know if I need help, ok?"

"Are you sure? We'll talk later. Ah, there are your parents. Call your sister and brother and then we can eat." *Uh oh, I have to find a way to avoid that conversation. I'm not sure I can handle it.*

NUI

"LUNA, ARE YOU THERE?"

"Ehhh, yes Khun … I mean Mom, coming." Oh shit, no time to change out of the cocktail dress back into my regular clothes. Very carefully, I unlocked the door and brought up my hands to wai, only to remember at the last second that Luna wouldn't do that with her mom, and pulled back my hair instead. "Oh, hi, Mom, how are you?"

She looked up and grinned, "Hi honey, I'm fine, and you? What are you doing in that outfit? Going somewhere?"

"Erm, no, I just thought I'd try out an outfit for New Year's Eve. In case we're going out." I had no idea if that had been discussed, but at least it sounded reasonable and was the best I could come up with quickly.

"I'm not sure yet. We'll decide later." She glanced over my shoulder and saw the mess on the bed. She didn't comment but raised an eyebrow. "You had a good day? Has Bo left?"

"A little while ago. And yes, good day, thank you. Very interesting."

"Oh really? Want to come to the kitchen and tell me about it? And can you please turn down the music a bit?"

"Sure, just give me a minute."

Back in my shorts and t-shirt, I looked at the dress pile and shrugged. It could wait.

Walking into the kitchen, I saw that Luna's mom had started to put out some cooking ingredients. A large pot of water stood on the stove, boiling, with a big bag of spaghetti next to it. Luna was right, it was going to be a pasta night.

"What can I do to help?"

Luna's mom stood there for a moment like she hadn't heard correctly. "You want to help me cook?"

"Sure, what are you making? Do you need me to cut anything?"

"Are you ok, sweetheart? What did you do today?" She sounded worried.

"Nothing much and yes, I want to help. Is that ok?" Why did she sound so surprised? Did Luna normally not offer? Maybe I should have asked her. I always enjoyed cooking with Grandma and experimenting a bit with flavours.

"Of course it's ok. Here, why don't you cut the tomatoes and cucumber? We're having Spaghetti with a salad on the side.

"Yum, do you want me to make the sauce? How about a spicy arrabbiata?"

Luna's mom spun around fast and put her hands on her hips. "You, what? Since when do you know how to make that? What is going on?"

Oh no! Busted already!? And we're not even at dinner yet.

"Erm, I think I saw it on a food show once but I also watched Nui's grandma cooking. She makes a spicy version of it, sort of like a Thai version," I replied tentatively. "But don't worry, we can use some pre-made sauce if you like."

"Hmm, yes, today we'll use that. I'm not sure we have all the ingredients to make a fresh sauce." She sounded slightly embarrassed. "But you can set the table. Just the three of us. Dad won't be home until later." Thankfully she had already put out placemats, glasses and dishes, as I didn't know where everything was.

For a while we worked side by side without speaking. I thought it was very relaxing. Luna's mom was so pretty and elegant with her blond hair casually pulled back. She wore an apron over her wrap dress and had a glass of white wine by the stove, from which she took occasional dainty sips.

"What did you do today, Mom?" I asked politely.

"Well, we had our fundraising committee today, and I have to work out the catering plans for the bazaar in two weeks."

"Is that at Dad's hotel? Can I help? Do you need volunteers for the day?"

"Ok Luna, what's going on? You've never been interested in any of my charity work."

"Well, I thought at least I'd get to see Dad for a while that day. He'll be there, no?" *Gosh, what has Luna been doing all this time?*

"Ah honey, yes he'll be there, but he has to work, though I'm sure he'll pop over for a bit," Luna's mom sounded sad. "We'll have a lot more time in Bali. Do you still need to get anything for that?"

"No, I think I'm good. I have plenty of clothes anyway," I assured her.

"Ok, something is definitely off. What happened today? Was meditation ok?" She sounded very concerned now.

"No, nothing happened. Really!" I was desperately trying to figure out why she was so surprised. Though it went against my instincts, apparently I had to be less polite around Luna's mom in order to appear normal. It was going to be a difficult evening if I had to watch every single word.

LUNA

THE ENTIRE FAMILY SAT AROUND THE DINNER TABLE. NUI'S parents were in their early fifties, just a bit older than my own. Nui's mom had a short, no-nonsense ponytail streaked with grey, and was wearing a light green shift dress. Her dad wore khakis and a white shirt and looked like a younger, darker version of his father, Khun Bpoo.

The food smelled delicious and I was surprised to find I was hungry, despite the knot in my stomach. Luckily there were stir-fried vegetables, brown rice and a broiled whole fish as well as a chicken dish. At least I wouldn't have to pretend to like meat.

Everyone helped themselves and started eating and talking simultaneously. Nui's father and grandfather shared a beer, the rest drank water. It was very noisy, with everyone laughing, gossiping, teasing each other and chatting, except me. I felt like a cuckoo in the nest, and it was overwhelming to observe the family dynamics, especially now that I understood everything they were saying. I stayed quiet, too afraid of making a faux-pas. My eyes were tearing from the chillies, at least that's what I told myself. Meanwhile, Joey continued to circle the table but wouldn't come near me.

Finally, Nui's father had enough, "Joey, stop this nonsense, sit down! What's gotten into him? Nui, what did you do to him? Get him to sit down or put him in the backyard. He's driving me nuts."

All eyes were on me. *Oh shit...*

"Erm, Joey come on here," I patted my knee half-heartedly. *Come on Joey, you know Luna so don't make such a big fuss, please!* "You know, maybe he's just hungry?!" I grabbed a piece of chicken and held it out to Joey.

"Nui! We don't feed Joey at the table. You know better than that." Khun Yaa and Mae were shouting at the same time. Shocked, I dropped the meat and Joey scuttled forward gobbling it up with a big slurp, then sat down to wait for more. Paa and Khun Bpoo shook their heads. Duen and Tum just giggled, probably glad that I got told off instead of them.

I finally felt the tears spilling over. Khun Yaa and Mae looked at each other and then at me, concern in their eyes.

"What's wrong, Nui, are you ok?" Khun Yaa asked softly. Everyone waited, the room all of a sudden totally quiet.

"I'm ok, just tired," I hiccupped.

The women clearly didn't believe me, but Mae intervened. "Ok, Duen you clean up tonight and Tum can take Joey for his walk and you go to bed soon, Nui."

"Why do I have to do the dishes?" Duen complained. "Today is Nui's turn and she hasn't even done the laundry yet. I want to watch Thai Idol." *So much for sisterly love.*

"Well the sooner you clean up, the sooner you can watch

your show. Nui will do the laundry tomorrow and take your turn cleaning." Mae pointed out.

The rest of the dinner was fairly subdued compared to a few minutes earlier. At least Joey had decided to stop moving around and growling, though he still regarded me carefully from a couple of feet away. At the end we all wai'ed to Khun Yaa to thank her for her cooking.

I walked down the hall to Nui's room. There was a small chest of drawers opposite the two beds. Duen was a bit shorter than Nui and favoured pink so it was easy to guess which drawer belonged to whom. I flipped through the folded clothes and randomly pulled out a long t-shirt and underwear. Holding on to my phone I quickly skipped across the hall into the bathroom to take a shower and brush my teeth. It was only seven thirty, but I was completely exhausted and felt jittery from the dinner. There was no key, just a tassel. *What the heck am I supposed to do with that? How do I lock the door?* Taking a wild guess, I hung the tassel outside. I figured maybe that was how Nui's family knew the bathroom was occupied? At least I hoped it was.

I quickly texted Nui. 'How do I lock the bathroom and which towel is yours? And your mom said I had to do laundry?' No reply. They probably were sitting at dinner, and Mom didn't allow us to use our phones while we were eating.

I took off my clothes and had the shock of my life. It hadn't even occurred to me that I would have to handle Nui's naked body intimately. *Eew!* It was one thing to look at someone in a bikini, but to wash and put lotion on another body felt like a total invasion of privacy. Even worse, she would be doing the same to my body! I felt like crying again. I didn't consider myself a prude, but the idea grossed me out. *Don't look! Don't think! Ignore! Ignore!* I kept repeating the words over and over, but of course, it didn't quite work that way. I still had to soap up and I couldn't avoid the mirror altogether. Keeping an eye on the door, I took the quickest shower of my life and grabbed one of the yellow towels to dry off. I couldn't make myself put on any lotion. Instead, I quickly slipped into the t-shirt to cover up. *I don't like the brand of lotion or the smell anyway,* I rationalised. *Oh God, and now I don't know which toothbrush is Nui's. That's just yuck! I want to go home*! Each time I looked in the mirror, I was stunned to see Nui's face instead of mine. *Just get through the night and tomorrow you'll be back in your own bed,* I tried to think positively, failing miserably.

Back in my room, I finally received a text from Nui. 'How is it going? You ok? Use the tassel. My towel is yellow, Duen has pink and Tum has green. Sorry, should have told you. Laundry—the washing machine is on the back porch, just get all the hampers from each bedroom.'

'Joey knows something is off and he's been acting all weird. What do I do? And your grandma keeps watching me like a hawk. I'm gonna go to bed, I'm exhausted. What else did you forget?'

'It'll be fine. There are some special treats for Joey in my bedside table. Give him a few and he'll come around. See you tomorrow.'

I tried to research out-of-body experiences on the internet, but the adrenaline rush was wearing off, and my eyes kept drooping. Finally, I gave up.

NUI

L<small>UKE</small> <small>BURST</small> <small>INTO</small> <small>THE</small> <small>KITCHEN</small> <small>RESCUING</small> <small>ME</small> <small>FROM</small> <small>THE</small> awkward silence. "When are we eating? I'm starving," *Thanks Luke.*

"Did you wash your hands?" His mom asked.

"Mo-om! Of course. What's for dinner?"

"Grab some sodas and we can sit down".

Luke brought bottles of Coke and Sprite to the table.

"Eh, I think I'll just have water," I got up to get some water from the dispenser.

"Worried about your figure? Another diet?" Luke sneered.

"Well, better than having rotten teeth from all that sugar. Don't you know that you can use Coke to clean drains and toilets? That says it all."

"Oh, and when did you become Ms Know-It-All?" Luke laughed.

"I just keep my eyes and ears open, unlike someone I

know." Luke really was very similar to Tum. Obnoxious and annoying. Must be a teenage boy thing! Best to simply ignore him. It was kind of phony for me to chide him, when I drank sweet Thai tea by the gallon, but he didn't need to know that.

"Stop it, both of you!" Mom intervened. "I want to enjoy my dinner in peace."

"Do we have any chillies?" I asked.

"Chillies?" Mom looked incredulous, "I thought you didn't like spicy? And volunteering and cooking? What did you do with the real Luna?" She joked but nodded at the cupboard. "Flakes are in there."

"She probably messed up something and is just trying to earn brownie points," Luke suggested knowingly, like that was a common occurrence with Luna.

"I did not! What's wrong with helping people and being nice?"

"Nothing wrong with that but it's not you! You're too grumpy for that." He smirked.

"Oh yeah, as if you would win a Mr Nice award." He really pissed me off now. *Did they have this kind of conversation every night? Not nice.*

The rest of the dinner was quiet, at least by my standards. *How weird. It's so hard to get a word in edgewise in my family.*

After dinner I didn't volunteer to do the dishes, as Luna's mom would probably have thought that odd too.

She suggested we watch 'Love Actually'. I briefly ducked into my room to clean up and check messages. Oops, I guess I should have told Luna about the bathroom stuff. I hoped Joey was going to be ok.

Luna's mom had cued the movie and was walking in with a glass of white wine. "Want to have a sip?" She asked.

"No thank you. I'll just have water".

Luke had retreated to his room to do whatever brats did on their own. We settled on the couch.

"How are you getting on with your essay?" Luna's mom asked. "Isn't that due soon?"

"Yes, I was trying to work on it earlier, but we can't really figure out the approach. I think Luna, I mean Nui and I pretty much have the same experience."

"Why would you think it different? Your lives are pretty similar aren't they?"

I looked at her. *You have no idea*!

"Actually I think our lives are very different. We go to the same school but nothing else is the same." That our motivation for the meditation class and the end result was beyond what we had expected, wasn't something I cared to share.

"Well, I always thought that people are more alike than not. Especially now that more and more people get to travel and experience different cultures. And with the internet there are hardly any boundaries anymore."

"I guess. Anyway, we still have to figure out how to write it. We're meeting a bit earlier at the temple tomorrow, if that's ok with you?!"

"Sure, honey. Just get it done soon so we can have some fun during our trip and you don't have to worry about homework. By the way, your dad and I talked about your comments the other day and we thought it might be a good idea to go home over Songkran. What do you think?"

"What comment?" I was clueless.

"You know, when you said that you wanted to have a more permanent base."

"Ohhh, you mean like moving to the US?"

"Well, not permanently yet, but at least we can see the family and maybe take an early peek at some colleges."

"Erm, yeah, that would be great. Thanks, Mom."

"You don't sound very excited about it, Luna. I thought this was what you wanted?" Mom seemed disappointed by my lukewarm reaction.

"No, no. I think it's great, it was just a surprise," I quickly reassured her. *Lucky Luna, I wish I could go. And she says her parents don't understand her. Mine wouldn't be so accommodating!*

25

LUNA

I JERKED AWAKE, MY HEART PUMPING TOO FAST. DAYLIGHT danced across the ceiling in strange patterns that I didn't recognize. *Did I forget to close my curtains?* I heard a snuffling noise to my right. Spooked, I turned, only to realize I was looking at Duen's face, mouth open, snoring slightly. *Huh?* Slowly the previous day's events started to resurface. A quick peek at my watch revealed a small, brown hand. Groaning, I pulled the cover back over my head. Damn, I had hoped it was all just a bad dream. My brain felt fuzzy. Duen's turning and occasional mumbling had woken me up several times during the night. I wasn't used to sharing a room. Besides, I didn't smell like me, the sheets didn't smell like mine and the bed was too hard and too small for my restless tossing. Each time I tried to sleep, it took me ages, thoughts spiralling like a dog chasing its tail. Worried, excited, despairing, curious, hopeful, anxious—back and forth, up and down the entire emotional scale. I said a silent prayer. *Please let the reversal work so that I can sleep in peace tonight.*

But first I had to get through the morning. I tiptoed out to use the bathroom and almost tripped over Joey who had made himself comfortable in front of the bedroom door.

"Morning, Joey!" I was hesitant to pet him after his behaviour last night. He stretched and tentatively wagged his tail. "Oh, so you recognize me now? Just give me a sec and we'll go out, ok?" I ducked into the bathroom, brushed my teeth and dressed in shorts and a t-shirt. This time I appraised Nui's body more closely. *Hmm, so this is what it feels like to be petite and skinny. Nice. Oh well, that's never going to be you Luna.* I shrugged.

Khun Yaa was already in the kitchen cooking breakfast. The rest of the household wasn't there yet.

"Good morning, Nui. Feeling better? Do you want pork or shrimp with your congee?"

Ugh, neither! Just the thought made me nauseous. *How can people eat that gooey mess for breakfast?*

"Um, actually, I feel like some cereal or fruit or just some toast? Do we have any?"

"You know we don't eat that western food for breakfast! It's not good for you. Too much sugar and you'll be hungry again in an hour!" Grandma looked at me disapprovingly. "Did Luna put you up to that? You can have some papaya, but you have to eat some congee too," she decreed.

Yikes! My mom would never make me eat things I didn't like.

"Erm… I'll just take Joey for a quick walk. Be right back!"

I dashed back into the bedroom to grab a few of the dog treats Nui had stashed away. Joey willingly followed me to the front door where I had seen a lead last night, but as I bent down to clip it on he backed away.

"Come on Joey, no time to play games, we gotta go!" I tried to bribe him with a treat which he snatched quickly but still didn't allow me to snap on his lead. Instead, he grumbled.

Grandma peeked out from the kitchen.

"Is he still acting up? Since when do you need a lead for Joey and why was he sleeping outside your room last night?"

I shrugged pretending to be equally baffled.

"Be right back!" I couldn't let myself get drawn into explanations.

Outside, I instructed Joey, "Ok, you better stay close. I'm worried about the Soi dogs and don't want you to get into any fights, ok? You get some treats if you behave!"

Soi or street dogs were strays that roamed throughout Bangkok unchecked. They scavenged for food, often in packs, or lived off hand-outs from residents. My family had been warned about them from the first day we arrived in town. Mostly, they left people alone, but occasionally we heard of some aggressive dogs attacking other dogs, and even people.

Sure enough, there were several dogs resting under the awning of one of the little shops lining the street. I made sure to keep a safe distance between us, as I didn't know how Soi dogs would react with another dog on their turf. It must have been too early for them to get excited about Joey, or perhaps they knew him. He simply ignored them. I wanted to stay on the main road instead of getting lost in the confusing side alleys, but Joey had other plans. He turned left and walked a few steps into Soi ten looking back at me to check that I was coming.

"Come on Joey, I don't know that way. Can't you just walk here, so we don't get lost?"

He refused to budge, waiting for me to follow.

"Is this the way Nui normally takes you? Fine, but you better remember the way back, and we're not going far, ok?!" Letting him take the lead, I was completely surprised when just thirty metres into the Soi we came to a small pocket square and park.

"Ok, ok, you were right, this is better than walking in the street." Joey scampered over to do his business under the trees. I turned away, pretending not to be aware of the stinky pile.

"Hey nong, nong, you need to clean that up!" An angry voice called out. On the sidewalk along the park were a couple of food stalls serving soup and fried dishes. A short row of picnic tables with blue and red plastic stools under grey umbrellas had been set up for customers.

"Come on, clean that up, we are eating here. The Soi dogs are bad enough; we shouldn't have to put up with your dog's mess as well. We should call the police. This is getting out of hand!" The cook, an older lady, wiped her face and got increasingly worked up while simultaneously stirring her wok.

"You're right," one of the male customers in front of her chimed in. "It's a disgrace that people want to have pets but not look after them. All dogs should be banned in Bangkok and someone needs to get rid of those Soi dogs too. They are vicious and rabid."

Oh man, what a way to start the morning. Are locals always this angry? And Joey is a good dog. I had to check myself, as only moments before I was worried about the Soi dogs myself.

"I am really, really sorry and yes, of course I'll clean it

up. Unfortunately, I forgot to bring a bag. Can I get one from you and I'll take care of it?" For once, I was glad that all street food stalls used plastic bags for their take-aways. Generally, they overdid it and packed every bit of food separately, but it came in handy now. The stall owner harrumphed but waved me over and handed me a plastic bag, "Better think of it next time, nah?!"

"Yes, I will, thank you very much," I wai'ed to mollify her.

"Don't worry about it. Pi' Ohm is always in a bad mood in the morning," a smooth voice whispered in my ear. I turned and came face to face with the most handsome guy I had ever seen. Warm, dark eyes crinkled at the corners with a mischievous grin. Thick, wavy hair that looked blue-black in the sun, lightly tanned skin, a bit of stubble and bright, even teeth. He was maybe a foot taller than me but with Nui's tiny frame, that didn't mean much. He was dressed casually in a white button-down shirt with the sleeves folded back, washed out jeans and comfortable sandals. He was, in short, gorgeous! I realized I was checking him out and blushed.

Flustered, I automatically replied in English, "Oh, thank you, but I know I should have thought about it myself."

"Tough morning?" he responded in English without missing a beat. I had the feeling he knew what had gotten me all muddled up.

"Uh, not really." Switching back to Thai, I was embarrassed and tongue-tied.

"I'm Channon," he introduced himself.

"I'm Lu… I mean Nui!" In my confusion I almost wai'ed to him.

"Nice to meet you, Nui. Do you come here every morning? Maybe I'll see you around?"

"Sure, that would be nice." *Nice*? *How lame.* Inwardly, I cringed.

"Eh, Nui, I think your dog decided it was time to go home." Channon pointed at Joey casually walking back down the Soi.

"Oh shit! Joey, wait!" I dashed off after him, only at the last minute remembering why I was holding a plastic bag in my hand. "Ah double shit!"

Channon was laughing out loud, "Go! I'll take care of it! See you around."

"Oh God, thank you so much. See you."

I raced after Joey but could have saved myself the stress as he was proceeding at a leisurely pace toward home.

"Damn it, Joey! Now I look like a complete idiot. And he cleaned up your mess too. I'm so embarrassed." Joey clearly couldn't care less and once home, he headed straight for the doors to the patio in the back. I let him out and returned to the kitchen.

I washed my hands at the sink and joined Mae, Paa and Grandfather at the table. Duen and Tum hadn't shown up yet.

In front of me was a bowl of rice porridge, next to a small plate of cut papaya. Grandma pushed chillies, fish sauce, shredded pork bits and some shrimp my way. Yikes! How people could eat this in the morning was beyond me. I nibbled on the fruit and tried a few bites of congee without the condiments to placate Khun Yaa. It tasted bland, but I refused to add any of the other stuff. Khun Yaa looked at me with raised eyebrows but didn't say anything. I was still flustered from my encounter with Channon and kept my head down going over our conversation in my mind. Before I knew it, I had finished the entire bowl. Me, the non-breakfast eater!

"Nui, remember that we have to prep Tum tomorrow." Mae said.

"Huh, prep for what?"

"Nui! You know how important this is for him and us. Krit's exemption for the weekend was finally approved and he'll be here tonight."

I had absolutely no idea what she was talking about.

"Uh, of course, I haven't forgotten." Time to get out of here and let Nui sort it out.

Standing up to leave the kitchen, Khun Yaa coughed, "Haven't you forgotten something?" She pointed at the dishes. "And you still haven't done the laundry either. Did you feed Joey yet? What is wrong with you, Nui? You've been out of sorts since yesterday."

"Umm, nothing. Really. I gotta go." I quickly picked up the bowl and plate and put them in the sink and rushed out. Peeking into each bedroom I dumped all the clothes in one hamper and went to the back porch cramming everything into the washing machine. How do I turn this damn thing on? And where does the detergent go? I never had to do laundry at home so didn't know how the machine worked. Just then Khun Yaa appeared from the living room.

"What are you doing Nui? Why are you staring at the dryer? This is getting out of hand! You and I are going to sit down later and talk." Her voice didn't leave room for dissent. "And you still haven't fed Joey either, have you? You know he's your responsibility. How can you forget to feed your own dog?" She tutted and shook her head.

"Erm, I'm so sorry Khun Yaa but I'm really running late now." I hoped she'd offer to do the laundry for me and feed Joey.

"Go, but we'll talk later." She shooed me out of the way.

Sure, Nui can sort it out with her later. I was glad I wouldn't have to face her.

I grabbed Nui's bag and rushed out. Walking a tightrope all evening and morning had left me frazzled.

The skytrain was crammed, even at seven in the morning, and I had to wait for the second train before I managed to squeeze myself into a carriage. I finally understood why they had to keep the train so cold with so many bodies crushed together. Elbows in faces and steps on bare toes didn't make for a great commute. I'd hate to have to deal with that every day, especially as I had lost my usual five-foot eight advantage of looking over people's heads.

26

NUI

B<small>Y THE TIME</small> I <small>ARRIVED AT THE TEMPLE IT WAS ALREADY PAST</small> seven thirty. I didn't see Luna anywhere, which was odd. Normally she was pretty punctual. *Considering how freaked out she was yesterday, she can't have forgotten we are switching back today. Wonder if my parents needed her to help at the shop this morning? But she would have texted me. I'll give it another five minutes.*

Looking around I noticed people skirting around a Thai girl, who was typing on her phone. There was something familiar about her. Just then, the girl looked up and seemed puzzled having me stare at her. A tick later, I could literally feel lightbulbs going off in both our heads.

"Oh my God! Luna? This is so weird!" I started laughing as I strolled towards her. "I seriously didn't recognize myself. How bizarre."

"It's not funny Nui, it's freaky!"

"Oh, come on, you gotta admit it's pretty strange looking at yourself. Anyway, how did it go? Did you like it? Everything ok?" I had so many questions. "I really like your mom, she's so nice. It was pretty funny though, she was shocked when I offered to make the pasta sauce. I guess you don't cook much, do you?"

Luna rolled her eyes. "Duh, big surprise."

I laughed. "Oh, and she mentioned a bazaar at the hotel. I told her I'd help."

"Damn it! Why did you do that? It's just some old expat ladies wanting to sell their second-hand stuff. Mom's always involved in some charity do."

Just as I suspected, Luna had probably avoided any kind of engagement, more or less on principle.

"Why wouldn't you want to help? It's for a good cause, no? Mai pen rai, you decide what you want to do," I shrugged. "So how did it go at home?"

"Oh God, it was so weird. Joey definitely knew something was off. He was barking and growling at me at first and your grandma was suspicious and kept watching me the whole time. There were so many things that were tripping me up. You didn't tell me about the laundry thing. I put the clothes into the dryer by mistake and Khun Yaa had to take over."

"You did what?" I laughed. "You mean you don't know the difference between a washer and dryer? Seriously Luna? That's hysterical." I snorted, wiping away tears.

Luna was annoyed and a little embarrassed, "So what? We always had people doing our laundry. And you didn't tell me about feeding Joey either, and then this morning I got yelled at when I didn't clean up after him. How was I supposed to know all that? I've never had a dog."

"Geez, Luna, you really live in a different world, don't you? Did you go to the park? That was probably Pi' Ohm. Forget about her, she's always grumpy. I avoid her."

"Yeah, that's what Channon said too!" Luna looked away, shyly.

Did she just blush? I didn't even realize my own face could flush like that. Interesting!

I was curious. "Channon? Who's Channon?"

"Just some guy who was there and he seemed to know her." She quickly changed the subject. "Your mom said you have Tum's prep tomorrow, and Krit is coming home tonight. Any idea what that means?"

"Oh shoot, I totally forgot. I definitely need to be home for that. He's going to be ordained as a novice monk on Sunday and tomorrow we need to prepare him for that. We have a neighbourhood party with lots of food and everyone goes to the temple for the ceremony. It's a big deal. Do you want to come?"

"Maybe. Depends on how long it takes. I want to be home for New Year's Eve. And I definitely want to sleep in on Sunday, I'm exhausted." Luna yawned to emphasize her point.

"It's from noon to five but the ordination itself is early. Let me know later if you want to come."

"I'll have to talk to Mom first, I don't know what she has planned. Anyway, so what are we gonna do now? Mom probably thinks we're in meditation now, right?" Luna asked. We were still standing in front of the temple entrance,

"Let's go to the spirit house and then grab some food," I suggested. "I'm starving. Khun Bo only had some fruit and Cornflakes for me and I didn't want to ask for anything else. Do you always eat so little for breakfast?"

"Ha! Khun Yaa made me eat a bowl of congee." Luna

countered. "I almost choked. And shrimp and pork? Yuk! How can you eat that in the morning?"

"Ahh, now I'm really hungry," I grinned, dismissing her complaint. "Let's go!"

27

LUNA

I ALWAYS ENJOYED THE PEACEFUL TEMPLE GROUNDS, THEY provided a true oasis in this chaotic city. The contrast was even more glaring afterwards as we crossed the pedestrian bridge into the maze of Siam Square, a warren of little shops and stalls, with alley after alley of individual boutiques, pharmacies and food shops.

Nui knew a little place that served breakfast bowls. The ingredients made them sound more like lunch to me, but whatever. I ordered a black coffee and water at the counter while Nui went for her Thai tea and noodles. Ugh, I still felt bloated.

The waitress brought our food over and put Nui's noodles in front of me. Talk about stereotyping. Disgusted, I pushed the bowl towards Nui and grabbed my coffee.

"We need to talk about the essay. You're in Bali next week and we won't have much time to sit down and finalize it. How do you want to handle it?" Nui asked, while dosing her noodles with fresh chillies, vinegar and fish sauce and expertly mixing it with her chopsticks.

"Nui, can you please go easy on the food? I don't want to put on any weight, and I don't have your metabolism, ok?!"

Nui looked up from her bowl, "What do you mean? This is nothing, and it's much healthier than your sugary cereal."

"But you're eating for my body, so take it easy, ok?"

"And you better eat something real, I don't want to lose weight, ok?" She countered.

I had to look away. I took a sip from my cup. Yikes, instant coffee! But better than nothing; I desperately needed a caffeine hit.

"So, do we write separate reports and then just put them together? I'm not sure what's best, especially with what's happened to us." Nui asked.

"I think we should keep it general—explain the sequence, mention what Ajaarn told us and then the experience itself, except the out-of-body part," I suggested. "We can't do more than that. Our conclusion is that meditation is universal and has benefits for everyone, regardless of background."

"Ok, how about if I write the set-up part and you write the conclusion and we'll put it together when you're back from Bali?"

"Yeah that should work," I mulled it over, "So, do we say that because people meditate for the same general purpose, they also get the same results? Or can people use it for different purposes? I know we are the only idiots who took it too far." I had to add.

"Don't tell me you're still pissed off." Nui rolled her eyes as she slurped her broth. "I think it's pretty amazing that we managed to do this. I mean, what were the chances? And nothing really bad has happened, so why are you so angry?"

"I'm not angry, I'm terrified that we won't be able to go back!" I bit my tongue to avoid shouting at her.

Nui conceded: "Yeah, I'm a bit nervous too, but why do you always worry about things that haven't happened yet?"

"You know, not all of us can have your 'mai pen rai' attitude." I snapped at her.

"Look, we made it this far and a few more hours won't be that difficult. Gosh, Luke was right, you are really grumpy," she shot back.

I stared at her, furious now. "How dare you bring Luke into this? This whole thing was your idea in the first place. So, you better figure out how we reverse it and we'll pretend nothing ever happened." Ironically, now I *was* feeling grumpy, but also tired and nervous, and I just wanted to be me again.

"Well, excuse me! I couldn't have switched if you hadn't wanted to do it too, ok? So, get off your high horse and don't put this all on me!" I had never heard Nui speak like that, and it was creepy seeing the words fall from my own lips. *Is this how I look when I'm in a bad mood?* I felt tears coming on. *What have I gotten myself into?*

Nui took a deep breath, "Listen, let's just get through today, and by this evening we'll be back to normal, ok? I don't want to fight with you and we need to do this together. It's only for a few more hours and we'll laugh about it this afternoon, ok?"

I bit back another sharp comment. After all, I *had* gone ahead with the idea, and it really didn't matter anymore who came up with it first.

"So, where's Mom this morning?" I changed the subject.

"I'm not sure. She said she had a meeting at ten and she'll be back around three."

"Ok then, let's write some notes now before we go home."

For the next hour we both kept our heads down and worked on the essay, acutely aware that one wrong comment could blow up into another fight.

NUI

Kʜᴜɴ Bᴏ ᴡᴀs ʜᴏᴍᴇ, ʙᴜᴛ ᴏᴛʜᴇʀᴡɪsᴇ, ᴡᴇ ʜᴀᴅ ᴛʜᴇ apartment to ourselves.

"Hello girls, do you want a snack or a drink?" She asked when we walked in.

"Thank you Pi' Bo, that would be great. Then we have to study."

Her eyes widened. "Khun Luna! You speak Thai?"

Though she had asked in English, I had automatically responded in Thai. Damn, I had forgotten I was meant to be Luna.

"Um yes, Nui has been teaching me a bit." I quickly turned and pushed Luna into her own room.

"Shit. I can't believe I just did that. Sorry."

"Mai pen rai, Khun Luna!" Luna smirked. "Told you, it's difficult to keep things straight! But more food? You can't be serious." She shook her head, then flopped back onto the bed and stretched like a cat. "Can't wait to sleep in my own bed tonight."

Yeah, so much for you wanting to experience the other side, I thought, cynically. *Guess, you prefer your cushy life, after all.*

After Khun Bo dropped off some fruit and fresh coconuts, I locked the door.

"So how are we going to do this? Same as yesterday?" I asked.

"I suppose. I don't know what else we can do." Luna shrugged.

Ajaarn Anurak's taped voice sounded the same as always, but I could immediately tell it wasn't having its usual effect on me. I caught myself holding my breath trying to concentrate on his words. Every little sound from the street was distracting, when I was normally able to tune it out. Even Luna's inhale and exhale sounded exaggerated.

Uh oh, this is not the way it's supposed to be. Ajaarn's reminder to be 'here and now' didn't work either. *Why can't I relax?*

By the time we came to the 'light of compassion' part which normally deepened the trance I knew I wasn't going anywhere today, much less out of my body.

I opened my eyes. Luna was looking right at me, lips tight.

"It's not working, is it?" She whispered.

"No, not for me," I admitted. "Maybe we're just too tense right now."

"Oh yeah, and how do suggest we relax? I thought meditation is supposed to have that effect." She swallowed hard. "Shit, shit, shit! What now?"

"What if we wait a bit and try again later? We could watch a movie."

Luna shook her head. "I can't sit through a movie right now. I feel itchy all over. Let's go to the pool, I need some air."

I changed into one of Luna's swimsuits and she wore one of her bikinis as it was the only thing she could adjust for my smaller frame.

Luna didn't even sit down but dove right into the water. I almost had a heart attack.

"Luna! Are you crazy? I don't know how to swim. And wear some sunscreen! I don't want to get any darker!" It was so weird looking at my own body from the outside. *Do I have a good shape? I kind of like being tall and white and curvy like Luna.* I had never really thought about it before.

Luna came up for air and actually grinned.

"What do you mean you don't swim? See, you're doing just fine!" She turned around, kicked off, and for the next twenty minutes swam laps before collapsing into the lounge chair next to me.

"Are you mad, Nui? Why in the world are you hiding under a towel in this heat?"

"What? Oh, I forgot. You *whiteys* all like to tan but we don't."

"Yeah, I know. I'm lucky if I can find a plain body lotion without those skin whiteners here. You guys are nuts. So, get rid of the towel please. You're in the shade, anyway." Luna rolled her eyes mocking me.

"You know Luna, I keep thinking, what do we need to do if we can't switch back? There are so many things that are different for us."

"Don't start! You're the one who said it would be easy! I told you we should have tried to switch back yesterday. You're freaking me out." Luna was visibly upset and almost vibrating with frustration.

I tried again. "But, maybe we don't have to learn everything from scratch and instead let some things just come naturally. Sort of like, we speak both languages now. And the way you just jumped into the pool? I would have never done that! Pools and oceans scare me."

"I don't even want to think about staying this way. We have to make it happen. We can't be stuck like this. Let's go inside and try again, ok?" Luna jumped up and grabbed her towel.

I was still mulling it over as I followed her to the elevator. *What if... what if... what if... If only we could ask somebody for advice, but who would even listen to us, much less believe us? If we weren't able to get back into our own bodies, would I have to live with Luna's family forever and she with mine? As much as I complained about my life sometimes, I simply couldn't imagine being without my family.*

Luna disappeared into the bathroom to rinse off the chlorine. At home, by default, I had to take quick five-minute 'wash and go' showers, but that clearly didn't apply to her. When she finally reappeared, she looked like me but smelled like Luna. I shook my head.

We sat on the floor and nodded to each other. Let's do it! Luna switched on the last session we'd recorded, but pushed stop almost immediately.

"Hold on, do you think we should maybe start right at the beginning, to get back into the flow?"

"I'm not sure. The last sessions build on the earlier ones so I think it's ok to start at the end. After all, that's when we managed the 'OBE'."

"OBE? You mean 'out-of-body experience'? Seriously?" Luna smirked.

"Well, we gotta call it something, don't we? You have a better word?" I had to grin. Not all humour was lost yet.

"How about 'The Freaks'? Or 'The Body Snatchers'? Or the 'Space Walkers' or …?"

"Hahaha. That's funny." Actually, it wasn't particularly witty, but it felt good to laugh a bit.

"Ok, here we go." Luna sobered quickly and pressed start.

LUNA

AJAARN ANURAK'S SOOTHING VOICE FILLED THE ROOM. I definitely felt a bit better than during our earlier attempt, but still didn't drift off as I'd come to expect. Instead, random thoughts pinged around in my head. *What if this is permanent? Why did I agree to this? Will I have to go to the temple tomorrow? I'm going to miss Bali!* That thought alone stopped me from getting anywhere near a trancelike state.

Exasperated, I huffed out a breath and looked up.

Nui was staring at me, her eyes wide. Her voice shook. "It's still not working, is it? I keep thinking of all the stuff we have to do if we are stuck like this."

"I know, same here! Shit, what now?" My throat was tight, and my eyes started tearing up. "I'm scared Nui!"

"Me too! I am so sorry. I really didn't think it was even possible." Nui finally admitting that we had gone off track was shocking as hell, but at least I wasn't the only one freaking out.

"Well, I agreed, didn't I?" I tried to be fair, even if I wasn't happy about it.

It must have made Nui feel a little less guilty as she became all pragmatic.

"Well, it is what it is now, so let's try to be practical and figure out what we need to do. It's probably best if we go and see Ajaarn tomorrow; hopefully he can give us some advice."

"Tomorrow is your big family thingy, isn't it? Will you, I mean I, be able to get away?" If it was me I would just sneak out but I knew that Nui felt differently about family obligations.

"Oh shoot, forgot about that again! No, you're right, you have to be there both days so I guess the earliest we could go is Monday?" Nui amended.

"That's not gonna work either. Remember, Bali on Monday. Damn it, that means I will miss the entire holiday with Dad!" I was getting depressed just thinking about it. "And what am I supposed to do all week while you're gone?"

"Hmmm, I hadn't really planned anything specific. Something always pops up. My parents might need me in the store or they ask me to babysit my cousins or go to the temple with my grandparents. I haven't made plans with my friends yet. I think we just need to get through the weekend and hopefully we can get away for a little while at some point and try again."

"Oh God! How am I supposed to handle all that? You need to write me a checklist. There's bound to be some disaster!" I pushed my hands down on my skull as if that could prevent my head from exploding.

"What, you think it's going to be easier for me to be with

your family in Bali? Does that mean that I have to go and actually swim in the ocean?" Nui sounded offended.

"Ha! Bali beach holiday compared to working and babysitting during my holidays? You think that's a real contest?"

"Welcome to my life! You said you wanted to see how the other side lives," Nui countered sharply. "Besides, you know how I feel about the water, so for me it's not going to be that easy, ok?"

"Whatever."

Our emotions were all over the place. One minute we were optimistic and determined, and the next we were at each other's throats. It was time to regroup.

"Time out, Nui. Fighting isn't getting us anywhere, so let's do this. Let's play twenty questions as a starting point. Then you can walk me through what I need for tomorrow and Sunday. You have to be there! Tell my mom that it's a new cultural experience and you've been invited. What do you think we should do about our phones? Switch, or keep our own? Not sure what's better really. What if I get a message from someone I don't know, and I can't reply? But you will need an international phone plan for Bali."

"Stop, stop, stop! Go slow. It's probably best if I take yours. If I get messages for you, I'll just forward them. You reply to me and I'll send them. It'll be slow, but at least we won't mess it up. Your right thumb will unlock the phone and the password is 1103. And I'll mark my contacts, so you know who they are, ok?"

"Ok, my password is 2102. While you do that, I'll pack a bag for you for Bali. At least that part is easy. It's only five days so you don't need much."

I pulled my carry-on bag from the closet and threw in a few dresses, shorts, t-shirts and tank tops, sandals, hat, a few swimsuits, some costume jewellery, underwear, a few cosmetic items. They weren't necessarily my top choices, but there was no reason for Nui to wear my favourite items. Ok, that was petty, but I wasn't feeling very charitable at that moment.

"Start talking. What's your favourite food?" I fired off the first question.

"Gaeng Keow Wan Kai, Green Chicken Curry"

"Uh oh, problem! You know I don't eat meat."

"But chicken is not really meat, it's white." Nui objected.

"It's still an animal and I don't eat those. You eat veggies and fish, don't you?"

"Duh, fish are animals too, so that doesn't make any sense. Anyway, you know Khun Yaa, she can cook anything, and we always have vegetables and rice or noodles, so you'll be ok. Just be careful of the chillies." Nui added, cheekily.

"Here, you can just ask Khun Bo for what you want, she won't cook any meat for you though."

"Damn. I guess I'll have to manage without." Nui shrugged.

"Ok, what about drink?" I asked.

"I normally just drink water, ginger or Thai tea."

"No coffee? I need caffeine in the morning."

"There's a Starbucks near Soi ten. They open at six thirty so you can get one for your walk with Joey. Just don't get me addicted, and you'll have to finish it by the time you get home otherwise my parents will ask why you're drinking it."

"Ok, I can manage that. That reminds me, what about money? How much money do your parents give you? Will it be enough to buy the coffees?"

"Duen and I usually get one thousand Baht per week, Tum a little less, but if we need extra, we just ask them. What about you?"

I jumped up to open the drawer of a dresser where I had stashed away some money. "Hmm, one thousand isn't much. I better take some cash from here. Luke and I usually get around five thousand."

"Wow, your parents are pretty generous. Ok next, any allergies?" Nui's turn to ask.

"Nope. You?"

"Not that I know of."

Questions and answers ping-ponged back and forth.

My turn. "Clothes? No scratch that, we have to make do with what's in our closets anyway. Ok, what else? TV or books? I don't watch a lot of TV unless it's a movie with Mom."

"I don't either, except the news. I read a lot, but mainly international news and politics. Most of it is online. We don't have a lot of books at home, but I have a library card if you want to go and pick up something." Nui opened her wallet to show me the card.

I waved her off. "I'll just download the Kindle app on your phone. That way I can read from my own library and add new books. You'll need to take my Kindle with you, otherwise my parents will wonder why I'm not reading. Same log-in as my phone.

"Oh, speaking of family," Nui said. "You need to be careful. Paa is always trying to pull me into discussions about politics. He likes to provoke me. Better stay away from that."

"Well, that's easy, I don't know anything about Thai politics anyway. Ok, what about your friends?"

"Apple, you know. I'm pretty sure Toey and Dearn will be there tomorrow. I grew up with them, but they go to another school now. I'll point them out to you tomorrow. I haven't seen them that much lately so they are probably mad at me and a bit jealous of you because you and I are spending so much time together, just so you know." Nui scrolled through her photo album to show me a picture of the girls.

"Oh, great. So I have to cover for you tomorrow *and* pretend that Luna is a bitch?" I summarised, as I walked into the bathroom to pick up my favourite shampoo and body lotion. Too bad I couldn't take them with me to Nui's house.

"Don't be silly. They'll be fine. But it's probably best you don't see them next week. We go way back, so it could get confusing for you."

"Let's see what they say tomorrow. Ok, who else will be there?"

"My Aunt Varaporn and Uncle Karl—he's German. He runs a local tour company and arranges all the itineraries for foreign visitors. I think he's quite successful. They've been married for ten years or so. Grandma and Grandpa weren't very happy at first; they were worried about the whole Thai women/foreign man cliché, but they are ok with it now. I sometimes babysit their girls. Eve is six and Jenny is four. They are very sweet. You'll like them."

"Yeah, I think I can deal with little girls. Anyone else?"

"I don't know. Mom's parents can't make it. They live in Chiang Rai and it's too far for them. I'll have to tell you about anyone else when I know who's there, ok?"

"Ok, what else?"

"Can't think of anything. What about Bali? Do I have to go into the ocean?" Nui fiddled nervously with her phone and I saw her shudder briefly.

"I don't know what hotel Dad has booked but if it's anything like the last one, you'll have a great pool and won't need to go to the beach. And if I can swim as Nui, then you can definitely swim as Luna. Just try it. But remember that I don't cover up in the sun like you do. Put on some sunscreen and you'll be fine."

"Yeah, pool hopefully will be ok," I replied, making mental notes. "And yeah, yeah, no towels in the sun. I got that."

"Ok, what else?" I finished packing and sat down to sip some coconut water and mark my own phone contacts for Nui.

"I'm not one hundred percent sure what the plan is for tomorrow, but it'll probably be the same as when Krit became a monk. Grandma and Mae will be up early to start cooking. Normally, a few of the neighbours come over to help. You can just get up like normal and take Joey out. You'll have to ask Mom or Khun Yaa if they need you for anything. I'll come to the house around noon, ok?"

So far everything seemed clear. I motioned for Nui to continue.

"Everyone will arrive around twelve to eat, then we all go to the temple. I'll explain the rest tomorrow. People will probably leave by five or so, since it's New Year's Eve. Then we just clean up. If anything changes, I'll find out tomorrow when I'm there. Any questions?"

"Ha! Maybe a million or so, but I guess I'll have to wing it like last night. Just make sure you're not late, ok?"

"No, I definitely don't want to miss it. Will your mom be ok with that?"

"Don't see why not. She's probably busy with her bazaar thingy anyway, and Dad will be at work. Mom had asked if we wanted to see the fireworks from the hotel tomorrow night so just go along with what she decides, ok?"

"Sure, no problem."

"Ha! Famous last words. You know, isn't it strange that we have to do a crash course like this? How come this never came up before?"

"I know, but I suppose friendships develop over time."

"That's why I don't have any close friends, I never got the chance. You done with your phone?"

Nui nodded. "Yup, all ready. Just forward me whatever you get, ok?

Before I could get to my feet, I was hit with a wave of dread. Caught up in the twenty question game, I hadn't really thought about the consequences of our failed switchback. I swallowed hard and again felt tears threatening to fall. Nui apparently didn't have the same issue. She looked quite content with staying in my body and going to Bali. *No wonder, compared to me she has an easy ride ahead. This sucks!* I felt at once bitter, cheated and anxious. Biting back a nasty comment, I tried to steel myself.

"I better get going, it's three already."

"Ok, good luck, and I'll see you tomorrow at noon."

Nui got up and hugged me. I reciprocated half-heartedly.

I was just about to open the front door when Mom walked in.

"Oh, hi, Mo… I mean Mrs Taylor. How are you today?" God, I missed her and really wanted to hug her.

"Oh, hi, Nui. Very well, thank you and you? What have you girls been up to?"

"Nothing much really, went for a swim and worked on our essay since Luna will be away next week."

"Ah yes, that reminds me. Luna, you need to pack your bag soon," she said over my shoulder. "We have a very early start on Monday."

"Already done!" Nui sounded smug.

"Wow, what have you done with the real Luna?" Mom teased her.

I had to catch myself to not roll my eyes. Leave it to Nui to score bonus points with Mom. *Hey, they are actually my points,* I realised. The thought made me smile.

"Oh, Mrs Taylor, I have invited Luna to come to my brother's ordination ceremony tomorrow and Sunday since she's never been to one. Are you ok with that?"

"At what time?" Mom asked.

"Tomorrow from noon to five and on Sunday it starts at eight in the morning."

"And Luna agreed to get up that early on New Year's Day?"

"Yes, she said she might not get another chance."

"Ahem, I'm standing right here. I can speak for myself," Nui interjected. "Yes, I'd love to go, Mom. I'll be home in plenty of time for dinner. Is that ok?"

"Let's talk later. Remember there's also Dad's family brunch with the owners on Sunday at noon."

"Oh!" Luna hadn't mentioned that. "But I could come straight from the ordination to the brunch, no? That should work, right Nui?"

"I'm sure it will be fine."

I wanted to linger but that would only make the good-bye harder. I took a deep breath. "Ok, I better run. Text me if anything comes up, ok? Bye Mrs Taylor. Nice to see you."

"Bye Nui, and Happy New Year."

NUI

As soon as Luna left, her mom asked, "Is Luke home? I need to talk to both of you."

"I don't know, I haven't seen him. I think he's at football practice. Are you alright?" She seemed distracted.

"Ah yes, of course. I have to make some phone calls. Can you let me know when he's back?"

"Sure!" I could tell something was bothering her.

She headed to her small office near the kitchen while I returned to my room to check Luna's phone and messages. It felt like snooping, but it was no more invasive than handling her body.

Luke announced his arrival half an hour later by slamming the front door. Sounded like someone else was out of sorts too.

I walked over to her office. "Mom, Luke's back."

She was on the phone. "Can you call him?" She mouthed.

I knocked on his door, "Luke, Mom wants to talk to us."

"I want to shower first!"

"You can take one after, I think it's important. Come on."

Luke grumbled but followed me back.

Khun Susan had moved to the dining room and motioned us over.

"Ok, kids, I'm afraid I have some serious news. I spoke to your Aunt Jane today and she has been diagnosed with breast cancer and has to have surgery as soon as possible." She swallowed hard then continued. "As you can imagine, we're all very upset and Uncle Tom cannot deal with the children right now on his own. I promised I would go there to help until we know more. I'm flying to Chicago tomorrow morning and I'm not sure yet when I'll be back."

Though I didn't know who Aunt Jane was, I could tell that Luna's mom was deeply upset.

"I'm so sorry to hear that. Yes, of course, stay as long as you need to. Luke and I will be ok and we have Dad and Khun Bo here too, so don't worry about us."

"Thanks Luna. I don't want to interrupt your routine too much. Thank God next week you're still on holiday, but the week after that you'll need to be quite self-sufficient and make sure you're doing your homework, ok?"

"No problem, Mom, we'll handle it. Sorry to hear about Aunt Jane. Hope she'll be better soon." Luke added and hugged his mom.

"Thanks guys. I'm very proud of you. Your dad and I decided that it's best you still go ahead with the Bali trip. You haven't had much time with him this year, with the move and all. He's booked you rooms in the hotel for the next two days. You can have dinner there tomorrow and see the fireworks. On Sunday, you can attend the brunch and then leave for the airport Monday morning. That'll make things much easier.

Khun Bo will pop in to check on things, but otherwise, she'll have the rest of the week off. Khun Pak will take me to the airport and then come and drop you off at the hotel, ok? Ah, so many details to organize. I better get on with it! We'll have an early dinner tonight so I can finish all the arrangements, ok?"

"Sure, Mom," Luke and I said, simultaneously.

Dinner was pretty subdued but Luna's mom tried to put on a brave face. I couldn't imagine what it would be like for Aunt Varaporn to be sick with Jenny and Eve at home but entertaining thoughts like that weren't helpful.

After dinner, Luna's mom went back to packing. Khun Mark came home early but we didn't talk much as he was equally pre-occupied with the departure. I called it a night at nine and went to my room.

Checking the bag Luna had packed I added an extra dress for dinner and brunch at the hotel. I decided against texting Luna with the news as there was nothing she could do about it, and she'd only get upset. I worried she might freak out considering how upset she was earlier, and hoped she'd be calmer the next day. I felt a tad uneasy with my decision. *Are you sure you're not just saying that so she won't try and torpedo your Bali trip? Well, what could she do? Tell her parents?* I didn't want to analyse my own motivation too closely and instead switched on the TV.

LUNA

Closing the front door behind me I felt sick to my stomach. I stood still to calm myself before hitting the elevator button. Nui and I had lost control of our snowball and it was now hurtling downhill and gathering speed. What seemed like fun and games had suddenly became all too real. I wouldn't see my family until they returned from Bali. I hated that Nui called my mom 'Mom'. And on top of that, Nui would enjoy *my* spot on the beach. It was so unfair. What was I supposed to do in her stead? Work and babysit? *Stop it Luna, you wanted to experience a traditional family life. Yeah, but as me, not in someone else's place. Shit, shit, shit, why did we have to do this crazy mind swap?* Another thought popped into my head. *Hey, maybe you'll get to see Channon tomorrow.* A little tingle inside almost made me smile.

It took me forty-five minutes to get back to Nui's house.

Walking down the Soi I tried to remember all of Nui's instructions. Joey met me at the door wagging his tail.

"Hi Joey! Recognize me now? At least that's something." I whispered, as I scratched his head. "Who's home?"

There was noise and laughter coming from the kitchen. Were they already celebrating?

I stopped at the door and saw the entire family gathered around the kitchen table. Everyone was talking and laughing, including a newcomer. He grinned at me and before I could embarrass myself, he solved the puzzle.

"Hey sis, where have you been? Come and say hello." Krit, Nui's older brother!

I felt shy and just waved at him, 'Hi."

He looked taken aback. "What, I don't even get a hug?"

I wasn't used to hugging handsome, eighteen-year-old guys, even if technically Krit was my brother. Besides, Nui hadn't said anything about her relationship with him.

I walked over trying not to blush and he pulled me into a bear hug.

"Welcome home. How are things?" I mumbled against his chest.

The awkward moment was over, and the family conversation resumed at full speed. Mae and Khun Yaa kept putting food in front of Krit, and Nui's paa offered him a beer which he declined. He was planning to see some friends in town and didn't want to drink too early.

"So, Tum, ready for your big day?" Krit asked.

"Of course!" Tum puffed himself up. "I can't wait to see all the presents. Did you get me something?" *Uh oh, did I have to get Tum a present? Note to self – check with Nui.*

Krit laughed, "You know it's not about the presents, right?! I thought you learned that from your teacher."

"I know that, but I can still look forward to the presents, can't I?" Tum replied, cheekily.

"Yes, you can. But, at least pretend that it's for merit. And you, sis, what have you been up to?" Krit turned to me, "Gone on any more crusades against the government?"

"Oh, nothing much really," I frantically tried to think what Nui would say.

"Nui has been getting very deep into meditation. She and her friend Luna have been to the temple every day for almost three weeks to study," Mae volunteered.

"Wow, that's different." Krit raised his eyebrows in wonder. "How come?"

"Eh, we have an essay due on how meditation affects people of different cultures, so this was our practical experiment."

"Sounds deep to me." Krit finished his drink. "Khob Khun krub Khun Yaa, I've really missed your cooking. I better take a shower and get ready. My friend is going to pick me up soon. Mae, what time do we start tomorrow?"

"Grandma and I start early. Nui will go with Paa to the shop and Duen will help us here. You can sleep in tomorrow, but we'll eat at twelve thirty latest."

"Ok, great. Good to be home. Oh, by the way I've invited a friend for tomorrow. I haven't seen him in a while and he lives in the neighbourhood. He said he'd like to come to the temple too."

Perfect timing! I jumped in. "Me too. I've invited Luna. She's never been to an ordination."

"She's welcome to come, but will she understand what's going on if she doesn't speak Thai?" Mae asked.

"Oh, she's learned a lot since you last saw her, and I can translate the rest for her, not a problem. Thanks Mae." One issue solved.

I finished eating my rice, green curry and morning glory. The chicken bits had gone to the side on my plate. In my peripheral vision I could see grandma glance at my plate and shake her head in disapproval, but thankfully she didn't say anything about my 'new' eating habits. Not sure how long that was going to last; food was her pride.

"Nui, you must be at the shop tomorrow eight thirty, latest, to help Paa while I'm here. There was a leak after the thunderstorm yesterday and we had to clean most of the shelves and they have to be restocked. Pop will be there earlier to get started but we need to be open by ten."

"Sure, no problem."

Dinner was finished much earlier than apparently normal, but we all had a long day ahead and would try to go to bed early. This time I had kitchen duty. The washing and drying I could just about figure out but didn't really know where everything went. Thankfully, Grandma was still bustling about and ended up putting the utensils and dishes where they belonged. Krit's arrival must have distracted her from her earlier threat to interrogate me. Just in case, I quickly left the kitchen before she could bring it up. I even remembered to feed Joey this time, and as an apology for the night before I took some treats for our nightly walk.

Krit had left by the time I got back. A new towel, blue this time, hung on a hook to dry. I took a quick shower, still not quite daring to look too closely at Nui's naked body. I was in bed by nine, mentally rehearsing the things I had to do the next day and feeling sad about missing our family holiday. *This sucks*!

32

NUI

I SLEPT IN FITS AND STARTS AND WAS WIDE AWAKE BY SIX.
Luna's parents were having coffee in the dining room and I
could hear Khun Bo already in the kitchen. She probably had
to clean and lock up after we had all left. Luna's dad said he
would go to the hotel later for New Year's Eve preparation
but would wait until Khun Susan had left. I realized they
probably had forgotten about the ordination, but if she left by
eleven, I could still make it on time.

I grabbed the bowl of cereal that Pi' Bo had put out for
me, wishing it was congee. Luna's mom was writing instructions on what to do while she was gone.

"I'm not sure who to delegate this to, Mark. I know your
people are all set with the event order, but I suppose I'll have
to ask Sonia to make decisions on behalf of the committee."
She distractedly nodded at me while continuing her conversation with Luna's dad.

"Is that the bazaar you mentioned, Mom? I'll be there and I'll fill in wherever I can," I volunteered.

"Thanks, sweetie. I'll ask Sonia to assign a task for you on the day, ok?" Mom smiled. "Maybe you can be the go-between for the hotel and the organizers."

"Erm, sure, I'd love to. By the way, I can still go to Nui's brother's ordination, right?" I thought it best to bring it up while I was in her good graces.

"Do you really have to, today of all days, Luna? Khun Pak is supposed to pick you and Luke up after he drops me at the airport. You can use the pool at the hotel and have lunch there."

"But, Mom, I only will get to see this once and I promised Nui. Luke can take my luggage with him and I'll come to the hotel by skytrain in time for dinner, ok?"

"I suppose, but make sure you're there by six, ok?"

"No problem."

Khun Susan eventually took off at eleven, and though she wasn't my real mom I still felt teary-eyed when she hugged and kissed me goodbye. "I'll call you as soon as I land. Look after your brother, ok? Love you!"

"Love you too." It felt extremely strange to say this to anyone but my own family, but it seemed appropriate.

33

LUNA

I SLEPT BETTER THAT NIGHT, MAINLY BECAUSE I WAS WORN-out. Joey had moved into the bedroom at some point and was curled up on the floor next to my bed.

Only six-thirty and there was already noise coming from the kitchen. Grabbing shorts and a t-shirt, I dashed into the bathroom to brush my teeth and get dressed. Joey was waiting for me when I got out. I remembered to take my wallet and a couple of plastic bags.

"Morning Mae, Khun Yaa. I'm going to take Joey out. I can help you when I'm back."

"We're ok here, and we have Khun Pichamon and Khun Pang coming to help. The kitchen gets too crowded." Grandma waved me off.

I figured they must be the neighbours that Nui had mentioned. *Too many names to remember.*

The pack of Soi dogs was back but they barely lifted their

heads as we walked by. Pi' Ohm was at her stall, but it was Saturday and still too early for her regular customers; only five seats were occupied. *Maybe she'll be nicer if I buy some food from her.* Thai omelette seemed to be the best option, even if she put quite a few chillies in it.

"Good morning Pi' Ohm. Sabai di mai kha?"

"Hrmph sabai di. What do you want?" she grumbled.

"May I have an omelette please? And see, I remembered the bags this time." I waved the bags like some great trophy, feeling silly.

Another mumble but her face remained stoic. I found it hard to read Asian expressions at the best of times and without verbal clues I was lost. *Suit yourself! At least I tried.* I turned around and had a distinct sense of déjà vu staring into those beautiful brown eyes. *How does he manage to sneak up on me like this?*

"Good morning, Nui. You're up early on a weekend," Channon grinned.

"Oh, hi, good morning. Well, Joey still needed to go out." I stammered. "Oh, and thanks for cleaning up after him yesterday. I'm so sorry about that," I added, blushing.

"No problem. Glad I could help. You ordered breakfast? Can I join you? It's so boring to eat by yourself."

"Oh, erm, sure." I felt tongue-tied.

Joey was still content to wander around the little park, so I sat down and almost immediately, Pi' Ohm called me to pick up my order.

"I'll get it," Channon offered.

He had a bowl of noodle soup which actually smelled quite good, even if there were meat balls in it.

"You must live around here if you come to the park every morning?" Channon asked. He expertly picked up noodles with his chopsticks, put them into the spoon and slurped them together with the broth. Not your typical Western style of eating, but I thought it was cute. *Get a grip, Luna.*

"Yes, just around the corner on Soi fourteen. What about you?" The omelette was excellent but had quite a kick with those chillies. I carefully dug some out and pushed them to the side.

"I'm staying with friends nearby right now. I'm an intern at the pet hospital on Soi nine. Do you know it? Maybe you take Joey there?"

"Oh? Why are you doing an internship there?"

"I'm going to be a veterinarian, but I had to postpone my first semester at Mahidol to get my military service out of the way. The new semester starts in March, so I thought it would be good to get some hands-on experience."

"A vet? That's cool! How did you decide on that?"

"It's something I've always wanted to do. I love animals and if I can be around them all day *and* help them, that's even better. What about you? You're still in school, aren't you?"

"Yes, twelfth grade at BIS. I'm not a hundred percent sure yet what I want to do after but I'm interested in politics and journalism." I repeated what Nui had told me. Personally, I hadn't made up my mind yet or even given it much thought.

"You still have a bit of time I suppose. Maybe you should come to the hospital one day and see what we do there. It's not just about medicine, we also do training and even adoption. And you like dogs, right?" Channon winked at me and I felt heat rising to my face.

Is he flirting with me? Stop. Reality check! He's flirting with Nui, not me. Somehow, that thought was deflating.

"Sure, I'd like that. Soi nine is very close and we still have another week off."

"Come next week and I'll show you around. We could

meet here or at the hospital. Speaking of. I better go. Happy New Year, Nui. See you next week."

"Bye, Channon."

I stood too, to collect Joey and walk back home. *Shower, then shop, but first coffee.* I tried to finish it quickly before getting home and ended up burning my tongue. *Ouch! Next time I'll do this the other way around. First coffee, then breakfast with Channon?* I smiled. *Getting ahead of yourself, Luna?*

There was a racket coming out of the kitchen when I got back. *Can they even hear each other?* While Mom and Grandma were busy with the neighbours, I slipped into my room to grab some fresh clothes. Naturally, the tassel was on the bathroom door. Duen was still in bed so it had to be one of the boys. I knocked to let him know that there was a line.

"Five minutes." Tum.

"Hurry up! I need to go to the shop."

"I get extra time because it's my special day!" He declared.

"Ha! In your dreams! You're not getting any cleaner anyway so hurry up." *Gosh teenage boys were really all the same. Thank God Luke had his own bathroom.*

Uff! I had been so caught up in meeting Channon that I'd completely forgotten my own family for a while. Not sure if that was a good or bad thing.

"Hurry up Tum, I'm going to be late." I was sure he lingered on purpose just to annoy me, something my dear brother would do.

"You're supposed to be respectful to a monk!" Tum complained.

"Ha, you're not a monk yet so that doesn't count."

The door finally opened and a whoosh of hot air rushed out.

"What have you been doing in there? Looks like a steam sauna."

Tum ignored me and wandered off to his own room.

I showered and dressed in a plain blue skirt, white t-shirt and flip flops, figuring I could change later for the temple if I needed to.

Duen was awake but still in bed. "Nui, can I borrow your blue dress for today, you know the one with the red flowers?"

I had no idea what dress she was talking about but figured that sisters most likely shared clothes regularly.

"Sure, go ahead. I gotta go to the shop. See you later."

Dashing out, I quickly stopped in the kitchen to let Mae and Grandma know I was on my way. Two other women were busy pounding chillies in a stone mortar and cutting vegetables at the table, but since I didn't know them I simply wai'ed to both and backed out.

"Nui, before you go, put Joey into the backyard, so he doesn't get in the way," Mae called.

"Ok, bye."

Joey didn't seem too keen on the idea but at least there was shade in the yard and his food and water bowls were there too, so he'd be fine.

NUI

BY THE TIME I FINALLY LEFT THE HOUSE I WAS SERIOUSLY late. Luna's dad had asked me to make sure Luke was ready when the driver came back from the airport run. And, of course, the little idiot hadn't finished packing and was playing computer games. I felt like screaming at him, but knew that wouldn't help, so instead I grabbed the iPad out of his hand and refused to hand it back until he had closed his suitcase. Running out the door, I remembered I needed money from Luna's stash to give my family as a gift for the ordination. There was no time to get an extra present for Tum right now. I'd make up for that later or tell Luna to buy him that new Monopoly Fortnite game I had seen recently. I knew he liked both games so the combo would be perfect for him even if he wouldn't be able to use it until he was back from the temple.

I debated taking the skytrain or a taxi, but figured

Saturday morning traffic wouldn't be a problem, and it would be faster in a taxi. Besides, I'd had a few texts from Luna and preferred to read them in a car. Naturally, that didn't work out, so I jumped out of the cab and onto a moto-taxi instead. I just had to make sure Luna didn't see me, in her body, arriving on a bike; she considered them 'death traps'. All the while I was still trying to figure out how to break the news her mother had left, gently.

LUNA

THE MALL WAS ONLY A FEW SOIS DOWN THONG LO AND THE temperature wasn't too high yet. It was quite a nice stroll.

The Pantry sold basic kitchen pots and pans, dishes, glasses, some hardware items and household linen. It wasn't fancy, but had a good selection at reasonable prices. It was also in a convenient location and was doing quite well, according to Nui. The door was still locked but Pi' Pop heard my knock and let me in.

"Hi Nong Nui. How are you?" She smiled. "Big day today for the family."

"Hi Pi' Pop. Yes, the house is already getting busy. What do you need me to do here? Is Paa around?"

"Yes, he's in the back sorting out deliveries. We have to put the store back together now the leak has been fixed. You can help me with the shelves over here. It'll be quicker if we do it together."

"Sure, no problem."

For the next hour, Pop and I moved around putting merchandise back where it belonged. It was mindless activity for me but I was intrigued by some of the items. I never knew there was such a variety of woks and steamer baskets. Those alone took up two shelves. Mortars and pestles in twenty different materials and sizes, rice cookers, cleavers, cutting boards, and some items I wasn't familiar with, but I couldn't ask Pop what they were; my ignorance would have been obvious.

By ten the store looked presentable and Pi' Pop opened the doors. I still hadn't seen Nui's dad, but figured he'd call me if he needed to. Custom was slow but Pi' Pop predicted a rush as people were going to be cooking family dinners for New Year's Eve. I texted Nui to come to the store at noon. No response. I wondered what she was up to. There hadn't been anything particular on the schedule that morning.

The next two hours flew by quickly, the shop became busier as Pop had predicted. I wrapped up purchases and helped customers find things in the shop. Restocking had made it easier for me to locate the items now.

At noon, Nui's paa came out of the back to say we would have to leave. No sign of Nui yet, and I was getting nervous. *Where is she?* I sent another text. Again, no response. *She better be at the house, otherwise there's going to be trouble.*

I felt sweaty and dusty by the time we arrived home. I would have loved to take another shower, but there were already people standing on the front porch, and the entrance was wide open with more guests spilling into the hallway. *So much for a break!*

Nui's paa jumped right in, shouting greetings left and right, slapping shoulders and shaking hands. I had absolutely no idea who these people were, but smiled and pretended to be equally excited to see them. I wai'ed a lot too, to be on the safe side.

There must have been at least forty people in the house. The air-con was cranked up high but didn't make much of a difference, as the doors to the backyard and front were wide open. A few picnic tables and stools had been arranged in the yard and women were carrying bowls, plates and glasses to set up a buffet. The living room was packed with older people and Tum was holding court.

"Pi' Nui!" Two arms wrapped around my waist. "I missed you!"

A second pair of arms went around my legs, almost tripping me, and a small voice piped up: "Me too, me too!" I looked down at two beautiful girls around five years old. *Ah, they must be Jenny and Eve, Nui's cousins.* They were absolutely gorgeous. Big blue eyes, lightly tanned skin and wavy dark hair. *Thailand's next supermodels!* I grinned and bent down to hug them. "Hi girls. I've missed you too! How are you?"

"Can we play with you Pi' Nui?" The older one asked.

"Of course, but first I need to see if Mae or Khun Yaa need help, ok? Where are your parents?"

"Mae is in the kitchen and Papa is not here yet."

"Ok, give me five minutes and I'll meet you in the backyard. Can you find Joey for me? He's probably scared with all these people here. We can put him in my bedroom." They dashed off to rescue him.

I had to squeeze by people in the hallway to look inside the kitchen, which was packed with women fussing around, gossiping and laughing at full volume. I saw Duen somewhere in the middle. There was no way I could add anything to it, so I backed out. *Ok, now what? Where the heck is Nui?*

"Hey sis, have you met my friend yet?" Krit threw an arm

around my shoulder. "Channon, this is Nui; Nui, this is Channon."

OH MY GOD! No way! This is a trick, right?

Channon burst out laughing, "Believe it or not, Krit, we had breakfast together this morning. Hi Nui, long time."

Krit's expression was priceless. "Ooh? How come? Something I should know?"

"Just coincidence. We happened to be at Pi' Ohm's at the same time when I took Joey out. It was so hectic here this morning and there was no time for breakfast. How do you two know each other?"

"Channon and I overlapped at military; he was in one of my training classes. He's now working at the pet hospital on Soi nine, so I told him to come by."

"Nui is going to come with me to the hospital next week. She wants to see what we're doing there, right Nui?"

Krit raised an eyebrow. "Really?" He sounded suspicious.

"Yes, really." *Since when do I have to ask him for permission? Oops, maybe Nui would have checked. Serves her right for not being here.*

Just then, I felt a tap on my shoulder. Turning around I faced myself. *Yikes, this is freaky.* I shuddered involuntarily. Hearing my own voice was equally bizarre.

"Hey Nui, I'm so sorry I'm late. Something came up. I'll tell you later."

She was wearing one of my favourite light blue dresses and I felt completely underdressed and icky now, especially standing next to Channon. *She told me this celebration was casual, so why has she dressed up?* I was peeved.

She smiled at the guys and greeted her own brother. "Hi, you must be Krit, right? I'm Luna, Nui's friend."

"Hi Luna, nice to meet you. Wow, where did you learn to speak Thai like this?" Krit was impressed.

"Oh, I've been hanging out with Nui and practising. Still working on the tones though." Nui downplayed our newfound language skills.

"Hello, I'm Channon, Krit and Nui's friend." He introduced himself and smiled at her.

"Nice to meet you too. Am I late?"

"No, no we're just starting, come with me and I'll explain what's happening," I replied.

Before we could turn around, a rocket shot from the living room and launched itself at Nui.

She laughed and bent down to pat Joey's head and ears, "Oh hi, Joey, there you are. Have you been a good boy?" He wiggled with delight.

Krit scratched his chin. "How strange. I've never seen him behave like that with a visitor. You must have gotten to know him quite well, Luna?"

"Something like that." Nui mumbled.

Channon was laughing. "Maybe she's a dog whisperer."

Eve and Jenny, hot on Joey's heals, stopped in their tracks when they spotted Nui.

Nui noticed them and grinned. "Hi girls, you must be Nui's cousins, Eve and Jenny, right?"

They smiled back shyly and politely wai'ed, but curiosity trumped caution. "You have eyes like us!" Jenny pointed out. "But why is your hair so yellow?' Classic child talk. I grinned.

Nui laughed. "I don't really know. It's always been like that. But I like yours better. So pretty."

The girls accepted the compliment as a given. "Do you want to play with us and Nui?" Eve asked, eagerly.

I intervened. "Give us a minute girls. I need to talk to Luna first. Why don't you go ahead and save us a spot, ok?"

I pulled Nui towards the back of the house; we had things

to discuss. We ducked into my, well, *her* room, Joey almost tripping us up in his eagerness to stay close.

"Who is Channon?" Nui immediately asked. "Is this the guy from Pi' Ohm's? Why is he here and why am I his friend?"

"He's Krit's friend really, but I didn't know until just now. I ran into him at Pi' Ohm's this morning again and we had breakfast together, ok? Nothing to it."

Nui wasn't distracted that easily, "Hmm, and he already calls you his friend? He's really handsome," she added with a wink. "Just be careful when Krit or the family is around, they are very protective that way."

I rolled my eyes, "Don't worry, there's nothing going on. He helped me out with Joey yesterday and I agreed to go to the pet hospital with him next week. Quit stalling. Why are you so late?"

"You know your Aunt Jane in Chicago?" Nui began.

"Yeah, why? What's up?" I motioned for her to speed up whatever she had to tell me.

"I didn't know if I should text you or tell you in person, but she has been diagnosed with breast cancer and has to have surgery."

"Oh my God! Oh no! She's Mom's only sister." I sat down on my bed with a heavy sigh. Though I had only met Aunt Jane a few times, I really liked her, and I knew she and Mom were close. "That is terrible news! And her kids are still so young. How is Mom handling it?"

"She is pretty upset. She left this morning for Chicago to help them."

"She what?! Mom left, and you didn't tell me? I didn't even get to say goodbye! How could you?!" I was at once angry and worried. "I can't believe you did this to me."

"I'm sorry Luna, but what was I supposed to do? I could hardly ask your mom if it was ok for Nui to come over to say goodbye, could I?"

Logically, I knew she was right, but I still felt like crying for both Mom and Aunt Jane.

"Still… How long will she be away for?" I sniffled.

"She said she'll let us know when she gets there. It will depend on the situation, but at least one week, if not two. She doesn't know yet. She said she wanted us to go ahead with the Bali trip anyway since you hadn't seen your dad much lately. So, tonight and tomorrow, Luke and I are staying in the hotel and we'll leave from there for Bali on Monday. I know this is all screwed up, but it came out of the blue. There was nothing I could do about it."

"This is getting worse by the second. What the hell did we do, Nui? We gotta switch back, now. This has to stop." I jumped up to lock the bedroom door, only then remembering there was no lock on this door either. I felt like tearing my hair out. *Can nothing go right these days?*

"I know, I'm really sorry Luna. I wish I could make it all go away. I don't think we have time to meditate right now, we need to get back or people will come looking for us."

"I can't just keep pretending; I'm too upset!" Deep down, I knew complaining wouldn't change anything, but it felt good to vent anyway. "This is so screwed up!" *Come on Luna, pull yourself together. You can do this.* "So, what comes next?"

"So, while people are eating, the family will go to Wat Pasee for the pre-ordination. It's only a few minutes by car but tomorrow we'll walk there in a procession. I just need to see if I can get away tomorrow 'cause there's the brunch too."

"You better be here!"

"Yes, yes, I'll definitely try, but what do I tell your dad?" Nui shrugged indecisively.

"Don't just try, tell Dad that the family expects you. It's a great honour to be invited. Make something up. You know better than I what it means. He'll buy it if you say it's about Thai culture."

"Fine! Ok, so today you go with the family. There will be a bit of chanting and praying by the monks. And then the hair-cutting. You don't need to do anything else. Just take your cues from Krit and Duen. The whole thing shouldn't take more than an hour. When you come back here, people will give Tum some gifts and Mae and Paa will give him the orange robes. And then everyone leaves. So, pretty easy," Nui explained.

"If it's only for the family, will you be able to come? After all, you're a farang now." I couldn't help the dig.

"Mae and Paa should be ok with it, but we'll have to ask anyway, for form's sake. If not, I'll stay here and play with the girls and you'll be back in an hour anyway."

"And tomorrow? That's a much bigger deal, no?" I was nervous I might commit some terrible faux pas.

"Tomorrow will be the actual ordination. So, everyone walks from here at eight. It's more formal. I'll have to show you how to wear a Thai skirt." Nui got up to open the closet. "They are wrapped around a few times. You can either wear a blouse or a t-shirt with it. It'll be hot when you walk."

She shook out a beautiful dark red silk fabric. "Basically, it's an open piece that you wrap around your waist. Then you tie it really tight and you fold over the top, so the tie doesn't show." She started to demonstrate when the door banged open.

Duen poked her head in. She looked at Nui in Luna's

dress and Thai skirt and started giggling. "What are you doing, Luna? That looks pretty funny. Is this some new fashion trend?" Turning to me. "Nui, Mae and Paa want to get going. Why are you crying? Are you ready?"

I wiped my eyes. "It's nothing. I'm coming."

We left Joey in the bedroom and squeezed through the crowded hallway. The noise was worse than if we were standing in the middle of a busy intersection.

I tracked Mae down near the front door and quickly asked her if it was ok for Luna to come. She probably didn't hear me but nodded anyway, "Let's go, let's go. We don't want to be late."

Channon was standing next to Krit and apparently was coming too, though I didn't know what his reason was. He glanced at me and Nui a few times, probably wondering why I had glassy eyes. I couldn't worry about that right now.

A tall blond man, Uncle Karl, carried Jenny in his arms and Aunt Varaporn held Eve by her hand. We all piled into cars, Paa driving his parents, Mae and Tum. Krit had Channon, Nui and myself, and Duen rode with Uncle Karl and his family.

The ride was short, and the ceremony went by in a blur. I couldn't concentrate. Krit had to nudge me when it was time for me to cut Tum's hair. Sitting back down, I noticed Nui wiping her eyes, furtively. This was a much bigger deal for her than I thought. We stopped at a klong behind the temple to put the collected hair on a lotus leaf into the water, supposedly for good luck. By the time we got home, the party was in full swing. Nui and I finally got to play with the girls for a while, but by five o'clock everyone started to drift off to get ready for their New Year's Eve celebrations. Songkran, the official Thai New Year, was in April, but most people took the opportunity to celebrate both. Nui had to rush off as well and we didn't have time for another chat, but maybe that was for the better. I was still upset and needed time to process everything.

36

NUI

I STOPPED AT THE HOTEL'S FRONT DESK TO GET MY KEY. THEY said that Luke's room was next to mine but the connecting door was closed. Thankfully, my luggage was waiting for me. I jumped into the shower. It was huge, but probably normal by hotel standards. All kinds of soaps, shampoos and conditioners were lined up on a shelf, and I let myself indulge, dancing under the spray. *I could get used to this, but who knows when I'll get another chance? Duh! You're going to Bali.* I had to laugh. I studied myself, or rather Luna, in the mirror. *Hmm, I kind of like having some curves instead of my own flat body and chest. I wonder what she thinks about my body.* Running my hands over her body did feel invasive though and I quickly finished dressing. It felt odd wearing a bra; I usually couldn't be bothered and didn't really need to. I was glad Luna had done the packing as I would have forgotten. Her hair took much longer to dry than mine and I didn't quite know how to style it as mine fell straight down, naturally. I would have to allow extra time in future. *Hang on Nui, you're switching back as soon as possible. Don't get used to this.*

Luna's mom had texted from Taipei, but was now in the air again, on her way to Chicago. She was due to land at nine tomorrow morning, Bangkok time. I felt sorry for her having to spend New Year's Eve on a plane alone while worrying about her sister.

Dinner was booked at the Italian restaurant for eight o'clock. Five minutes before, I knocked on the connecting door.

"Let's go, Luke."

———

GIANNI, THE MAÎTRE D' WELCOMED US LIKE FAMILY. "LUNA, Luke! Welcome to Ravello! I'm so happy that you picked my restaurant for tonight. I've reserved the best table for you, naturally." I had seen Gianni in action before. He greeted everyone in the same effusive manner and guests really liked it. Luna had explained that the majority of the staff were Thai, but the restaurant managers and main chefs were farangs, to give the hotel a multi-cultural touch. *Guess that's why the prices are so high and only expats and affluent high-society 'hi-so', can afford it.* I mentally admonished myself. *That's hypocritical Nui; you're taking advantage of it too.*

"Your father said you should go ahead and order. He'll be here shortly." Luna's dad was probably doing his rounds, checking that everything was in place for the evening. At eleven all guests would join the countdown party in the lobby, which had already been cleared of most furniture. I had never been to a fancy New Year's Eve party before and was looking forward to it.

37

LUNA

K<small>HUN</small> Y<small>AA</small> <small>AND</small> M<small>AE</small> <small>ORGANIZED THE CLEAN-UP.</small> B<small>Y SIX</small>-thirty we all finally sat down. The men had beers and everyone else sipped home-made lemonade. Channon was still there; he and Krit were going out later to a New Year's Eve party.

"What are you doing for New Year's Eve, Nui?" Channon asked.

"Erm, no plans really. It's been a long day." Besides, I had expected to be at the hotel with Mom and Dad.

"Nui, why don't you go with Krit and Channon? Just come home right after midnight, ok?" Mae suggested. "Krit will look after you, won't you Krit?"

"Huh? I don't think so. They are going to a private party," I stammered.

"Chai, you should come, Nui. We're only going to a friend's house on Soi eleven. They always have a big party on

New Year's Eve and we'll watch the fireworks from there. It's pretty casual," Krit concurred.

"Yes, come Nui!" Channon chimed in. "Better than sitting at home on New Year's. No offense." He smiled at Mom.

"It'll be good for you to get out a bit; you've been studying so hard lately. Have a bit of fun," Mom insisted.

I couldn't believe it. Nui said her parents were overly traditional, yet her mom was basically kicking me out to go and party! Maybe she was worried because of my meltdown the night before.

"Err, I'm not sure, and I'm pretty tired too."

"Oh, come on sis, I haven't seen you in a while and it'll give us a chance to catch up. It won't be a late night, anyway. I have to go back to Hua Hin tomorrow. Take a nap if you want. We'll leave by eight-thirty, ok, khrup?" Krit persisted.

"Hmm, I guess." *Uh God, what have I let myself in for?*

As soon as I got to my room, I texted Nui. "I'm going to a party with Krit and Channon. What should I wear?"

I was too keyed up to nap, so I decided to take a long overdue shower. I could still hear the family talking in the kitchen.

Nui's response was brief. "Fun. Mom ok with it? Def the red stretchy dress!"

NUI

GIANNI SEATED US IN A SMALL ALCOVE THAT OVERLOOKED the restaurant. "Very sorry to hear your mom won't be able to join you tonight."

"Yeah, she had a family emergency," Luke explained.

"Allora, we'll make sure you have a good time, anyway." Gianni positively beamed. "We do have a set menu for tonight, but you are, of course, free to order anything you like. I'll give you both menus and you can decide. And I'll get some bread and water for you in the meantime."

It felt nice to be treated like a VIP. Other guests were glancing our way, probably wondering who these kids were.

"What do you feel like eating, Luke?"

"I'm just going to have some Parma ham without the melon, and then spaghetti Bolognese. And then tiramisu. I don't like all the fancy food on the set menu."

The menu was six courses which was also too much for me, but I liked the sound of some of the dishes.

Gianni returned with bottles of still and sparkling water. A waitress behind him set down a breadbasket and poured olive oil on our bread dishes and topped it up with some balsamic vinegar.

"Allora, have you decided?"

Luke placed his order.

"Gianni, can I just have a few things off the set menu, not the whole thing?" I asked.

"Of course, you can, what would you like?"

"I'd like the beef carpaccio please."

"Ha! So, you're eating meat again Luna?" Luke snorted. "I knew your vegetarian fad wouldn't last."

Damn, I had completely forgotten that Luna was vegetarian. But, if she can decide what to eat, why can't I?

"I've decided to try it again once in a while," I shrugged, as if it wasn't a big deal.

"Yeah, right!" He smirked.

"Sorry Gianni. So, I'm having the carpaccio and then the pan-fried sea bass with the cannellini mash. Not sure yet about dessert. I'll decide later, ok?"

"No problem. I'll get that started for you. Do you want anything else to drink?"

"Can I have a coke, please?" Luke asked

"No, you cannot!" Luna's dad materialized beside Gianni. "You'll be up all night."

"But, Dad! It's New Year's Eve. I have to be up at least until midnight. Please!"

His dad relented, "Ok, just one. Luna, you want one too?"

"No, thank you. I'll just have water."

"Did you order already?"

"Yes, but just an appetizer and main course. The whole menu looks too much."

"Ok, Gianni, can you bring me some Parma ham and melon and then I'll have the lamb. And a glass of the house red. Thank you."

"Prego." Gianni filled Khun Mark's water glass and left.

"How was the ceremony, Luna? Did you enjoy it?" Luna's dad asked, while dunking some focaccia into the olive oil.

"It was really interesting. The entire neighbourhood was there to celebrate. Tomorrow, I have to leave here by latest seven-fifteen for the ordination. We're going to the temple at eight."

"I'm sorry Luna, but I don't think that's a good idea. It's going to be a late night and we have the brunch tomorrow, so you need to be here at noon. I have to work in the morning, to be ready for Monday." Khun Mark shook his head apologetically.

"But, Dad! I promised Nui. Her family is expecting me and I'm not going to get another chance to see this." Luna would kill me if I didn't go.

"I know, Luna, but circumstances have changed, and I need you here for Luke." He stood firm.

"But that's not fair. All he'll do anyway is go to the pool or play computer games. I won't be gone long. Please! I don't want to disappoint Nui. And you always said we should learn more about the local culture, kha." I'm not sure I would have dared to argue like that with my own paa, but it was important for me to be at the ceremony, for my own family.

"Why do you keep saying kha Luna?" Luke asked but didn't wait for a response. Instead he turned to his father and surprised me. "Dad, I'm twelve years old and I don't need a babysitter! And you're here anyway if I need you."

"Alright, alright. Ganging up on me, huh?" His father grinned. "Fine, Luna, you can go, but please be back by noon. We're hosting the family of the Thai owner representative and you can't be late for that, ok?"

"Sure, Dad. Thank you. I'll be here on time. By the way, what time do we leave on Monday, and where are we staying?" *Better change the topic.*

"We're on the nine-thirty Thai Airways flight, so we leave here by seven-thirty, sharp. There shouldn't be too much traffic at that time, and we're in business class so we can go through fast track."

"And where are we staying?"

"We're in Jimbaran, at a new hotel right next to the Four Seasons where we stayed last time."

"Oh, good so we're on the same beach! I liked it there," Luke approved.

"You guys are clearly spoiled," His dad shook his head but smiled. "Next time you'll fly in eco and we're staying in a three-star."

"As if!" Luke scoffed. "You gotta have some benefits from working in the hotel industry, at least that's what you always say."

"Touché! But I don't see *you* working for it, Luke."

"Duh, I'm still in school."

"A kid who doesn't need a babysitter anymore, right?" Khun Mark countered. "What about you Luna? You looking forward to it too? I'm sorry Mom can't be there, but we'll have a good time anyway, right?"

"Sure, Dad. It'll be great. Just wondering, how many years do you have to work in the hotel industry to get all those perks?" *Perks sounded good to me, especially if they involved travelling.*

"Well, that depends on the company you work for, and to

some extent, your level of seniority. Why are you asking? Did we finally convince you to join the business after all?" He winked at me.

It had never occurred to me before, but while talking to Luna's dad, I realized that a hotel job might be a good way to travel. After all, that's why Luna had been to so many places.

"Maybe. I haven't really thought about it. What would I have to do?"

Luke rolled his eyes and mouthed an exaggerated 'No!'. Apparently it wasn't the first time the subject had come up.

Our first course arrived, and Luna's dad launched into his spiel with relish. He never even commented on my meat dish.

"Well, it totally depends on what you are interested in doing. You know, your mom and I both went to hotel school and had summer jobs in hotels. That's probably the fastest way. We could take a look at some schools when we're in the States for Songkran. What are you thinking about?"

"Oh, just looking at some options. Nothing specific yet," I hedged.

"You know, you could always do an internship in a hotel first, to see if you like it. And it helps that you already speak a few languages."

"Ha, you could make beds and do the dishes." Luke laughed, his payback to me for encouraging his dad.

"Luke! Show some respect. Do you have any idea how hard it is to make those beds that you like to sleep in?"

"Sorry, Dad. I just don't see Luna doing it."

"It's a good idea to work in each department in the hotel for a little while. You get to appreciate how hard everyone works, and how it all ties together."

Wow, I had no idea Luna's dad would get so passionate about this. Somehow, I had assumed he worked in hotels to make big money, and didn't really care about the rest. No wonder his people liked him.

"That sounds like an idea."

"Think about it, Luna. If you wanted to go to a Uni with a hospitality programme, there are some good ones in the U.S."

"Ok, let me think it over. Maybe an internship is a good idea."

Our second course arrived and the conversation became more general. The food was excellent. I felt full, and declined dessert.

Khun Mark had to leave to make another round of the hotel, but would meet us for the countdown. The lobby was packed with elegantly dressed people sipping wines and cocktails. A seven-piece live band was playing in the background and some guests were dancing. It all looked very glamorous.

Luna's dad brought me a half glass of champagne to toast at midnight. Luke got a flute too but his contained sparkling water. The New Year couldn't have started on a more exciting note. It was going to be epic. I fell asleep with a grin on my face.

39

LUNA

THE DRESS WAS MUCH SHORTER AND TIGHTER THAN I WOULD normally have chosen, but on Nui's small body it looked perfect, and sexy. *Is this how actors feel when they are in costume?* I messed around for a while with Nui's limited selection of earrings and bangles, but decided less was more especially with such an eye-catching dress.

Krit gave me a thumbs up when I walked back into the kitchen, and from his appreciative smile, I could tell Channon liked what he saw too. I stood up straighter.

Neither wanted to drive as they'd already had a drink and figured there would be police controls all over the city tonight. Though Soi eleven wasn't that far away, it took us almost an hour by taxi to get to their friend's house. All the restaurants and clubs on the street were packed, and hundreds of people were jostling and jaywalking every which way.

"Skytrain would have been faster," Krit grumbled. We finally left the cab and walked the last stretch to the house. The strappy heels started to pinch my toes. A guard at the door checked us off on a list and waved us through to the elevator.

From the outside, the building didn't look like much, but stepping off on the twenty-third floor, we entered a new dimension. A massive open space with lots of windows and several balconies was divided into living and dining areas, and a staircase at the far end led to another floor above.

"Wow, this is huge." I was seriously impressed.

"I know! Sirichai comes from big money. The family owns several department stores here and in Chiang Mai. Come, I'll introduce you," Krit grabbed my arm and walked into the room.

At least fifty people were standing around chatting, while some kids chased each other around. Uniformed waiters slipped in and out of the crowd offering drinks and canapés on trays. We approached a small group standing near the entrance.

"Hi Sirichai," Krit greeted a tall Indian-looking guy dressed in designer clothes.

"Hey guys, so glad you made it. Krit, Channon, come meet my parents."

"Eh, Sri, this is my sister Nui. I hope you don't mind that she came along." *Great, now he makes it sound like I begged to go!*

"Hi Nui, good to meet you. Nice dress. How come Krit never told me about his beautiful sister?" Sirichai's smile felt creepy, like he was sizing me up.

"Thanks for having us. You have a very nice home. And likewise, how come Krit never told me about you either?" *This came out sharper than I intended but what the heck?*

Two can play that game! I had learned to do small talk with the best of them at Dad's functions.

Krit raised an eyebrow at me in surprise. *Oops, maybe that was rude*? But it was justified, I decided.

Channon laughed. "Score: Nui one, Sri zero. Guess, Sri, you gotta polish that charm a bit."

Sri's eyes narrowed. "Oh, don't worry. I'm sure I'll get even."

Geez, please don't tell me he took that seriously. Why do guys always have to be so competitive?

After we greeted his parents—a stately, older Indian couple dressed in a beautiful embroidered sari and silk kurta respectively—we were free to mingle. Channon and Krit knew a few people in the room and I was content to just listen and watch. More guests arrived and the waitstaff set up a big buffet close to the kitchen. It looked like this was a combined business/private function for the parents.

Krit and Channon made sure I didn't feel left out. It was nice to have two guys looking after me. *I could get used to having a big brother... and friend.*

Sri was entertaining with his parents but stopped by occasionally to make sure we had enough food and drinks. I stuck with sodas but figured at midnight I'd allow myself a glass of champagne.

Perhaps it was the stress of the past few days, or being surrounded by so many people all the time, but I began to feel a bit woozy and decided to get some fresh air and a minute to myself. Leaving Krit and Channon to their conversation, I stepped out on one of the balconies. Ugh, Bangkok wasn't the place to get fresh air, especially not in the city centre. The noise from the parties below reached all the way up to this level. Yet it felt good to have a moment. I heard the sliding door open behind me.

"Oh, there you are. I was looking for you, Nui. Are you having a good time?" Sri asked. "Here, I brought you a drink." He handed me another soda with a lime wedge.

"Yes, thank you. It's a lovely party, but I needed some air. I'll come back inside in a minute," I assured him.

"Happy New Year, Nui, in case I don't get to say it later." He leaned forward.

"Yes, Happy New Year, Sri. Why don't we go back inside?"

"Oh, come on, don't I at least get a kiss? After all it's New Year's Eve. Everyone should kiss someone on New Year's Eve, it's tradition!" He moved forward again and bent down. I shuffled back until I hit the railing behind.

"I'm sure there's someone who'd be happy to kiss you at midnight. Let's just go inside, ok?"

"Don't be such a tease Nui. You come here all dressed-up, and drink and eat my food, and then go off on your own, practically begging to be rescued. And now you're playing hard to get? Who do you think you are?"

My mouth dropped open. *Is this guy for real? Did he really think I would kiss him just because his parents are hosting a party? And where did he get the idea that stepping onto a balcony was an invitation for harassment?*

"You know, I better go. Thanks for having me."

I moved to pass by him, but he grabbed my elbow and turned me around.

"Come on, one kiss is not going to hurt you."

I felt, rather than heard, the sliding glass door open.

"Nui, Krit was looking for you," Channon announced, firmly.

"I was just coming, right Sri?"

"Yeah, whatever," Sri brushed passed me.

I could hear Channon stage whisper to him, "Nui two, Sri zero!" *Guys!*

He turned to me. "What happened?"

"Oh, nothing really, but thanks for the rescue. I better find Krit."

I hadn't touched my soda but handed it to Channon. He took a sip and grimaced.

"What's this, Nui?" Channon looked disappointed.

"What do you mean? It's soda!"

"As if. There's at least a good shot of vodka in here. You can't tell?"

"What?" I stared at him. "No way. I didn't ask for any vodka. Sri brought me the…" I trailed off. *Was that why I was feeling so dizzy?*

"What? Are you saying Sri spiked your drink? How many of these have you have? I'm going to kill that bastard!" Channon was fuming.

"I don't know. You were there. Every time he came around, he brought a fresh glass. I am so sorry, I didn't know."

"You have nothing to be sorry for. That son of a ... Krit is going to be furious. I think it's best we leave."

"It's almost midnight, let's just wait the few minutes and then go. We were planning on leaving right after, anyway. I don't want to cause a scene with everybody here. Nothing has happened. I'm just not feeling so great, ok?"

"No, it's not ok, but if that's the way you want to play it, fine."

Channon was seriously upset on my behalf, which I thought was very sweet. He was right of course, Sri deserved to be called out on his behaviour, but I didn't feel it was the right place or time.

"You're sticking with me and I'll get you a glass of water now. Are you feeling ok?"

"I'm a bit nauseous but I'll be fine and we're leaving soon anyway. Thanks Channon, and thanks for rescuing me." Maybe it was the alcohol, but without thinking, I stood on tiptoes to kiss him on the cheek. He turned his head just then and my lips brushed against his, accidentally.

OMG! What are you doing Luna? I jerked backwards and bumped into the glass door. Channon grabbed my elbows to steady me.

"Oops, I'm so sorry Channon!" I blushed furiously, but hoped the dim light outside and Nui's darker skin would hide it. "I didn't mean to do that!"

Channon grinned. "Don't worry, Nui. Guess you're not used to alcohol. Sri's loss, my gain," he winked. "Let's go back inside and we'll leave in a few minutes." He took a firm hold on my arm and didn't let go until we were standing next to Krit, who gave us both a questioning, if not slightly suspicious look.

"Later," I mouthed at him. He draped his arm around me, and I leaned in. It felt nice to have his support as I didn't feel too steady on my legs.

It was just a peck, Luna. No big deal. But I still felt embarrassed and a tiny bit disappointed that it wasn't more.

Two minutes to midnight and people started drifting outside. I pretended to be too hot so we stayed near the glass doors. We wouldn't be able to see any fireworks but that was ok with me. Rockets were already going off all over Bangkok and someone started the countdown: "Ten, nine, eight, seven, six, five, four, three, two, one; Happy New Year!" Hip, hip, hurrah! People hugged and kissed, and one thought went through my head: *What am I doing here? I am supposed to be*

*with Mom and Dad and Luke and not drinking spiked drinks,
pretending to be Nui.*

"Happy New Year, sis." Krit gave me a hug.

"Happy New Year, Nui." Channon raised his glass to me.

Hmm, maybe this isn't so bad after all.

"Happy New Year, guys. Thanks for letting me tag along
but I'm ready to go if you are."

"Sure, let's say goodbye to Sri and we can go," Krit
agreed.

"Maybe it's best we just leave. He's busy with his family
right now. We can always explain later." Channon was eager
to leave as well.

"Yeah I guess that's fine. Ok let's go. It will take us a
while to get out of the street and find a cab, anyway."

The three of us piled into the elevator and walked out into
the Soi. People were dancing and throwing their arms around
strangers, clearly drunk. Krit and Channon sandwiched me
between them and we slowly made our way down to the main
street. Even if we couldn't get a cab, we would be able to use
the sky train which was running until two that night.

We eventually made it home by one, and we knew that we
had to be up again by six-thirty. Not enough sleep for me,
especially with a fuzzy head.

"Channon, why don't you take the couch instead of going
back and forth to your friends? You can borrow some of my
clothes tomorrow. At least you can get some sleep," Krit
offered.

"That would be great." Channon sounded relieved about
not having to make the trip twice.

The house was quiet. It had been a long day, especially
for the grandparents. While Krit helped Channon settle, I
simply brushed my teeth, set an alarm and fell into bed. I was
exhausted and tipsy but couldn't turn off my thoughts. What a

day. I was still stuck in Nui's body; went to a temple with her family; Aunt Jane was sick; Mom was on a plane; Sri's harassment, and then the kiss with Channon. I felt like a popcorn machine with new kernels constantly exploding around me.

40

NUI

I FELT TEMPTED TO SKIP THE CEREMONY WHEN MY ALARM
went off at six. My family wouldn't know if I'd missed it, but
I knew I'd feel guilty. I had also promised Luna I wouldn't let
her muddle through it on her own.

The night had not been as restful as I'd expected. Odd and
strangely lucid dreams had kept me in a semi-conscious state.
They started to fade as I glanced up at the ceiling, but I could
still recall a few bits and pieces lingering in the back of my
mind. I was hobbling along the razor sharp ridge of a moun-
tain in flip-flops with Luna behind me. There was no rope or
guide and I could feel my feet bleeding, but I didn't dare
looking down. In the distance was our goal, the Statue of
Liberty, which somehow was sitting on top of the Chinese
Wall. Bangkok's Giant Swing sat further along the wall. We
held hands as we teetered along, neither of us surefooted, and
both in danger of slipping into the abyss that loomed on either

side. I didn't need Dr Freud to explain it all to me. The dream reminded me that I needed to fetch the *Adventures beyond the Soul* book I'd picked up at the bookstore, from home. I didn't want Luna to find it as she might accuse me of having tricked her into the mind-swap.

Reluctantly, I dragged myself out of bed. I skipped the shower and dressed carefully in a simple shift dress that was meant for Bali but would work for the temple just as well, with a scarf to cover my shoulders. There wasn't much I could do with Luna's bed-hair but pull it back in a tight pony-tail. By the time I left, I was already late again, which was very unusual for me. I hated waiting and normally made sure I didn't keep others standing around either. On the way out of the hotel, I grabbed a muffin from the courtesy cart in the lobby to munch in the taxi.

LUNA

OUCH! THE PHONE ALARM CLANKED LIKE A CHURCH BELL between my ears. My head hurt, and my mouth tasted like dry cotton. It took me a moment to remember why I was feeling so miserable. "Bastard!"

Joey put his paws and head on the bed and I stroked his ears. "Not you, Joey. That guy, Sri. Happy New Year to you! Let's hope it starts off better than the last one ended."

I checked my phone and found a 'Happy New Year' message from Nui, but nothing yet about Mom in Chicago. Too early for that.

Duen was still sleeping. I figured I'd feel better after a shower and some water. Why in the world had I set the alarm for this ungodly hour on New Year's Day? Slowly, other noises in the house penetrated the fog. Tum's ordination! Oh, and Channon stayed last night! I grinned and then flushed at the memory of my accidental kiss. *Just pretend nothing happened and get through the ceremony, somehow.*

Mae and Khun Yaa were already chopping and cooking in the kitchen. *Gee, this ordination thing really is a lot of a work.*

"Good morning and Happy New Year." I hugged both, figuring Nui would do it too.

"Good morning Nui. Happy New Year to you too. Did you have a good time last night?" Mae asked.

"Yeah, it was ok."

She took a closer look. "Did you drink at the party? You look like you're hungover." *What is it about mothers? Do they have a sixth sense or what?*

"No, no I'm just tired and need some water. Then I'll take Joey for a quick walk." I quickly backed out of the kitchen, yawning. *This was going to be a looooong day.*

"Morning Nui, how are you feeling?" Channon was rubbing his eyes. He was wearing shorts and a t-shirt he must have borrowed from Krit. *Hmm, nice. Oh ok, now I'm* awake. *Maybe this year IS starting better already.* I grinned to myself.

"Ah, you're smiling, I take it that means you're ok." Channon misinterpreted my grin.

"Um yes, sort of. I think I just need some water or orange juice."

"Give me a second and we can take Joey out together and get some juice. You're probably dehydrated."

Channon disappeared into the bathroom and I went back to the kitchen to get another glass of water. I wasn't sure if Mae or Khun Yaa had seen Channon in the living room so wanted to forewarn them.

"Channon stayed here last night and we're taking Joey for a quick walk. We'll be back in fifteen minutes, ok?"

"Channon stayed here, and now you're going for a walk together?" Khun Yaa raised her eyebrows.

"It was too late for him to go home and come here again this morning, so Krit suggested he stay."

"I see. Just be back soon, we have guests arriving and we need to get the cars ready." Grandma turned back to the stove, too preoccupied to delve deeper in the subject.

———

I FELT BETTER AFTER DRINKING A BOTTLE OF ORANGE JUICE AT the local 7/11.

"Um, Channon, about Sri last night? I think it's best if you don't say anything to Krit. He'll just get worked up, and nothing really happened, ok?"

"Actually, I think he should know. I'm pretty sure he would want to take it up with Sri. That was unacceptable behaviour."

"Yeah, I know, but there's nothing he can do about it now. He's going back to training this afternoon and I don't want him to be worried or mad, ok? I'll tell him when he's back. It's not like I'm going to see Sri again anyway, so let's just forget about it."

"If that's what you want, fine, but promise me you won't go out by yourself. It's not safe." Channon instructed.

"Oh, come on, it's not like I go to parties all the time. Besides you can't live life in a bubble. Things happen, so let's consider it a lesson."

Channon's lips twitched. "When did you become so wise? Just promise to be careful in future, and if there's a problem, you call me, ok?"

"Yes, sir!" I teased him, but secretly I was thrilled that he was being so protective; it felt nice.

We walked home in silence and the rest of the morning flew by. Two pick-up trucks had arrived, and neighbours were helping to set up a bar and band in one, and a decorated chair in the other. *Thai customs are just plain weird. Why people want to drink this early on their way to a temple is beyond me.*

I just had enough time to change into the Thai skirt and brush my hair. Neighbours and family arrived and helped themselves to food from the kitchen. Some people looked barely awake. Why they scheduled the ceremony for New Year's Day, of all days, was beyond me. It was most likely Thai superstition, or creating merit for yourself. I shrugged and nodded to myself, and drew a weird look from Duen.

Nui was still missing.

NUI

THE TRAFFIC GODS WERE AGAIN AGAINST ME. THE TAXI HAD dropped me off at the mouth of Thong Lo, and I had to more or less run the rest of the way. I was panting by the time I arrived at the house.

Luna looked a little peaky but at least she had remembered to wear the Thai skirt. Jenny and Eve were holding her hands but she glanced at me over the girl's heads with pinched lips. Probably annoyed with me for being late again.

Krit carried Tum, dressed in his white robes, out of the house, and deposited him in the chair on the truck.

"Is Tum sick?" Jenny asked with a concerned frown.

I grinned and before Luna could make up some fake reason, I explained, "No, no he's fine. It's just that his feet can't touch the ground until he's in the temple, so Krit has to carry him."

Jenny nodded like that made perfect sense, not even

surprised that a farang knew the answer. People filled their cups at the bar and a three-piece band started playing Thai tunes. Off we went. The mood was contagious and Luna seemed to loosen up a bit as we shuffled-danced along. The procession took almost a full hour. I was grateful for the early start, after all, this would have been torturous in mid-day heat, even for me.

A monk was waiting for us, blessing the entire group as we walked around the temple three times as instructed. After Tum was carried into the temple, Paa and Mae washed his feet and gave him the orange robes. Tum had to say some prayers and was formally accepted as a novice monk into the temple. He would stay there for almost a month. The rest of us gathered again behind the bar car to walk back home. Quite a production for such a short ceremony, but the ordination was a big rite of passage for Thai boys and men. Most people left then to sleep off the drinks and previous late night.

While Luna went to the bathroom, I quickly grabbed the book out of my bedside table and stuck it into my backpack. I was petting Joey when Luna returned.

"Did you hear from Mom yet?" Luna asked.

"No, nothing yet, but if her flight was on time she'll have only just landed. I'll text you as soon as I know, ok?"

"You know, I was thinking, since the mind swap is out-of-body anyway, do we even have to be in the same room to try it again? Maybe we could do this from a distance while you're in Bali, no?" Luna looked at me expectantly.

"Hmm, maybe. We could try, but we'll be back Saturday night anyway. And we should both try to meditate on our own, so we don't have to start from scratch."

Luna narrowed her eyes, "What exactly are you saying Nui? You don't sound so keen to make the switch. Are you afraid it might mess up your holiday in Bali?"

I protested, "Of course not. I want to switch back. I was thinking, maybe you can find out if Ajaarn Anurak is at the temple, so we can go and see him on Sunday?" I got up and grabbed my bag. "I really have to go now Luna. I'll be late for the brunch."

"That doesn't really answer the question though, Nui. Fine, I'll find out when Ajaarn can meet us, just in case. Make sure you have your phone with you. I'll definitely need your help this week."

"Of course. By the way, I think your dad is way cool and the work he does is so interesting. I'm thinking about going into the hotel business."

As expected, Luna was surprised by the out of context comment. It was enough to distract her from questioning my hesitation about a remote mind swap.

"Nui! Stop saying things that I will have to deal with later. I have no interest whatsoever to work in hotels so don't encourage Dad, ok?"

"I'm not, I was just asking him about it. And besides I'm not the only one who can mess things up, ok? What about Channon?"

"What about him?"

"Well, he's hovering around you all the time. Is there something going on that I should know about?"

"No, nothing, and the only reason he's hovering is because of what happened last night!"

I was shocked when Luna told me about Sri's behaviour. "Oh shit! I can't believe Krit's friend would do that to you. I'm so sorry!"

"Good thing Channon was around, huh?" Luna had to rub it in.

"Fine, fine. Ok, I really have to run. Take care and text me! I'll see you on Sunday!"

4 3

LUNA

I FELT AT A LOOSE END, AND SUSPICIOUS OF NUI'S REFUSAL to try a distant switch back. *She changed the subject awfully fast. And now I am stuck here for six days without her. How am I supposed to survive that?*

My mood didn't improve when I came back to the living room. Krit was saying goodbye to the family. Aunt Varaporn and Uncle Karl had the sleepy girls in their arms and were also on their way out. Krit came over to give me a hug. "Take care, Nui. I'll see you in a few weeks, ok?"

"Drive safely. See you soon!"

Channon walked over. "Ok, I better leave too. See you tomorrow at Pi' Ohm, Nui? Maybe you can come to the hospital with me after and I'll show you around?"

"I have to see if Mae and Paa need me for anything, but yes, I'll probably see you there." At least one positive thing to look forward.

Channon waved as he walked out with Krit and all of a sudden, the house seemed too empty. Two neighbours were still in the kitchen, but with Tum, Krit, Channon, Nui and the rest gone, it felt lonely. *Yesterday you were complaining about having too many people around, and now you don't like the quiet. Make up your mind.*

"Mae, do you need any help? If not, I'll take Joey for a walk. He's been cooped up all morning."

"Go ahead. We're almost done anyway."

I decided to take a slightly different path and walk over to the pet hospital to take a look. It turned out to be less than ten minutes from home. Joey must have recognized the place and wasn't keen to get closer. He planted himself at the bottom of the driveway and refused to walk further.

"No worries, Joey, we're not going in. I just wanted to see where it is."

As we turned to leave, a van drove up, two young guys jumped out and opened the rear cargo door. I could hear some whining, and watched as they carefully picked up what looked like a small husky on a tarp or blanket. Its fur was covered in black grime and it appeared to be very weak and skinny. *Poor puppy! Why would anyone have a husky here in Bangkok?* Even I knew it was not the right climate for the breed. The dog briefly lifted its head and looked straight at me. I felt rooted to the spot. Piercing blue eyes drilled into me as if they were trying to send a message. The men grabbed the blanket tighter and hustled the dog inside. For some weird reason, I felt guilty as we slowly walked back to the house.

Too tired to do much else, I decided to try meditation again. The house was quiet and the adults were probably resting as well. I had no idea where Duen was. I put my head-phones on and pressed start.

NUI

I WAS LUCKY AND CAUGHT A TRAIN IMMEDIATELY. IT GAVE ME just enough time to shower off the sweat from the procession. Luna's mom had texted to say she'd arrived in Chicago. I forwarded the message to Luna to reassure her.

"Luke, you ready?" No response. The brunch was set up in the interior courtyard of the hotel, between two restaurants. Chefs in white jackets and toque hats manned stations around the outer area. There was seafood, a grill, sushi, a breakfast stand with eggs, waffles and smoothies. I didn't know where to look first. Inside the European restaurant were more sections with bread, cheese, cold cuts and salads. Chefs behind the open kitchen counter were preparing pasta and meat dishes on demand. Luna's dad was hosting a table in the private dining room and waved me over. Thankfully, they were still standing around, sipping champagne and chatting.

"Mom Luang Teerawat please meet my daughter Luna.

She just came back from an ordination ceremony, that's why she is running a bit late."

Oh! I hadn't expected a descendent of royalty. I automatically wai'ed with my fingertips touching my eyebrows and a low bow.

"Well, Mark, looks like your daughter has very well adapted to Thailand—ordination, perfect wai, and next you probably tell me that she speaks Thai too," ML Teerawat smiled at me.

"I do indeed, Mom Luang Teerawat. I wish you and your family a very happy New Year," I responded in Thai.

Khun Mark's mouth dropped open. "What in the world? Luna, since when do you speak Thai? I had no idea."

"Oh, I've been practising with Nui and our meditation was also in Thai, so I picked it up, I guess."

"Well, Mark, maybe it's a sign that you need to stay in this country." ML chuckled. "Let me introduce my wife, Thanpuying Wassana."

Who are these people? Thanpuying was yet another royal. Again, I wai'ed. The others turned out to be a son and daughter and their spouses, plus two grandsons.

Considering they were real high-society, they were all pretty casual and relaxed, but I felt a bit starstruck. The family was way above my social stratosphere and I didn't think we would have anything to talk about at all. *Hang on, they think you're Luna, so they probably don't have any expectations. This could actually be interesting.* Luke was already talking to the boys, most likely discussing football teams. We went to different stations to pick up some food.

I ended up sitting between Luna's dad and ML, presumably filling in for Luna's mom.

"So, Luna, why you are so interested in Thai culture?" ML asked, as we started to eat.

"Hmm, I think Thailand is a very interesting mix of so many different things." I said, feeling shy.

"Yes?" ML raised his eyebrows questioning. "What do you mean by that?"

I was trying to figure out how to best frame my thoughts without letting on what I personally thought of the issues in our country. Luna had always said that the contradictions and contrasts in Bangkok were mind-boggling to her, even if they seemed completely normal to me.

"Well, I suppose Bangkok is a pretty modern city, but there are also so many traditions and customs that everyone seems to observe. I wonder sometimes how it all fits together."

"You and me both, Luna. I wonder how the next generation will deal with the modern world while observing our traditions. I already see a lot of changes and not all of them good."

I hadn't expected him to voice his misgivings so openly, but felt emboldened.

"Yes, I agree, but we also shouldn't stop progress just because it's new."

"That's true, but not many visitors make an effort to understand our unique culture. They come to enjoy the beaches and weather and hospitality. They bring their money but also leave a lot of bad habits behind for our youth to pick up. I'm glad to see you're not one of them."

What I'd really like to do is get the inside scoop from ML. I'll never get this close again to someone that high up. Just ask!

"Mom Luang Teerawat, as you said, I'm interested in the country and I was wondering if perhaps I could interview you at some point about your insights on Thailand and where it's heading. I'm sure you have so much background information and many thoughts about that. I could use it for a school essay."

I jerked as Luna's dad kicked my foot under the table, stopping my unconscious jiggling. I quickly looked at him and he was shaking his head at me with a frown. I wasn't sure if he meant my question or restlessness or both.

ML hadn't noticed the interference. "I'd really like that Luna, but I'm afraid I cannot talk about politics with you or anyone else for that matter. You might not know, but I used to work for the crown and it prohibits me from discussing such things. I'm sure you understand."

"Oh I'm so sorry, I didn't mean to suggest anything improper."

"Of course not, you couldn't have known that," ML waved off my concern.

Damn, he really would know all the dirt about what's really happening in this country. What a coup that would be for an article.

ML continued, "But let's not get too heavy on this subject. What do you enjoy most about your new home? I understand you have lived in many places already."

"Yes, Dad dragged us around a bit," I grinned. "I don't know exactly how to put it, but to me, Bangkok has a heart or pulse unlike other cities we've lived in." At least Luna and I agreed on that.

"That's a beautiful way of phrasing it. You're quite the poet. What do you want to do when you finish school?"

"I'm not a hundred percent sure yet. Originally, I thought of becoming a journalist, but the hospitality industry seems very interesting too." *Ok, that was not exactly what Luna said, but since she hadn't made up her mind, I might as well fantasize a bit.*

"Well, you could always become a travel writer and

combine the two, couldn't you? You've already travelled widely, and you speak a few languages from what I understand. That would surely give you an advantage."

"Let's see. Thankfully I don't have to make up my mind right now," I said.

THE REST OF THE BRUNCH WENT BY QUICKLY. ML AND HIS family were extremely kind and didn't seem to mind speaking with two kids. Luke and his new friends were discussing when and where to meet up for football.

We said our goodbyes in the lobby and then went to the pool to relax. As soon as we sat down, Luna's dad launched into me.

"What were you thinking Luna? You can't ask ML about politics, you know that! A) it's impolite, B) he's my boss and C) you know better than to get involved in a country's politics. We are guests here! How many times have I told you this before? And watch your table manners, you've been fidgeting so much lately. What's gotten into you?"

Uh oh! He was seriously annoyed. *How was I supposed to know that that subject was off limits? Does anyone care about politics in this country at all?*

"I'm sorry, Dad, I forgot. And he was so kind, I didn't think he minded me asking," I grovelled.

"And where's this new found interest in Thai life and politics coming from anyway? Don't you think you're taking this whole immersion thing a bit too far, Luna?" He wasn't fully appeased.

Luke snorted, but when I shot him an angry glance he casually got up and dove into the pool. *Good riddance!*

"I'm really sorry, I wasn't thinking." *Divert, divert,*

divert. "Dad, do you think it's a good time to all call Mom now?"

He gave me a look that made it clear he didn't buy the diversion for one second, but then exhaled loudly and picked up his phone.

I blew out a relieved breath. *Crisis averted—for now.*

LUNA

THE PHONE IN MY HAND VIBRATED. I STILL HAD MY headphones on but must have dozed off instead of meditating. I felt a bit disoriented, but overall better.

Nui's message confirmed she had spoken to Mom and she would update me tonight.

So, now what? I wondered. *A full week ahead with nothing planned.* Though it was tempting to hide in my room, I figured should probably see what the family was up to.

Khun Yaa sat at the kitchen table peeling lotus root. "Hi Grandma. Where is everyone? Need any help?"

"No thank you, Nui. I'm almost done. But come and sit with me." She cut the roots into slices and put them into a bowl of water. I could smell vinegar. Maybe to prevent discolouration?

"I think we all can use some ginger and lotus for digestion

after the last two days," she patted her round middle. "Your parents have gone to the store to check on things but they should be back shortly."

Khun Yaa looked at me. "What's going on with you, Nui? You seem to have something on your mind these past days. You've been so quiet. Not your usual self. Want to tell me about it?"

She looked so concerned that I almost broke down to confide in her about our dilemma. Unfortunately, that wasn't an option.

"Oh, nothing really, but can I ask you something? I know you occasionally meditate, and I was wondering what it's like for you? You know Luna and I have been doing the lessons to see if our background makes a difference to how it works, but I don't have anyone to compare it to in my own culture."

"Oh, that's an interesting question." Khun Yaa stopped peeling and put her hands in her lap. "Yes, I've been doing this for many, many years, and for me it's a matter of grounding myself, especially if something has upset me."

I stared at her. "You? Upset? Really? You are the calmest person I know!" I couldn't believe she could ever be off kilter.

Khun Yaa smiled. "What you see on the outside is not always what goes on inside, Nui. I'm sure you know that." *Did I ever!*

She elaborated. "Some days, little things can bother you that are really not worth fussing about. Meditation helps me let it all go and focus on what is really important, and that is to be happy and grateful for my life and the people in it."

"Have you ever had an out-of-body experience when meditating?" I held my breath.

Her expression transformed and she looked positively

serene. "Yes, I have, and it's beautiful. You feel connected to everything around you and it's very peaceful. It has only happened once to me but I do remember it well." She seemed to relive the experience and I almost envied her.

"Oh wow, how did you do it?" I couldn't believe that Nui and I had had a source right here in her own kitchen and didn't even know it.

"I'm not really sure what prompted it, but I do remember being very calm. If you're really interested in this, you should talk to your other grandmother or Aunt May. They have a lot more experience with these kinds of things. Perhaps it has something to do with living in the Golden Triangle?" Her eyes twinkled.

The Golden Triangle was an area in the North of the country where Thailand, Laos and Myanmar met along the Mekong River. It used to be one of the largest opium producing regions and some claimed it still was. Was that what Grandma was referring to? I was pretty sure she wasn't implying that Nui's maternal grandmother had anything to do with that.

"Are you serious? How come I never knew that?"

"Have you asked before?" Khun Yaa laughed. "Come, enough of that, help me with dinner and then we can all have an early night."

I couldn't wait to tell Nui. Maybe we had found another source to help us if Ajaarn Anurak couldn't.

Dinner was light and went by fast. Nui's parents said that they wouldn't need me at the store the next day, which meant I was free to join Channon at the pet hospital and maybe I could find out what happened to that husky. *Any excuse to see Channon, right Luna?* I hated that I couldn't even trick myself into believing my own made-up reasons.

I took Joey out for his last walk around the block. Duen was away at a sleepover that night, and with both Krit and Tum gone, I had the bathroom to myself and took a long shower.

It was eight thirty when I closed the bedroom door and texted Nui.

NUI

NONE OF US FELT LIKE EATING IN A RESTAURANT AGAIN AND Luna's dad agreed to let us order room service and stay in our rooms. He ordered wake-up calls for all of us at six-thirty. After taking another shower I repacked my bag so I could just brush my teeth and go in the morning.

I was tempted by the beef and chicken for dinner. Even though Khun Mark hadn't said anything about my carpaccio the night before, I planned not to overdo the meat-eating in Bali, but surely I could get away with it through room service.

I was just digging into my beef stir fry when Luna texted. 'Call me.'

We face-timed and it was odd to see Luna sitting on my own bed with Joey next to her. She seemed excited. "You never guess what I found out."

"What?" I took another bite.

Luna squinted. "What are you eating? Don't tell me that's meat!"

Damn! Busted, even in my own room. How stupid.

"I was craving beef, and no-one needs to know, ok?"

"Oh, and who do you think signs the room service check? You are such an idiot. Dad will know. And you'll probably give me indigestion." She added with a grimace.

"And how was I supposed to know that? Maybe he won't look too closely?"

"Trust me, Dad will check that you didn't order anything crazily expensive, so you better be able to explain if he asks."

"Ok, ok, I'll think of something. By the way, I talked to your mom and she's fine. She said she'll call again after the surgery on Tuesday."

"Shoot, I forgot."

"See, that makes two of us. Mai pen rai. What did you want to tell me?"

"Khun Yaa said that your other grandma and your aunt in Chiang Rai had a few out-of-body experiences. Maybe we can ask them what to do?"

"You're kidding me. I had no idea. How come Grandma never mentioned that?"

"Ha! I asked the same thing and she said, 'Did you ever ask?' What do you think? Shall we call them?"

"Hmm. I think it would still be best if we talk to Ajaarn first. He knows us both, and if we can't get anywhere with him, we can still call Aunt May and Khun Yaai."

"Why would we ask Khun Yaa? She said she doesn't know."

"Khun Yaai not Khun Yaa, my other grandma—Mom's mom."

"Argh, you guys and your titles! Anyway, anything else? You ok for your trip?"

"Yeah, I think so. What are you going to do while I'm away?"

"Your parents said they don't need me at the store tomorrow, so I thought I'd go with Channon to the pet hospital."

"Channon again, huh? Just because he saved you last night, doesn't mean he's your knight in shining armour now."

Luna blushed.

"Do you have a crush on him?" I teased, but added a warning. "Luna, don't make things more complicated, ok?"

"I'm not. He's Krit's friend, and he thinks I'm you, anyway."

"Oh right, so you want me to start dating him when we switch back? What if I don't want to?" It obviously didn't occur to Luna that her actions would affect me too. I started to get annoyed with her.

"And I need to start eating meat again? What if I don't want to?" Luna snapped back. *Fair enough, though not quite equal in impact.* I could have argued my point but decided it wasn't worth getting into a fight for.

"Ok, ok! We both need to be careful. Let's not mess this up any more this week. Promise?"

"Ditto," Luna retorted and added a perfunctory, "have a good trip!"

———

I HUNG UP AND FINISHED MY FOOD. *DARN, HADN'T THOUGHT about the cheque.* I pushed the room service trolley outside and decided to give meditation another try. Within five minutes I knew I wasn't going anywhere; I was too excited about Bali. Time instead to catch up on the news, which I had completely neglected in the last few days.

LUNA

THE CONVERSATION WITH NUI HAD PUT ME ON EDGE AGAIN. We were both adapting too easily. Sure, there'd been some hiccups, but overall it wasn't as difficult as I had imagined. But how long would we be able to keep up this act? I felt uneasy that neither of us had put in much effort to reverse the situation. Granted, it had only be a couple of days, and hectic ones at that, but I definitely did not want to become too comfortable being Nui. After all, we both had our own families and lives to live. *But you wouldn't have met Channon otherwise. Hush, Luna!* I realized I was grinning to myself.

That night, I dreamed of the husky I had seen earlier that day and felt his eyes drill into me again. I'm not sure if Joey had reacted to my dream, or he just thought he'd get away with it because Duen was away, but in the morning he was lying on top of my bed with his head on my chest.

"Morning, Joey, how did you end up here? Ready to go

out?" I stroked his ears. It was only six forty-five, but I had promised Channon to meet him for breakfast and was eager to get going. I quickly showered and brushed my teeth, then rifled through Nui's and Duen's clothes trying to decide what to wear. *Stop Luna, didn't you promise Nui not to stir things up? But, I can still look nice, can't I?* Argh, if I continued those dialogues in my head, I was going to go mental. Bad enough that I was already two people in one, I didn't need conflicting voices in my head, too. In the end I choose a simple light blue cotton dress. Probably more dressy than Nui would have bothered with to take Joey out but I felt better for wearing it.

It was still quiet in the house. First things first: coffee!

I saw Channon sitting at a table when we arrived. He was joking with Pi' Ohm while digging into his noodles. I could have happily watched him for a while but Joey decided to greet Channon before detouring to the trees. Channon looked up and his smile send an instant tingle to my belly.

"Good morning, Nui. You look nice. Are you going to join me for breakfast?" Channon asked.

I wasn't sure I would be able to eat anything with him looking at me like that, but I nodded and turned to Pi'Ohm.

"Saswadee dee mai Pi' Ohm." She liked Channon and I must have benefitted by extension, since she actually semi-smiled at me.

"Yes, yes, happy! What do you want this morning?" *Hmm, maybe not quite so friendly yet.*

"Can I have the omelette please. It's very good." This time I could see a distinct twitch around her lips; she was warming up.

"So, how was the rest of the day?" Channon asked, as I sat down and took a sip of my coffee.

"Pretty quiet. Everyone was really tired, so we had an early night."

"Yeah, same here. Those were long days. Are you coming with me to the hospital today?"

"Sure. Joey and I stopped by there last night, but he balked at the driveway. I better drop him off at home first."

"No problem."

"I wanted to ask you something. I saw two guys take in a husky last night who seemed to be in pretty bad shape. I was really surprised. Isn't it too hot here for that breed? And they need to run a lot, don't they?" Pi' Ohm dumped a plate in front of me, I wai'ed to thank her but she had already turned away again. I started picking out the chillies.

"Oh please, not another one." Channon instantly fumed, his lips pursed in a tight line. "Some people should be locked up." He waved his chopsticks around. "You know 'Game of Thrones', right?"

"Yeah, what about it?"

"Well, then you know why we have such a huge husky issue here. Somehow, people got it in their heads that a 'wolf' would make a good pet. Next thing you know, the cute puppy grows up and becomes a strong husky who needs to run and exercise, and all of a sudden, it's too much work and they leave him out on the street. And of course, that poor dog has no idea how to survive here. It is such a disgrace!" Channon raked his hair in frustration. "If I ever catch any of those bastards…"

"Are you kidding? That's what's happening? A fantasy show?" Engrossed in seeing Channon so passionately worked up, I had stopped eating. I shouldn't have been surprised he had such a humane attitude, after all, he had rescued me as well. *Uh, oh, Luna. Careful.*

"Yup, and it's not the first time this has happened, either. Remember 101 Dalmatians? Every time there's a new film about pets, we see the same thing. People are just too stupid to see the difference between fiction and reality." He took a deep breath. "I'm sorry, I'm preaching, but I get so angry about this. We end up with all those abandoned dogs at the hospital, and you have no idea how difficult it is to find a home for a husky in Thailand. We already had to put several down because we don't have capacity for them all. And some are just too weak."

My appetite had gone and I pushed the plate away. "I had no idea. That's horrible. But where do they come from? There can't be lot of husky breeders here."

"Ha! If you have money, you can get anything you want in Bangkok. Just go to JJ market and look at the pet section there. And with a few hand-outs, everything is possible in Bangkok. That's another thorn in my side."

Chattuchak, or JJ as the locals called it, was the famous, huge outdoor weekend market, where you could buy everything from silver cutlery to clothes to plants to apparently dogs. I had gone with my mom a few times, but we had gotten lost in the little alleys. Hiring a guide was the only way to find specific items, and while most vendors were legit, I had heard of a lot of shady transactions going on too. As a tourist, you were almost guaranteed to buy at least some fake products. The hotel encouraged guests to hire respectable guides. I took a last slurp of coffee.

Channon shook his head, trying to calm down. "Enough of that. Let's go and check on that husky of yours and see how he's doing."

He returned our plates to Pi' Ohm and I went to get Joey. We dropped him at home and Channon quickly said hello to the parents and grandparents and explained that I was coming with him to the hospital to look around.

Good thing they knew Channon, as I wasn't sure Mae or Khun Yaa would have let me tag along otherwise. Grandma gave my dress a pointed stare, though. I chose to ignore it.

NUI

THE BEDSIDE PHONE RANG AT SIX-THIRTY SHARP. I SHOT straight up at the unfamiliar ring. *What? Where?*

"Good morning Khun Luna, this is your wake-up call. Do you want another call in ten minutes?" The operator asked, cheerily.

"Erm, no thanks. I'm awake."

"Have a good trip."

Yup, Luna was right. Everyone in the hotel knew your business if you were the daughter of the General Manager. I fell back and stretched like a cat, my hands not even touching the side of the bed. *Ah, this is the life!*

Bali! Yes! The thought propelled me back upright, grinning. There was plenty of time for another shower with no-one to fight for the bathroom. Bliss! I didn't really know how to dress for the flight, but since Luna had packed the bag, I figured anything would be appropriate. Compared to my own,

Luna's clothes were all bland—loose-fitting and in neutral colours. *Maybe she is self-conscious because she is bigger than us Thais? Yeah right, as if!* I snorted at the mere idea that Luna could possibly have any hang-ups.

Just before seven, I knocked on the connecting door, 'Luke, come on, time to go."

"In a minute." He sounded cranky. Like Tum, he was not an early riser.

I didn't know if or what we would get to eat on the plane, so I grabbed a croissant and two mini muffins from the lobby cart, just in case. Luna's dad had a cup of coffee in his hand and was speaking with one of the staff. When he saw us, he walked over and put his hand on my shoulder.

"Ready, Luna?"

I felt a bit awkward with his attention. As a Thai I was brought up to only touch family members or close friends and definitely not any unrelated males. I quickly bit into a muffin, nodded and ducked out from under his hand to follow Luke. Approaching the car, it all of a sudden hit me that I would be travelling with two foreign guys to another country for a whole week. My family would have had an absolute fit if they knew. This was a complete no-no in my culture. I tried to push the thought away. *They think you're family so there's no need to be anxious. You're safe with them, just enjoy it.* I still felt slightly uneasy.

A smiling bellman grabbed our bags and put them into a limousine. Luke wanted to sit up front with the driver, so Khun Mark and I had plenty of room in the back.

"Ready to have some fun, kids?" He asked.

"You bet!" Luke perked up. "Dad, can we go white-water rafting again? And I want to go parasailing this time."

His dad laughed. "Let's just get there first, ok?"

The drive to the airport was pretty fast, despite it being a regular work day. The toll-way in the opposite direction looked like a parking lot though. I didn't envy our driver having to go back through that.

I had never flown business class or internationally, so I hung back and followed Luke's lead. Unfortunately, I still managed to create an awkward delay. Luna's bottles of lotion and shampoo were too big to pass security so we all had to go back to check the bag, with Luke complaining non-stop that we now would have to stop at the baggage carousel in Bali. His dad was more understanding. I was a bit annoyed with Luna. She should have known and packed accordingly. Thank God Luna's dad was carrying all our passports; I hadn't even thought of that. It would have been ironic to blow my first foreign trip over a silly mistake like that. The rest was easy, even for a novice like me. The airline staff took care of everything for business class flyers. Boarding ahead of the crowd made me feel a bit smug, until I remembered that my next flight would most likely be in the back of economy to Chiang Rai to see Khun Yaai and Aunt May. *Life's not fair. Enjoy it while you can.* I sighed deeply, drawing a concerned look from Luna's dad.

Apparently I was the only one polite enough to follow the demonstrations of the flight attendants and reading the safety card. Everyone else had their heads buried behind papers or were listening to something on their headsets, which I thought was pretty rude. It took me a little while to figure out the controls for the seat and TV and I accidentally pressed the call button twice. The attendant just smiled politely and reset it. Luke rolled his eyes at my clumsiness but I shrugged it off as an accident. The flight was smooth and the big chairs were so comfortable, I almost nodded off after take-off, but I was definitely looking forward to ordering the spicy noodles on the menu. It was a total let down when the attendant told me had ordered a special vegetarian meal, which turned out to be steamed rice with some overcooked beans and carrots that tasted of nothing. *Damn it.* I wondered if I could ask for another dish but didn't want to risk drawing attention to myself. At least they had some hot sauce to spice it up.

LUNA

THE ANIMAL HOSPITAL WAS HUGE, MODERN AND SLEEK. IT was open around the clock and had specialized clinics, plus boarding and grooming services. According to Channon, they'd just completed a big expansion and they were now one of the top teaching hospitals in the country, affiliated with US veterinarian associations. He clearly was proud of his internship there.

Channon had to use the employee entrance and we met again in the lobby. He took my arm to lead me to the emergency counter, totally unaware of the shiver it sent down my body. His staff card allowed him to see the intake information.

"It looks like a husky was reported on Ekkamai Soi thirty in a restaurant parking lot, hiding behind some trash cans. The owner of the restaurant had two of his staff drop him off. Thankfully, he knew us, as he has a pet himself. Doesn't look like the husky has a tag or chip so they can't find the owner. He's in recovery. Want to see him?"

"Don't you have to work?" I asked.

"I don't start until ten, but I usually come a bit earlier to play with the dogs in the adoption centre."

"You'll end up adopting them," I teased him.

"I wish I could!" Channon nodded seriously.

We walked through to the recovery section which had about twenty cages on either side of a central corridor. Nearly all of them had one or two occupants. There were a few barks as we arrived, but overall it was fairly quiet. Most of the dogs were probably too weak to put up much of a fuss.

Channon stopped in front of the third kennel on the right.

"Here he is! They think he's about ten months old, not quite fully grown yet."

The husky was curled up in the corner on a blanket but lifted his head and tentatively swiped his tail across the floor. Cleaned up, his coat was a checkerboard of light grey and white with dark patches around the eyes.

Again, those blue eyes locked onto mine and I felt that same intense connection as yesterday and in my dream. *What's up with that?* I couldn't figure out why I felt so drawn to him.

"Poor guy! He's beautiful! What's wrong with him?"

"Mainly dehydrated and a bit malnourished but otherwise he seems pretty healthy. They'll probably keep him in observation for another night and then put him into the adoption centre to see how he gets along with the other dogs. Apparently, he'd had some of his shots already, otherwise he'd be in worse shape. I wonder why there wasn't at least a tag though."

"Well, like you said, if you can buy a dog at a weekend market I'm pretty sure there are ways around that too."

"True."

We contemplated the husky in silence.

"You want to name him?" Channon suddenly suggested. "I have to warn you though, once you give him a name, he's yours." He winked at me.

"I wish." And weirdly enough, I really did. I'd never owned a pet because we moved so much, but I actually felt a connection with this husky, as if he was calling me. *Hang on, you're Nui, not Luna; you can't make that decision. But what if...?*

"He does look like a wolf, doesn't he? And with those eye patches he could be a Bandit or maybe Raccoon or Lupin for wolf?" I wasn't sure why only English names popped into my head, but Channon didn't seem to find it odd.

"There you go, I think you've already adopted him."

"Wait, wait. I can't just adopt a dog. But you know what, let me ask Luna. You've met her and I know her family has been talking about getting a pet." I was thinking on my feet. Luke had asked a few times, and Mom and Dad were open to the idea, but they were concerned about the required quarantine in the next country. It had never really been a priority for me but seeing Bandit—*uh oh, did I just name him?*—made me reconsider. And if we could convince my family, Bandit would be with me. Nui would just have to play along until we were back in our own bodies. I looked at him again and made a decision.

"You know we're in Thailand, so he should have a Thai name. How about Chone? Can I come and see him again?"

"Chone it is!" Channon looked pleased. "Yes, once he's moved to the general area it would be great if you could spend some time with him. We're always looking for volunteers to play with the dogs."

"Hey, Chone, how do you like that?" Did I imagine it, or did he look more alert? *Wishful thinking, Luna!*

Turning back to Channon I said, "I guess I better let you go to work. What do you actually do?"

"I help out wherever I'm needed. I'll have to check at the front. Come on, I'll walk you out and show you the adoption centre on the way. You can pick up a form there and see what needs to be done." He grinned and again took my arm.

"Wait, it's not just up to me. Luna is away this week, but she'll be back on Saturday. I'll talk to her later today, so she can ask her parents, ok?"

We walked out together and detoured to the front desk where I picked up a form.

"Ok, thanks, Channon. Let me know how Chone is getting on, will you?"

"Will do or better yet come by later and see him again. I get off at six and I can let you in."

"Oh sure, that sounds great. Why don't you give me your number and I'll text you if I can make it?" *Did I seriously just ask him for his phone number? Pretty bold move, Luna.* I grinned. *Get a grip! I have a legitimate reason, don't I?*

We exchanged numbers and I almost skipped home.

NUI

WE LANDED AT JIMBARAN FOUR AND A HALF HOURS LATER and pretty much on time. Immigration lines were long, but at least the luggage was out already and our driver was waiting.

"I changed the booking since Mom is not here. Luke, you share the suite with me, and Luna, you have the connecting room, ok?"

"Why does she get her own room?" Luke pouted.

"Because she's older and needs her privacy, ok?" His father wasn't in the mood for complaints. "Deal with it. You're lucky to be going; I'm not going to have you spoil the next few days with whining."

Luke grumbled but knew there was a limit on how far he could push.

My room was huge and had its own balcony. I stepped outside to take in the view and could see the ocean just across the treetops.

The connecting door was open, and I peeked into the living room of the suite that was bigger than our kitchen and living room combined! *Wow, all of this for three people? Welcome to the other side.* Why the heck was Luna always complaining about her travels, if this was the standard she was used to? Clearly, she was spoiled but I was determined to enjoy every minute of it.

Her dad was unpacking in the bedroom at the far end.

"Thanks so much, Dad. This is fantastic. I really like this place."

"Glad to hear that. We'll walk around a bit later to see where all the outlets and pools are, and we'll have dinner by the pool, ok? Tomorrow we can go to the beach. It's walking distance from here and we'll have pizza there. I remember you liked that."

"Sure, Dad. I'm fine with whatever you suggest."

"Thanks, honey. I know it's not exactly what we had planned, but we'll have a good time anyway, ok?" He walked over to give me a hug and seemed eager for my approval. *What is it with this constant touching?* I quickly disentangled myself. He looked at me, curiously.

"Everything ok, Luna?"

"Of course. It'll be good! Where's Luke?"

"He went to see the pool. Why don't you unpack and then we'll walk a bit too? I want to get some air and stretch my legs."

"Sure, I'll be right back."

The compound was massive. There were three large pools including one for adults only. We found Luke near the water-slide. His dad told him to be back in the room in half an hour to get ready for dinner. There were tennis courts, a gym, a kids' club, a restaurant near the pool area and another one on

the lobby level. There was also a little boutique selling beach
essentials. It did feel good to walk around a bit even if the
flight hadn't been all that long. The gardens smelled delicious
with white Jasmine trees in full bloom.

LUNA

A KNOCK ON THE DOOR STARTLED ME.

"Are you there Nui?" Khun Yaa shouted, "I need your help."

"I'm coming!"

She was in the kitchen stirring something for lunch, that smelled delicious. Khun Yaa would forever be associated with food for me. So different from my own grandma in the UK who only cooked because she had to, and wasn't too good at it either. I grinned. It's actually nice to have someone taking care of the family like that. I promised myself I'd help her a bit more this week.

"What can I do, Grandma?"

"Eve and Jenny are coming over for lunch. Their parents have to go to some meeting and their nanny is not back yet from her New Year's trip to Chiang Mai. Can you look after them this afternoon? Grandpa and I have to go to the temple."

"Of course, happy to." Just the distraction I needed.

"Their driver will drop them off in a bit and Karl will pick them up around five."

"No problem."

The doorbell rang promptly at noon, immediately followed by a stampede and high-pitched calls, "Pi' Nui, Pi' Nui, we're here."

The girls careened around the corner and crashed into me, almost toppling me in their excitement. Joey beat a quick retreat.

"Woah, woah! Easy girls!" I laughed and bent down to give them both a hug. They really were beautiful little girls with big smiles on their faces. "Don't forget to say hello to Grandma".

"Khun Yaai! Mommy said to say thank you for having us." Eve nudged Jenny who nodded and piped up; "What's for lunch, I'm hungry?"

Grandma laughed. "That's my girl. You can help Nui set the table and we can eat in a few moments. Nui, your parents are coming, so there'll be seven of us."

"Duen not back yet?"

"She's staying another night at her friend's house."

The kids entertained us during lunch with their non-stop chatter. We helped Khun Yaa clean up, and Nui's parents went back to the store.

"Ok girls, what do you want to do this afternoon? Go to a movie or play here or go to Ocean World?"

"All of it!" Eve commanded.

"We can't do all of it today, but we can do one today and another thing next time. So, what do you want to do first?"

"I think we all need a little nap first before we do anything." Khun Yaa faked a wide yawn and looked at Jenny whose eyes were definitely drooping.

"That's a great idea. I'm actually a bit sleepy too, and so is Joey, see?" Joey had escaped the danger zone and was dozing with one eye open in the corridor.

"Why don't we go to my room? Duen is not here and you can lie on her bed, and then we'll go and get some ice cream, ok?"

"Yeah!" They chorused.

Ahh... if only everything was this easy.

They were out like a light and I nodded off for a few minutes, still trying to figure out what to do about Chone.

An hour later Eve popped up like the jack-in-the box. "Can we go and get ice cream now, Pi' Nui?"

"Sure. Just use the bathroom before we go, ok?"

I figured we might as well take Joey. The girls proudly held his leash even though he was walking by himself ahead of us.

We sat in the shade at the local 7/11 slurping mango popsicles. "So, what's next?"

"I don't know, what do you want to do?" Eve asked.

I wiped away mango juice which was dripping down their faces onto their hands, and it gave me an idea.

"How about getting our fingernails painted?"

"Yeah!" Both jumped up in excitement. "Can we get a foot massage too?"

Uh oh, don't get carried away..

"Let's see if they have can take us."

There was a little salon on the main road just between Soi eight and six that I passed every time I went to and from the skytrain. Sure enough, on a Monday afternoon, they could accommodate all three of us at the same time. The girls were treated like princesses and the manicurists even added some sparkles on top of their pink nail colour. Thankfully, they had forgotten about the foot massage. I would need to get more cash from Nui as soon as she was back. Breakfast and coffee each morning were adding up too.

We got back to the house around four and the girls decided that karaoke was next. I found the soundtrack from Disney's Frozen on my phone. They sang and acted it out in tandem switching roles and inventing some new words which cracked me up. The afternoon had really flown by. It was so easy to look after them and they were adorable and affectionate. Their father came to pick them up just after five, as promised, and we agreed they would come back again later in the week, or I would go to their house.

And here I was worried about filling my schedule this week. At this rate I would be running out of time soon.

NUI

I TOOK A SHOWER WHEN WE GOT BACK FROM OUR WALK. NOT having to constantly fight for bathroom space was a luxury that I couldn't resist. With all the complementary toiletries on the shelves, I thought it strange that Luna had bothered to pack her own. *Too precious to use the free gifts? Yup, definitely spoiled!* At seven, the three of us walked downstairs to the main restaurant. We managed to get a table outside and the waiter offered us some mosquito repellent, which we all used liberally. I'd never had much of an issue with mozzies, but I had gotten more bites in the last few days than in my entire life. Luna's body apparently attracted them in droves.

"By the way, Luna, since when do you eat meat again?" Khun Mark asked after we placed our order. "It's fine of course, but I was curious since Mom hadn't said anything."

"Oh, you mean the room service order last night? Actually, I ordered the wrong dish by mistake and I didn't want to wait anymore, so I just ate it."

I can't believe I just lied like that.

"As if! Admit it, you're giving up your veggie fad. What about the carpaccio the other day?" Luke jeered.

Damn it. Shut up Luke.

"You know Luna, if you want to go back to eating meat it's not a problem. You don't have to pretend otherwise, ok? I'm just surprised you didn't have any stomach issues after years going without it."

"Hmm, maybe I'll try it again occasionally, but I'll stick to fish and vegetables for now."

As we were eating, Luna's dad said: "You know there's something your mom and I wanted to discuss with both of you, and with her in Chicago now, it's become more relevant." He sounded serious.

"What's up, Dad?" Luke asked.

"Well, your mom and I thought that with Luna finishing high school and going to college next year, it may be time to look at settling back in the States. Originally, we wanted to wait another year until Luna graduated but with Aunt Jane being sick and the family needing help, we agreed it might make sense to move that date forward. What do you think?" He looked at us expectantly.

"Sure, whatever, Dad. They have a better football league there, anyway." Typical Luke!

No, no, no! Not now! Worst timing ever! Or... is it? Stop it, you can't possibly think this is good.

"Erm, are you serious? Mom only said we should check out some colleges over Songkran; she didn't say anything about moving yet." I was scrambling. "You're new to your job, won't that be an issue?"

"Well, it's not ideal to be honest, but family comes first,

Luna. I know you like Thailand more than the other places we lived, but you were the one who always wanted a more permanent location."

"Yeah, but if we leave now, I'd have to start in a new high school and then move again for college. So, it's really not permanent, anyway."

"At least you'd be in the US and could acclimate to schools there and be closer to your cousins. Mom feels she needs to be there for Aunt Jane."

"Do we have to decide right now?" I was close to panicking. "How soon were you thinking of moving?"

"We haven't made a final decision yet, but I want you to think about it, ok? We'll talk more when Mom is back and we know how serious the situation is."

"Oh, ok." *Oh damn. What do we do? Should I warn Luna now or wait until I'm back in Bangkok? Maybe nothing will come of it so there's no need for her to get all worked up. But what if they decide to move and we haven't figured out how to switch back? Do we tell them?*

My thoughts were going off in a hundred directions. And at the back of my mind a voice piped up, *What if you could move and study in the US? Wouldn't that be a dream come true?* Mentally I slammed on the brakes. *No way! I can't leave my family. But, what if? Stop Nui!* This back and forth was getting me nowhere. *Think of something else.*

"Uh, Dad, so what are we going to do tomorrow?"

"What do you kids feel like? Is there anything you want to do or see again?"

"Can we go parasailing please?" Luke begged. "Or we could try paddle boarding? Or go back to the white water rafting place?"

His dad grinned. "Ok, ok Luke, looks like you got it all

figured out. What about you, Luna? Anything you want to do?"

"I'm ok with whatever." I was distracted and couldn't think clearly.

"Ok, Luke, if I remember correctly, the Four Seasons has a water activity centre and we can check there for the paddle boarding. Let's talk to the concierge and then we'll decide."

Luke had finished his ice cream and his dad signed the cheque. We went back up to the lobby and managed to get an afternoon slot at four for parasailing. The place was only fifteen minutes away. Khun Mark said he'd ask the General Manager at the Four Seasons in the morning for permission to use the activity centre there as visitors.

If I had been more alert I would have insisted on getting at least some land-based activities on the schedule given my fear of water, but I was too preoccupied trying to figure out what to tell Luna about the new twist.

LUNA

AFTER THE GIRLS HAD LEFT, I DECIDED TO GO BACK TO THE hospital to check on Chone. *Admit it, you also want to see Channon.* I told grandma I wasn't hungry as the girls and I had had a snack. She looked unconvinced but didn't make an issue of it. I texted Channon to say I would meet him in the reception area.

There were still quite a few people with their pets in the waiting room. Cats, dogs, birds and what looked like an iguana in a cage. How an iguana made a good pet was beyond me, but some people kept snakes and spiders. *Mai pen rai—to each its own.*

Channon was running late, but I was content to sit and watch the animals. Apparently, Chone had already been released from recovery and was now kept in a single pen in the adoption centre until they could confirm that he got along with the other dogs.

As soon as we walked up to his cage, he started wagging his tail and then, to my surprise, came over to meet us.

"Oh my God, he looks so much better. This is amazing."

"He's still young and pretty strong and it looks like he hasn't lived on the streets that long. Some food, water and vitamins and a few days of rest and he'll be good as new." Channon confirmed. Chone put his nose through the mesh and I held my hand close for him to sniff.

"Hello Chone, I'm so happy to see you. We'll get you out of here soon, ok?" He looked like he fully understood and maybe he did.

"Ah, so you ARE adopting him?" Channon winked at me. A delicious shiver went all the way down my spine and I grinned back sappily.

"Well, I'll definitely try, but I have to wait until Luna is back on the weekend. You said he'd had some shots already?"

"Apparently so. They did the bloodwork and it looks like he's had all the core puppy vaccines. He'll need another round in a few months when he's fully grown. He's also been neutered so that's another checkmark off the list. Should make it easier to convince the family."

"Do you have any pets, Channon?"

"My family always had dogs but with the military and now vet school I don't think I have time for a dog. But as soon as I have my diploma, I will definitely get at least one dog. For now, I get my daily puppy love here." He smiled again. *Awww. Stop it!*

"Can I come and see Chone on my own?" *And you?* I felt myself blushing.

"Well, you could always volunteer here. That way, you can get a pass and see him every day." Channon suggested.

"That's a great idea. What do I have to do?" I sounded like an eager puppy myself.

"Just fill out the form. You can tell them how much time you have and what you can do. They'll want to see some references, but I can give you one, at least."

"That would be great. I'll do it tonight." *Gee Luna, tone it down. Don't be so obvious.*

"I'm done with my shift. Do you want to go and grab a bite or a coffee, or do you need to go home?"

Was he asking me out? Nah, don't imagine things. I'm just his friend's kid sister and we have a common interest. Reasoning didn't work; I was still excited at the idea.

"Erm, sure if you have time. Where do you want to go?"

"Have you been to 'The Blooming Gallery'? You know the bistro and florist place inside Soi eight? It's a nice, casual place."

"That sounds good. Bye, Chone, see you tomorrow."

He wagged his tail again as if he understood, then turned around and went back to his blankets.

"I think you just made a friend for life." Channon declared.

———

WE WALKED OUT OF THE HOSPITAL, AND FIVE MINUTES LATER, into a beautiful café that not only smelled but also looked great with hundreds of plants and flowers displayed and hanging off walls.

I stopped at the door to take it all in. "This is so pretty. I can't believe I've never been in here."

"It's fairly new. I like it and their food is good," Channon explained.

It wasn't crowded and we headed towards a high table

near the windows. On the way, we passed two girls who were staring at me. One of them looked vaguely familiar but I couldn't place her. She stood up and confronted me, somewhat aggressively.

"Nui! How have you been? We haven't seen you in ages! I guess you don't care about your old friends anymore?" She looked pointedly at Channon.

Huh, who is this? I was at a complete loss. Channon must have picked up on my discomfort.

"Hi, I'm Channon. And you are?"

His smile completely disarmed her. I almost felt jealous, but it worked.

"Oh, hi, I'm Toey, Nui's old friend and that's Dearn." She pointed at the other girl still sitting and watching us coolly.

"Nice to meet you both."

A lightbulb went off in my head. These were the two girls Nui had been talking about. They hadn't been at the ordination so we hadn't had a chance to meet before.

Thanks Channon for the rescue. Smoothly done. I grinned.

"Hi girls, I thought I would see you at Tum's ordination. I'm sorry you missed it." Let them try to put me on the defensive. Turning to Channon I said; "Can you give us a minute? You want to go ahead and order some food?"

Channon easily played along. "Sure, take your time. Want something to drink?"

"Just a lime soda is fine, thanks."

I sat down at the girl's table.

"I'm sorry I was spaced out walking in. How are you?"

"Ha, it was more like you only had eyes for Mr Handsome there, huh?!" Toey was still miffed but I could sense her curiosity too.

"Actually, we just came from the pet hospital. I went to check on a dog that was admitted yesterday; I was worried about him." *Give me a break, I'm not gonna have a guilt trip because you're jealous.*

"Oh, ok, but Dearn and I were just saying how we haven't seen you in so long. How are you doing and who is the guy?"

"Channon is a friend of Krit's and he's going to be a vet, so he's working at the hospital and was showing me around. I'd love to catch up with you. Why don't we meet this week sometime? You're still on holiday too, aren't you?"

"Yes. Why don't I text you tomorrow and we can plan a date, ok?" Toey finally smiled at me, apparently appeased.

"Great, can't wait."

Crisis averted. Better thank me for this one Nui!

Channon had ordered a beer for himself and a soda for me, and said some snacks were coming.

"Sorry about that. We went to school together but since I transferred to BIS I haven't seen them much. We'll catch up later this week."

"How do you like BIS? I went to a local school but hear good things about them."

"It's pretty good, very international, I was lucky to get a place."

"You must be pretty smart to have been admitted."

"Says the guy who is going to vet school!" I brushed off the compliment. "Are you from Bangkok?"

"Paa was originally from upcountry but moved here to work as a gardener for a landscaping company. They took care of the plants for a lot of the condo buildings here. He really had a green thumb and we always had a lot of flowers and plants around the house. Guess that's why I like this place." He glanced around. "He met my mom at one of the complexes he was working in. She was a receptionist but has now become a human resources manager for the company that handles all the estate essentials for the condos.

"You said he 'had'?"

"Yeah, he died in a stupid work accident three years ago. It's been really tough for my mom but she's ok now."

"I'm so sorry, that must have been hard. You were only what, sixteen? I can't imagine." I was sorry to have brought up the subject, but Channon seemed ok to talk about it.

"Yes, you grow up very quickly when you need to, and I had to be there for Mom."

No wonder he feels so protective of everyone.

"But enough of this. Let's talk about something more fun," Channon switched gears.

The evening flew by. Channon was easy to talk to and very entertaining. The stories about his military service were hilarious, although I'm sure it wasn't only fun. He also touched on some of the more gruesome situations he faced at the animal hospital every day. It distressed him how some people treated their pets.

"You know, it's always so easy to say that people are bad, but unless you know what they are going through, we really shouldn't judge. Of course, it's never right to mistreat any animal, but just look at the elephant issue."

"What elephant issue?" I had no idea what he was talking about.

"Let's not get into this right now. It always spoils my mood and I'd rather enjoy the evening." Channon deflected with a smile. "But if you're curious, just look up teak logging and elephant. It's a dark subject though." He warned.

I had forgotten to eat or drink and was simply staring at him. "I wish there was something I could do too," I blurted out.

"Well, you can start by adopting one pet!" Channon grinned. "But there are many other ways to get involved in animal issues."

"Hmm, let me think about that," I said, and I meant it.

We had eaten our way through calamari, pomelo salad and chilli potatoe chips. Channon ordered a burger for himself but I felt full and declined.

Toey and Dearn had left by the time Channon paid the bill, insisting he was the one who'd consumed most of the food and alcohol.

Though it was only a few blocks, he walked me home. This definitely had the feeling of a date. *Be careful, Luna, he thinks you're Nui. Maybe, but that's just on the outside.* Another voice in my head spoke up. *He's been talking to ME after all, not Nui.*

Channon said goodbye in front of the house but asked if I wanted to meet him again the next morning and come to the hospital.

The only definite item on my agenda was to visit the temple to see if Ajaarn Anurak was there, to ask if he could meet us on Sunday.

Khun Yaa cornered me in the hallway. "Why didn't Channon come in to say hello? Did you have a nice time?"

"He had to go and see some friends. And I need to call Luna. Do you know if Mae and Paa need me this week? I want to start volunteering at the pet hospital."

Khun Yaa smiled, "I'm glad you want to help, but remember that it's about the animals and not because Channon works there, ok?"

I blushed. "Of course it's about the animals. Speaking of, where's Joey?"

"Your parents took him to go to Khun Pang and Khun Pichamon's houses to thank them for helping with Tum's party. So you won't have to walk him later."

"Ok in that case I'll do a bit of homework and call Luna. Good night, Grandma."

I took a quick shower. By now I was more comfortable handling Nui's body. *Guess you can adapt to anything if you have to.* Sitting on my bed, I went online to check out the application process for volunteering at the hospital. It was very straight forward. I printed out the two pages. Since I wasn't eighteen yet, I would have to get a parent's signature and two references, like Channon mentioned. I wondered if I could ask Uncle Karl for the second one.

NUI

I RELAXED ON MY BALCONY BEFORE FACE-TIMING LUNA.

"Hey Luna, what's up?"

"Hey! How's Bali? Good flight? What did you do today?"

"Oh, not much, by the time we got to the hotel it was pretty late, so we stayed here and had dinner. Tomorrow we'll go parasailing and paddle boarding at the Four Seasons."

"That sounds like fun." Luna mumbled. I could tell she wasn't really listening; she was glancing at some papers. "Hey, listen, there's something I need you to do. Can you start talking to Dad about adopting a dog? There's this husky, Chone, who was just brought to the pet hospital. Channon and I went to see him, and if he doesn't get adopted, they may have to put him down. I really want that dog and you need to start laying the groundwork. I can pick it up when we switch back. Luke always wanted to have a dog, so he'll help. Ok?" She looked up for my response. *Does she expect me to take orders from her now?* I thought somewhat resentfully.

"Hmm."

"Nui? Did you hear what I just said?"

"Yeah I heard you, but your dad brought up something at dinner tonight, so I'm not sure if this is the right time to talk about pets."

"Why, what happened? Is Mom ok? Aunt Jane?"

"No, no, nothing about that, they're ok. But he said that he and your mom have talked about returning to the States sooner, to give you a chance to finish high school there before college, and to be closer to Aunt Jane to help her and the family."

"What? That's nuts! We've been moving around for the last sixteen years and now they suddenly want to move back?" Luna looked shocked and I finally had her full attention.

"I know! He said nothing has been decided yet, but he wanted us to think about it. Luke doesn't mind, but I said it would mean that I, I mean you, would then have to start at a new high school, and then again at a new college, and that it wasn't fair to pull me out now. That's what you wanted, right?"

"Yes, of course, the last thing I want is to move again now. We've only been here for six months. That's just not fair."

"That's what I said, but your dad made it clear that family is priority and it would mean a lot to your mom. He also said you always wanted to stay put in one place anyway." It felt somehow gratifying to throw her own words back at her, even if it didn't help the issue.

"Oh, it's pretty rich that he's holding that against me now. All this time it's been ok to move around without considering the family, and suddenly now it's a priority. The timing sucks. I know Mom is close to Aunt Jane, but we have to stall them. When did he say they want to move?"

"They didn't set a deadline and want to see first how the surgery goes. Did you meditate at all?"

"No, Jenny and Eve were here this afternoon, then I was at the pet hospital and had dinner with Channon."

"Dinner with Channon? What are you doing? Are you dating him? I thought we talked about that! Don't make it more complicated than it already is." I was starting to get fed up with her carelessness.

"I'm not dating him! Chill! He got me into the hospital so I could see Chone, and then we had a snack together! And by the way, Dearn and Toey were there too and now I have to see them this week to make up for you neglecting them!" Luna made it sound like she deserved a medal for handling Dearn and Toey.

"Luna, stop! You're taking over my life!"

"Oh yeah? And what about you? You're on holiday with my family in Bali after all!"

There was dead silence and we just stared at each other.

"Shit!" I finally whispered. "What are we doing? We're really messing this up, aren't we?"

"Damn it! You and I can't fight about this. We need to figure this out together asap." Luna agreed.

"I know! Ok, can you go to the temple tomorrow and I'll try to stall your dad. I'll also mention the dog. What's its name?"

"Chone. I told Channon that Joey wouldn't tolerate another dog in the house, so I would ask Luna to adopt him."

"Fine! I'll see what I can do. What else?"

"What about Dearn and Toey? What do I need to know before I meet them?"

I walked her through some basics of our childhood together until she felt comfortable enough to survive a coffee meeting.

But then she threw another curveball. "Oh, by the way, I am going to apply for volunteering at the hospital tomorrow, so I can see Chone on my own. I want him to get to know me better. If he's like Joey, he'll recognize me as Luna once we switch back, ok?"

"Luna! You're still doing it! What if I don't want to volunteer there? How am I supposed to explain that to Channon?"

"Oh yeah? Remember, you volunteered me too. If you don't want to do it, I can take over from you after our switch. But you should see the place, it's really worth it."

"Right, and maybe you won't even be here anymore but back in the US. Did you think about that?" I was ready to pull my hair out.

"Shit, shit, shit. You're right, there are too many balls in the air. How do we keep track of all that?"

"By lying as low as possible until we can sort it out. At least check with me first before you commit to anything else."

"Yeah, yeah, same goes for you."

"This is so exhausting. I'm gonna go to bed now, it's late here. Let's catch up tomorrow after you talked to Ajaarn, ok?"

"OK, bye." Luna disconnected.

I blew out a big breath. This switch was getting more complicated by the minute.

LUNA

I WOKE UP EARLY. JOEY WAS ON THE FLOOR. NUI'S PARENTS must have let him in last night while I was asleep.

Considering this was my holiday week, I was surprised by how eager I was to get going. Usually my mom would have had to kick me out of bed, but I had so many things to do today.

There was a text message from Nui already saying Mom had called again late last night. Nothing new otherwise.

I took my volunteer form with me to the kitchen to ask Mae for her approval. She, Paa and Nui's grandparents were having breakfast and I thought it might be wise to join them instead of running off to Pi' Ohm.

"Joey, we'll go right after, ok?"

The congee actually tasted quite good after two days of omelette. Mae and Paa were pleased I decided to volunteer and signed the forms without problem.

My departure got further delayed as I had to wait for Tum on his alms rounds that morning. I decided to skip coffee and go straight to the park.

Channon was just finishing his breakfast bowl.

"Hey Nui, I thought you weren't coming." He looked pleased to see me.

"No, no, it's just that I had to get my parents' approval and then Tum came on his round," I waved the papers at him. "Now, I need your reference and signature, then I'm going to ask Uncle Karl for the second one later today. How long does it take to process the application?"

"Wow, you're very efficient!" Channon laughed, "I think it'll be fast. They always need people to help out. Why don't you ask them yourself? Can you come to the hospital now?"

"Sure, I already had breakfast and I just need to drop Joey off." I felt a bit guilty for spending so little time with Joey, but once we were back, Nui would make up for it. "Ok, let's go." Channon got up.

"No breakfast this morning, Nong Nui?" Pi' Ohm called out.

"Not today Pi' Ohm. Already ate." She seemed to be warming up to me after all, though I still thought it was only because she liked Channon.

———

WE MET AGAIN AT THE FRONT DESK AFTER HE SIGNED IN AT the employee entrance. The staff at the counter promised to expedite the application as soon as I had the second reference.

When we walked into the adoption centre, I didn't see Chone. Channon grinned, "I have a surprise for you. Come on."

We passed the pens and stepped out into a grassy area

surrounded by trees and a chest-high fence. There were at least twenty dogs of all colours, breeds and sizes running around like mad and chasing each other and just having fun. And right in the middle of it, Chone was happily running along even though I could tell he was a bit slower than the other dogs. He was still not one hundred percent, but it was a huge improvement.

"Oh my God. This is amazing! I can't believe how quickly he's recovering. And he obviously gets along with other dogs. Hey Chone, over here!"

I don't know if he actually heard me, but he stopped in his tracks and looked over to where Channon and I were standing. And then, shockingly, he left his friends and came over to us.

"I can't believe it! He recognizes us." I was so excited.

"I think he recognizes *you*." Channon declared.

Chone stood in front of me looking up as if to say, "Where have you been? I've been waiting."

I bent down to let him sniff my hand and when he turned his head scratched behind his ears. He moved closer and pressed his body against my legs.

I kneeled down to hug him, "Oh Chone, I'm so glad you're better. You are a miracle. Do you know that I'm going to volunteer here so I can come and see you every day? And I'm trying to get you out of here as quickly as possible, ok?" I was rambling.

Channon laughed out loud, "I think he gets everything you're saying. Look at the expression on his face."

The morning was absolute bliss. I had no idea why I was so drawn to Chone, but it felt like I had known him forever. Maybe he was an old spirit in a new body. *Oh, don't get fancy Luna. Just because you're Thai right now, doesn't mean you believe in incarnation.* But if I was honest, I liked the idea.

Channon had promised to pick me up for lunch in the hospital café. I wish I had dressed a bit more carefully instead of just shorts and a plain t-shirt. I met some of the other volunteers who walked me through my chores. They cautioned me not to get too attached to the dogs as they could be adopted at any time. *Too late* I thought. *I better get Dad and Mom to make this happen somehow.*

Channon came back at lunchtime and brought a lead so we could take Chone into the restaurant with us. He was a true champion and behaved perfectly.

After lunch, Channon went back to work and I needed to go to Uncle Karl's office for the second signature.

5 6

NUI

AT BREAKFAST, LUNA'S DAD CONFIRMED WE WERE ALLOWED to use the activity centre at the Four Seasons across the street.

A group of instructors were standing next to paddle boards, kayaks and other beach equipment. Khun Mark had hired one instructor, Tom, for the three of us. Tom could have been a poster boy for a California beach commercial—brilliant white teeth, golden tan and a white blond mop of hair. His eyes were hidden behind black sunglasses.

"So, you're all first-time paddle boarders?" We nodded.

"And you're all good swimmers, right?"

"Yes," Luke and his father answered in synch.

"And you?" Tom looked at me.

"Erm, I'm ok, I guess. But could I wear a life vest anyway?"

"Sure, no problem. Let me get one for you." He walked over to a big chest.

The guys looked at me, puzzled.

"Luna what's wrong? You're an excellent swimmer." Khun Mark said.

"She just wants his attention, Dad." Luke laughed.

I rolled my eyes. "I do not. I just feel more comfortable with a life vest. It's none of your business anyway!" I knew that Luna had no problem swimming as me, but I didn't trust that change quite yet. *Better safe than sorry.*

"Kids, stop! You can wear one if it makes you feel better, Luna, though I'm really not sure why," Dad intervened but looked at me curiously.

Tom came back and handed me a vest. "Try this one. We have other sizes, but this should fit."

I felt like a klutz, but I didn't dare being on the ocean without support, even if we were close to the beach.

Tom walked us through the stance and grips and how to get back on the paddleboard if we fell over. I was pretty sure that would be me in a few minutes. *Why in the world did I agree to this? Testing a theory this way is pretty stupid. Just because I had Luna's body, didn't mean my brain automatically became fearless in the water.*

"Well, you can't learn boarding on the sand, so let's get in the water," Tom said.

"Stay close," he said to Khun Mark and Luke. "I'll watch Luna."

Luke just waggled his eyebrows with a knowing grin. I guess I asked for that.

To my surprise I found it pretty easy to not only get on the board but also to stand up and keep my balance. *Thanks Luna!*

"You're a natural, Luna," Tom said. "Look at Luke! I think he just wants to jump into the water." Luke was goofing off and he and his dad were laughing so hard that both had difficulties remaining upright. Once I got the hang of paddling and switching the grip, I quite enjoyed the rhythm. Tom had me follow him, and kept glancing back to make sure I was ok.

"This is fun!" I yelled. Naturally, just then a jet ski passed and caused a bigger swell that almost threw me off. We paddled for almost an hour before returning to the beach.

"Dad, can we do the jet ski next?" Luke asked.

"Tom, do you have any here?" Khun Mark looked around.

"Afraid we don't; we only use non-motorized equipment. The next jet ski rental is up the coast towards Seminyak."

"Dad, can we go?" Luke was all hyped up.

"Actually Luke, there's not enough time today. We could go for an early lunch before we go parasailing this afternoon."

Food always was a fail-safe idea to divert Luke's attention. He was instantly hungry at the suggestion of pizza. His father tipped Tom and we moved over to the beach restaurant. It was still early, but a few tables were already occupied. I ordered a fresh coconut and we decided to share two pizzas.

"So, Dad, what did Mom say about Chicago?" I asked. "You only mentioned that Aunt Jane is ok so far."

"That's pretty much all we know for now. They are operating this morning and the doctors will then decide if she's going to have radiation or chemo, or both."

"Did Mom say how long she'll stay?"

"It's too early for that Luna, we don't know yet how Jane will feel and cope after the surgery. Your mom thinks she'll be there at least until the end of next week, if not longer. I know it's not great, but your cousins really need her right now."

"Of course, Dad. I was just wondering."

The food was delicious, and it was very relaxing to sit by

the beach and listen to the waves. *This is the life. Enjoy it while it lasts. Next week you'll be back on Soi fourteen.* To distract myself, I decided to approach Luna's pet emergency.

"Dad, did you have any pets as a child? Did Mom?"

He laughed. "Why are you asking? You know I did. My dad always wanted a hunting dog, but each time we ended up with mutts from the local shelter. I think that was Mom's way of telling him what she thought of his hunting idea. But Dad was a push over when it came to dogs."

"Well, you know my friend Nui, right? She started to help out at this animal hospital near her house and they have a big adoption centre. She said there are so many great dogs there that have been abandoned because some people watch too much TV."

I dramatized what Luna had told me about the movie tie-ins. Both Luke and his father were appalled.

"Dad, we have to rescue one of those dogs." Luke jumped right in as I hoped he would.

"Guys, as much as I love the idea, you both know that we can't make that decision right now. Not with everything up in the air. What if we have to move back to the States soon? If I remember correctly it's very difficult to get a dog into the US, long quarantines and so on and that's just not fair to a dog. I'm sure there are plenty of dogs there too that need rescuing."

"Apparently it's not that difficult anymore. Luna, I mean Nui said that the laws have been relaxed and it's much easier nowadays. We could at least have a look at the dog and then decide, couldn't we?"

"Yes, Dad, let's do that when we get back, ok? You and Mom have promised that we would get a dog eventually. Might as well get one now!" Luke played right into the plan. Perfect.

"Ok, ok, we can go and have a look but no promises. Now let's finish lunch. I need to make some work calls before they pick us up."

Luke and I exchanged winks while his dad paid the bill. Step one—check.

LUNA

U<small>NCLE</small> K<small>ARL</small>'<small>S</small> <small>OFFICE</small> <small>WAS</small> <small>JUST</small> <small>OFF</small> S<small>ALA</small> D<small>AENG</small> <small>TRAIN</small>
station and I had to switch lines at Siam. I planned to stop at
the temple on the way back, as it was close to the
interchange.

The travel agency had a modern office on the second
floor of Silom Complex. While I waited my turn, I texted
Toey to see if she and Dearn could meet for coffee the
next day.

Uncle Karl was happy to sign the reference and I told him
a bit about the hospital and adoption centre.

"Maybe you should adopt a dog too?" I suggested. "Jenny
and Eve are old enough and I'm sure they'd love it."

He laughed. "Yes, I'm sure they would, but you also
know who would be taking care of the dog in the end.
Though I wouldn't mind. Maybe we'll come out and visit you

at the hospital after I speak with Varaporn. I think it would be good for the girls too."

"Thanks, Uncle Karl. I'll come and see the girls soon!"

"Thanks for your help yesterday. The girls adore you and I'm glad they get to play with their cousin."

"Why don't you call me after you talked with Aunt Varaporn and we'll set up a visit. I'm still on holiday this week so it's a bit easier."

"Sounds good. Ok, Nui, gotta get back to work."

"Thanks again, see you soon."

———

I WALKED TO WAT PATHUM VIA SIAM STATION. EVEN THOUGH it had only been six days, I missed the place and our morning sessions there. When I stepped through the gates, I remembered how calm and peaceful it was, despite the heavy traffic outside. This afternoon there were only a few worshippers at the spirit house. I wasn't sure how I was going to find Ajaarn Anurak. I asked one the lay helpers, but he just shrugged and said he didn't know the schedules or the monks. He suggested I wait for the supervisor who was expected back shortly. I stopped at the spirit house to say a few prayers even if I didn't have any incense or flowers with me. *The thought counts, doesn't it?*

Fifteen minutes later, I saw the young helper waving me over. An elderly man was waiting on the steps of the sala. I wai'ed and explained who I was looking for.

"Oh, Ajaarn Anurak? He's not here right now. I believe he is in the North at a retreat but let me check that. Can someone else help you?"

"That's very kind of you, but Ajaarn Anurak was helping

PLYAN

231

us with a school project and he gave us some lessons that we need to speak with him about. I hope that is ok?"

I was improvising and hoped that he wouldn't try to brush me off.

"Wait here." The man said and walked towards one of the side buildings. Five minutes later he was back. "Ajaarn Anurak is in Chiang Rai. He's leading a retreat for visiting monks from Europe this week." The man looked at some kind of schedule. "It says he'll be starting a new meditation class here late-January."

"Is there any way I can get in touch with him before then?" I figured I was breaking etiquette, but I had to ask.

"We cannot interrupt a retreat." The man replied sternly. "What could possibly be so urgent?" He seemed suspicious, probably wondering why a Thai girl would even suggest such a thing.

"I am so sorry, but it really is urgent. Do you know where the retreat is? Perhaps we can try to get in touch with Ajaarn Anurak after it's over? I know he has a cell phone."

"Well, I can't give you his number, but I can give you the temple number and perhaps they will pass on a message. Wait here."

Again, he went into the admin building and came back with a piece of paper with Wat Rong Khun and a phone number written on it.

"Thank you so much. This is very kind of you, and I very much appreciate your help." I wai'ed again and left the temple.

Getting back on the skytrain all I could think was, *what do we do now? What do we do?*

Toey had texted to say she and Dearn would be free on Wednesday afternoon. I really didn't feel like seeing them, but maybe it would take my mind off this mess. I confirmed four o'clock at a coffee shop on Soi six that Nui had suggested. I also texted Nui to say we needed to talk urgently. There had been no response by the time I got off the train.

NUI

THE PARASAILING CAMP SENT A CAR TO DRIVE US TO THEIR base.

"Dad, can I just sit and watch from the beach? I didn't really like it that much last time," I lied but I didn't fancy being high up over the ocean, only attached to a boat by rope.

"Can I get her extra time?" Luke jumped in immediately.

"Hold your horses, Luke. Maybe we'll split Luna's time. But you will have to go up as a tandem. You're only just old enough to be allowed up there, ok?" His father stayed firm.

They took their turns while I watched, and afterwards we sat on the beach for a while as Luke regaled us with his version of how *he* controlled the parasail. As if!

Dinner that night was fresh, grilled fish prepared by local fishermen on the beach. All in all, it had been a super-relaxed and fun day.

"What do you guys want to do tomorrow?" Luna's dad asked.

"Can we go to Ubud and see some of the temples up there?" I suggested.

"Boooring!" Luke immediately declined. "But we could go white water rafting there again, can't we, Dad? That was a lot of fun last time."

"That was fun!" Khun Mark agreed. "Are you ok with that, Luna?"

"Erm, sure but can we at least stop at one temple on the way?" *What is it with them and all these water activities?*

"Ok let's go back and make some calls. You can talk to Mom as well. She'll be up by now."

I had also received a text from Luna asking me to call her urgently, and I needed privacy for that.

The call with Mom was short as she was getting the kids ready for school and she wanted to be back at the hospital before Aunt Jane went into surgery.

I texted Luna. "Can you talk?"

LUNA

I WAS GOING TO DROP OFF THE VOLUNTEER FORM AT THE hospital before going home.

Maybe I would see Chone again too. That it happened to be six o'clock and the end of Channon's shift was pure coincidence. *Yeah right, Luna. At least be honest with yourself. You like him!* I conveniently ignored Nui's earlier admonition.

This time, I was allowed to go back to the adoption area by myself. Chone was still outside resting with his buddies under the trees. He came over and let me pet him.

"You are such a handsome boy, you know that? I can't wait to get you home. I hope Mom and Dad will be ok with it." I sat down on one of the benches in the run area and told Chone everything that had happened and the problems that were piling up. It felt good to just talk about it and I again realised what a crazy story it was. He looked up at me as if he understood every single word I was saying. Maybe he did.

"Hey Nui, looks like you're having quite the conversation with your friend here!"

Channon grinned and bent down to pet Chone. He had done it again; materialized out of thin air. That, or I had been too pre-occupied with my rant to notice him approach. *Did he overhear what I said to Chone? Gosh, it would be good to tell another person and ask for advice. No offense Chone!*

"Did you drop off the papers?"

"Yes, they said they would process them as soon as possible and I should be able to get a pass tomorrow. It'll be great to work here on a regular basis. How was your day?"

"Pretty interesting. I was allowed into the operating room today to observe some procedures. They really do amazing work here. I hope I'll be able to come and work here as a vet eventually."

"That would be cool."

We lapsed into an easy silence and watched the dogs. Shortly afterwards, the other volunteers started to bring the dogs inside for the night. I got up too.

"Are you joining me for breakfast again tomorrow?" Channon asked.

"Most likely, but I will definitely come here after I drop Joey off."

"Great. I'll see you tomorrow then!" Channon nodded, satisfied.

We walked out together, and he waved as he turned down Thong Lo. Unexpectedly, I felt let down, but it was time to update Nui.

NUI

"HEY LUNA, WHAT ARE YOU DOING IN THE BOYS' ROOM?"

"Duen is back so I can't talk in my room. How was today? Did you hear from Mom?"

"Just talked to her but she didn't have much time. She was going back to the hospital."

"Oh, ok. So, I went to the temple today and Ajaarn is hosting a retreat in Chiang Rai, and they don't know when he'll be back. All they knew was he's due to begin another class in Bangkok later this month." Luna said.

"Oh, damn."

"I know, they said they don't keep detailed schedules. I did get the phone number for the temple in Chiang Rai, but I'm not sure if I should call them. I mean, I know he was ok talking to us here, but if he's up there hosting all those other monks... What do you think?"

"Hmm, if they gave you the number then I think it's ok to call and find out. All they can say is no, right?"

"Yeah, I guess. But what would I tell him? I mean, I can't just say we swapped bodies and we need his help to switch back. I mean, if we could talk with him in person it might be different, but it's not like he is a 'switch' help line." Luna cringed at her own words.

"Let's find out when he's coming back. If they let you talk to him, just say that we have some super urgent questions we need his help with," I suggested.

"The way this has been going they'll probably say he's on his way to Timbuktu. Fine, I'll make the call but, in the meantime, I think we both really need to start meditating again. I haven't done anything, have you?"

"No, not really. I haven't had time yet, but I'll try another session tonight. Tomorrow we're going white-water rafting in Ubud, so we'll be gone the whole day. By the way, I talked to your dad about the dog, and Luke was really cool and jumped right in. Your dad said we could come to the shelter when we're back. He's definitely open to it but wants to wait until your mom is home. Can you send me a picture of the dog?"

Luna beamed. "Yeah, that's at least some good news! Thanks. And his name is Chone. I dropped off the volunteer application today. They said they are going to expedite it so I can go there on my own from now on."

"Luna! You volunteered me? Damn it!" My anger went right over her head.

"You'll love it, and if not I'll take over from you when we've switched back, don't worry."

"Yeah right, famous last words. Where have I heard that before?" Sarcasm didn't make a dent either in her 'me-me-me' attitude.

"Oh, come on, it's a good cause, and if nothing else you

can use the abandoned dog issue in one of your exposés, ok? And you volunteered me too so you can't complain."

"Slight difference; the bazaar is a one-off and yours is permanent."

Luna ignored me. "By the way, I've done a bit of work on the essay but not much. I think we'll have to make something up. Let's just hope Mr Campbell doesn't know anything about meditation."

"I won't be able to do anything tomorrow, but I'll tell your dad I need to finish it by Thursday, so you can have a look over the weekend."

"Tomorrow morning I'll be at the shelter, and in the afternoon I'll see Toey and Dearn, but yeah, I'll try to finish it up too and send it to you tomorrow evening."

"Sounds good. Night, and fingers crossed!"

"Night, Nui, I'll text you after I talked to the temple."

NUI

AT BREAKFAST, LUNA'S DAD TOLD US THE OPERATION HAD gone well, and Aunt Jane was recovering. Even though I didn't know her, I was happy to text Luna the good news on my way to the buffet.

The drive to Ubud took over two hours in heavy traffic. The guys snoozed, but I kept my eyes glued to the scenery. Farmers markets, craft shops, processions for some kind of Hindu holiday, it all was so exciting and foreign to me, even though I had grown up only a short hop away. What else had I missed by never leaving Thailand?

The van dropped us at the staging area on a hill above the river. Even from up there we could hear the roar of the water, which became louder and more ferocious as we descended a very long, rough natural staircase with only a rickety bamboo banister as a handhold. My toes were clenching my flipflops and I tried to take deep breaths to calm myself. *What were you thinking? Why did you agree to this madness? And why did Luna assume that Bali would be such a fabulous holiday?* For me it was pure stress, with all the water sports the family insisted on. It didn't matter that the paddle boarding had gone well, this white water thing was a whole different ball game. I should have just stayed at the hotel by the pool. *Come on, Nui, you wanted to have some new experiences, so get into the spirit.* The little pep-talk toned down the worst of my anxiety and when we arrived at the bottom, the river looked a lot more placid. The sound I had heard must have carried from higher up. *Maybe it won't be such a big deal.*

The rubber boat could hold eight people, including the two river guides. Everyone had to wear life-vests and helmets this time, so at least I didn't stand out. Our phones and wallets were locked into a waterproof cooler that was strapped into the boat. The guides demonstrated how to wedge one foot into the space between the side and bottom of the boat to anchor ourselves. Then they talked us through a series of paddling commands they would shout out to avoid hitting rocks and whirlpools in the river. Their warnings made me anxious again. *Breathe. It'll be ok. They wouldn't do this if it was dangerous, right?* Luke talked non-stop, twitchy with anticipation. The guides said the ride would be slightly shorter than normal; the river was running high and fast due to a heavy rainy season. There would be a picnic lunch at the end where the van would pick us up again.

The crew asked us to sit in the boat according to size and weight, though their formula seemed a bit random to me.

It started off mellow enough and I found myself enjoying the ride. Drifting down a wide river on a hot sunny day wasn't so bad after all. Emerald green rice fields and lush tropical jungle dotted the banks, and occasionally, a farmer waved at us as he tended the field with his water buffalo. Just as I became comfortable, the river started to narrow, the current picked up speed and whitecaps crested more frequently. The paddling instructions came quicker. I felt the pull of the current in my arm and back muscles. It was hard work. We were splashed as we dipped up and down the waves. Everyone in the boat was yelling and whooping. I got carried along with the excitement but gripped the paddle more tightly as if it was a safety bar.

We were coming up to the most difficult part of the ride; a narrow passage between huge boulders. It looked like we would get smashed if we hit either side. The noise in the boat died down and everyone silently followed the instructions which were coming even more quickly. The guides were trying to line us up with the gap between the rocks. Their shouts made it sound as if they were having a hard time or maybe they just wanted to add to the drama. We squeezed right into the gap which was indeed so tight, I could touch the rocks on my side.

As we passed through, the front of the boat dipped down over a small waterfall, invisible behind the rocks. We all jumped in our seats. I was caught off guard and before I realized what was happening, my foot became dislodged. I tilted sideways and fell over the rim of the boat. I didn't even have time to catch a breath before water crashed over my head. *Uff!*

The drop was so unexpected that I froze, expecting the life vest to do its thing and pop me up. Instead, I kept twisting and turning, bouncing off underwater rocks like a ping pong ball. Every time I hit one, I puffed out at bit more of what little air I had left. Time slowed. *This can't be happening! Do something! Get out, get out, get out! Someone help me!* I started thrashing round to push myself off the rocks to the surface but the roiling water kept me pinned down and my movements became more and more sluggish and lethargic. Random thoughts bounced around my head. *This is so unfair. All I wanted was a little taste of a nicer life. What will Khun Yaa ... I can't believe ... I wish...*

I had lost any sense of up and down, upstream or downstream and then nothing...

I CAME TO LOOKING UP STRAIGHT AT LUNA'S DAD AND brother hovering over me. *Huh?*

"Kuate arai khuen?" I croaked, but didn't wait for an answer. Instead, I rolled over and coughed up water.

"Oh my God! Luna are you ok? You scared the life out of me." Khun Mark grabbed me in a bear hug then held me at arms-length to check me over and eventually kissed my forehead. I could feel his arms shaking. *What the ...?* I tried to squirm out of his embrace.

"Hi, Mr Taylor. What happened? Where's Luna?"

He still held my arms and looked at me strangely, "What do you mean where's Luna? Honey, it's me, Dad! Are you alright? Where does it hurt? Did you hit your head?" Even his voice sounded shaky and he again pulled me into a hug.

I looked past him and saw a bunch of people I didn't know standing around watching us. We were on the banks of a river on a small rocky beach. *Who are these people?* I tried to make sense of the scene but my brain felt slow and fuzzy. Instead I asked again; "Kuate arai khuen?"

They all looked at me with blank stares. *Why is no one answering?*

"Why are you speaking Thai? Dad, maybe she has a concussion?" Luke suggested.

"Yes, we're going to the hospital to get her checked out,"

Khun Mark agreed. He appeared to be more in control having made a decision. "Did you notify the crew to call an ambulance?" He turned towards a guy holding a walkie-talkie.

The man nodded, "They'll be waiting for us."

"Ok, Luna, we need to figure out how to get you out of here. We're on the wrong side of the river for a car to pick us up. Do you think you can get back into the boat? They tell us the rest of the ride is very smooth."

"Sure, Mr Taylor, I'm fine really. Thanks for asking." *What am I missing? Why is he calling me Luna and where IS Luna?* I started shivering even though the sun was shining directly down on us. I looked down at myself and froze. *Arai wah?! You're losing it!* My brain couldn't compute what I was seeing. Goosebumps on white legs and arms, and an outfit that clearly wasn't mine.

"Man, you really must have hit your head, Luna! Do you have amnesia?" Luke acted concerned but I could see a barely supressed grin at the corner of his mouth. This was simply an adventure for him, but at least he provided some sort of clue. "We couldn't get to you in the boat when you went under, and then you got caught in a whirlpool. You almost drowned! Dad was amazing. He jumped right in and got hold of your leg and pulled you out. It was epic!"

"Really?" *Why was I in the water in the first place? Where are we? What am I doing here with you? And stop calling me Luna! Ok Nui, you better figure this out, and fast. Just pretend everything is normal for now.* Inside I was freaking out. *Did they drug me? Kidnap me? Brainwash me?* I started to hyperventilate.

"Stop Luke, don't you see you're scaring her?" Luna's dad interrupted. He turned to me. "Come on, honey, you'll feel better once we get you into dry clothes and have you checked out."

OMG, what are they planning to do with me? And where the heck is Luna? My imagination got the better of me and came up with increasingly alarming scenarios. People smuggling, slavery rings, drugs... But none of those things explained my white skin. Taking a deep breath, I decided I needed to find out more first, so for now I would have to go along with their plan.

I was a bit wobbly when I stood up, but otherwise felt ok. Mr Taylor helped me into the rubber boat and then sat right behind me holding onto my shoulders to anchor me. *Or did he want to make sure that I didn't jump overboard? Is that what happened? I'd been trying to escape?* Luke and the other people scrambled back on board too. Luna still hadn't shown up and I couldn't believe we would take off without her.

"Erm, Mr Taylor, shouldn't we wait for Luna to come back?" I asked, cautiously.

"Are you sure you're ok, or are you just making fun of me now, Luna?" Khun Mark sounded conflicted. I didn't know how to answer that so I kept quiet and just grunted. The river guides pushed off.

The rest of the journey went by without incident. We had to climb up a steep staircase with Mr Taylor holding on to me. We both were out of breath by the time we reached the top. An ambulance was waiting. Khun Mark said he would follow me to the hospital with Luke in a van. Seeing the medics started another wave of horrible images—organ harvesting, surrogate pregnancy... *Come on Nui get a grip. You've read too many horror stories and besides, they call you Luna, and her dad would never do anything bad to her.* Still, my pulse was racing.

At least the ride would give me more time to sort out what was going on. As I laid on the stretcher, the medics took my vital signs, which were all within range. My blood pressure was high but they said it was normal given the adrenaline rush of the accident. No broken bones, just bruises and shallow cuts, which they cleaned and bandaged. They bundled me in blankets and I finally stopped shivering. I still wasn't clear why I had been in a boat on a river with Mr Taylor and Luke in the first place. There was no way I would have gone off with them by myself without Luna.

As the crew wheeled me through the emergency door, I said a quick prayer that Mae or Khun Yaa would be there waiting for me. No such luck. *Oh God, Nui, you're alone in a hospital in an unfamiliar place with strange people. What have you gotten yourself into?*

The doctors performed a series of tests and took x-rays. Luckily, they decided that an MRI wouldn't be necessary. There would have been no way for me to lie still in a tube for half an hour in my current state. *Don't tell them about your head, or they'll make you stay in the hospital. At least you know Khun Mark and Luke.*

We were able to leave a couple of hours later. In the van, Luke kept prattling on about the accident and how I could have died. I tuned him out while I tried to sort out my muddled head and figure out where we were, but instead I fell into an exhausted sleep. My phone pinged as we pulled into the driveway of a hotel. The sign read Moevenpick Jimbaran, Bali, and the call was from... Nui? *Ok, now I'm officially in the twilight zone.*

LUNA

Somehow I had developed a real morning routine. Joey, coffee, breakfast with Channon and then the hospital to see Chone. *Don't get too comfortable Luna, you're switching back next week.* I felt a pang in my stomach, and immediately countered. *Who needs to think this far ahead?* Anyone hearing my own arguments would have thought me certifiable.

Nui's parents hadn't said anything about working at the store, and I figured Khun Yaa would tell me if she needed me at home. I felt a bit guilty for not offering to help more, but thought it best not to jinx it.

Chone became more beautiful every time I saw him. He had picked up energy and looked like he was growing overnight. I knew it was tricky to become so attached to him, but it was too late to worry about that. My biggest concern was that someone else might want to adopt him before we could convince my parents. I took a few photos and sent them to Nui to show Dad.

Channon was so easy to get along with and the staff clearly adored him. *Join the club.* But it was another relationship I had to be careful about. I felt bad deceiving him about my identity, but Nui was right, it would be impossible to explain the situation. *Oh Channon, by the way I'm actually Luna, only temporarily in Nui's body.* Just the thought of saying those words made me cringe. *What if he doesn't like you as Luna?* That idea was even worse!

Duen was out when I got back to the house. A good time to call the temple in Chiang Rai.

"Wat Rong Khun, sawasdee khrup."

"Sawasdee kha, I was wondering if I could speak with Ajaarn Anurak please?"

"What is this about? Ajaarn Anurak is in a retreat right now."

"This is Nui, one of his meditation students from Bangkok. Ajaarn Anuruk helped us with a school project and he said to contact him if we had more questions. I was wondering when he would be back in Bangkok, or if I could speak with him."

"Wait a moment." I crossed my fingers while I listened to recorded temple chanting.

"Ajaarn Anurak is hosting the retreat until Friday. After that he has received permission to visit his father upcountry. He should be back in Bangkok sometime next week."

"Oh! Is there any way to speak with him before he leaves?"

"I can take a message for him, but I don't know that he will be able to speak with you. Just be patient."

"Ok, khob khun maak ka." I gave him my number and hung up.

There was no way to predict if and when he would call, so there was no point in worrying about it. *Khun Luna! Getting all pragmatic now?* I snorted at the absurdity of it.

I still had an hour before meeting Toey and Dearn. The house was quiet; a good time to try a short meditation or at least see if there was any change to my last attempt.

Sitting back on my bed I started the tape and closed my eyes. Ajaarn Anurak's voice felt comforting as I went through the breathing exercises, and I relaxed. I had survived the last few days as Nui and felt much calmer. I didn't come close to having an out-of-body experience, but I didn't panic either.

I left in plenty of time but Toey and Dearn were already slurping iced coffee at the cafe. It was fascinating talking to two girls who had supposedly been my best friends since first grade. There seemed to be some kind of shortcut to the conversation, and explanations about most things weren't necessary, as they knew each other's backstory. I mainly listened, to be on the safe side, but I was a bit envious too. *It must be so nice to have friends like that.* I kind of implied that Nui had 'adopted' Luna because she was lonely. They felt sorry for her and suggested we all meet together the following week. I was humming to myself when I left.

My phone rang as I turned into Soi nine towards the hospital.

"Nong Nui? I am returning your call."

It took me a second to realize it was Ajaarn.

"Ajaarn Anurak kha? Oh, thank you so much for calling back."

"I don't have much time, but they said it was urgent. What do you need?"

The unexpected call-back left me dumbstruck.

"Yohm Nui. What is it?"

He sounded rushed, but also concerned.

I took a deep breath and my bottled-up anxieties popped like a string of firecrackers.

"Ajaarn kha, do you remember the project Luna and I were working on? And our conversation about our out-of-body experiences? Well... we did it. Nui and I switched bodies but now we can't figure out how to switch back. You have to help us!"

There was dead silence at the other end.

"Ajaarn Anurak kha?"

"Yes, Yohm Nui, I'm here, but I don't think I understand what you're saying. What do you mean you and Luna switched bodies?"

"I know it sounds crazy, but it actually happened. Remember how we talked about the connection to life energy and other people? Nui and I practiced on our own and then there was this thunderstorm and all of a sudden we were in the other's body. For the past week I have been living as Nui with her family and Nui is with my family in Bali right now. We need to get back into our own bodies but we don't know how. We've tried to meditate but it's not working. What should we do?"

"Wait. You're saying you're actually Luna? That's impossible. I know that people can raise their vibration to a high level, but I've never heard of anyone who's actually switched bodies or minds with someone else. Are you trying to play a joke on me?"

"No, no, Ajaarn Anurak it's really not a joke, I promise kha. We don't know how it happened, but it did and now we're stuck. Can you help us?"

I realized I was shouting in the middle of the street and people passing were frowning at me. If he didn't believe me, who would?

"Ok Yohm Nui, eh or Luna, calm down. Let's see what

really happened. I have to go back to the retreat right now. I am back in Bangkok next Wednesday and we can talk about it then. I will ask some of my brothers here if they know anyone who's come across this, ok?"

"Thank you kha. We are very worried."

"The best I can suggest right now is that you and Luna try to meditate again to calm down. No matter what really happened, I know that nothing can be done while you're so anxious."

"Yes, we realized that too, but it's very hard."

"I'm sure there's some explanation for it and we'll figure it out. I have to go now, but I'll see you next week. Come to the temple on Wednesday afternoon."

"Thank you kha, Ajaarn Anurak. We will. Good bye."

Though nothing had changed, I felt much better having talked to someone about our problem. Maybe I just had to accept I should deal with things as they came, instead of worrying about the future. *Luna, you're becoming positively zen! Where is this new 'it is what it is' attitude coming from?* I smiled to myself.

MY ID WAS READY, AND THE RECEPTIONIST HANDED ME A schedule for the rest of the week. I was to shadow Khun Pim for a few days before getting my own assignments. When I was back at school, my schedule would be more flexible, but for now, I would spend a few hours each day familiarizing myself with the centre and different jobs. Volunteering meant observing and training the dogs to obey basic commands, cleaning the pens and yard, taking them to the vet for check-ups, introducing and matching potential adopters to the dogs and answering questions about their behaviour. Channon came over after his shift and we decided to get a soda at a café nearby.

"What happened, Nui? You're smiling the whole time."

"What do you mean? Am I grumpy otherwise?" I teased him.

"No, of course not, but you seem different today. Happier, more relaxed."

I hadn't realized my emotions had been so close to the surface. If I felt better having talked to Ajaarn, I wondered if it would help to tell others as well, like Channon.

Don't go there Luna! I warned myself. Impersonating Nui was already difficult enough and needed my full concentration. *But wouldn't it be great if Channon knew he was getting to know Luna and not Nui? Stop it. He'll probably run away screaming and call a shrink.*

"Channon, do you meditate?"

"I used to. Why do you ask?"

"I'm just curious. Luna and I did this intense training at Wat Pathum and we both had some very strange experiences."

"What kind of experiences? I started when my father passed away and it really helped me to cope. Come to think of it, I probably should have continued but there never seemed to be enough time. Maybe I'll pick it up again."

"Well, this may sound strange, but have you ever had an out-of-body experience while meditating?"

"No, can't say I have, though I always felt very calm. Why? Did you?"

"Yes, actually, both Luna and I did, and it was really strange."

"Strange how? Good strange or scary?" Channon was curious.

Luna, what are you doing?

"It was pretty cool. You're kind of floating and see yourself from above but you feel connected to everything and everyone around you. Almost like there are threads running between people, and it's like there's some kind of exchange, not really words but more like vibrations, running along the lines. I really don't know how to explain it better."

"That sounds pretty awesome. I'd love to experience that sometime. How long did it take you to do that?"

"Well Ajaarn Anurak said it normally takes years of practising but for some reason Luna and I were able to get there pretty quickly. Not really sure why." No need to explain that it had been our specific intention from the beginning.

"Hmm, do you do it every time? Maybe you can teach me?"

"No, it doesn't work every time and I think the more you try the more you block yourself. I haven't been able to get back to it and now I'm kind of annoyed with myself."

"Why annoyed? If you already know you can do it, I'm sure it can't be that difficult anymore." Channon, as always, was philosophical about challenges.

"Ha! Easier said than done. You know how it is, when you really really want something and the more you push for it, the further it slips away. I suppose I'm thinking too much."

"Maybe you just need to remember how it felt?" *He really gets it. Can I tell him the rest too?*

"Hmm, maybe. You know, you sound just like Ajaarn. You sure you're not some kind of teacher yourself?" I tried to lighten the mood. I was getting way too close to spilling our secret.

"Hardly! Like I said, I haven't meditated in a long time. But now I'm curious."

"You should. Let me know how it goes."

We chatted for another half hour before I had to get going.

I still had to call Nui for an update, and I'd promised I would work on our essay.

THE FAMILY HAD FINISHED DINNER BUT WERE STILL SITTING around the table. Mae asked me to sit down.

"What have you been doing, Nui? We have hardly seen you these last few days?"

"Oh, I've been at the hospital helping out at the adoption centre, and this afternoon I met Toey and Dearn. I just picked up my ID for the hospital; they want me to come in for a few hours in the morning and afternoon for the induction."

"You've been spending a lot of time with Channon too, haven't you?" Khun Yaa said.

"Well, you know he works at the hospital. Why?"

"You know we like Channon, but remember you are only sixteen; you have school coming up and you need to concentrate on that." Mae added.

"Channon is Krit's friend and you were ok with me working at the hospital. So, why is this suddenly an issue? I only see him there, anyway." I was annoyed and maybe I protested a bit too much, but still.

"You're having breakfast and lunch with him and you missed dinner again because you were out with him. I don't want you to get carried away." Mae insisted.

"Oh come on! You know I won't have much time after next week anyway, and Channon is starting Uni soon."

"Why don't you ask him to have dinner with us tomorrow after you're done at the hospital. We'd love to see him again." Khun Yaa said.

Uh oh, what is this? Meet the parents? I would have

preferred to keep these two sides separate but there was really no good reason to decline.

"Erm, sure, I'll ask him. I have to work on our essay for next week. Can I use the boy's room? It's quieter."

"You just want to call your boyfriend." Duen giggled.

"He's not my boyfriend. Mind your own business. I just need some peace and quiet to finish this essay. You're always making so much noise."

"Girls, enough. Nui, go ahead and use the boy's room. And don't forget to walk Joey. He needs more exercise."

"Sure Mae, let me work for a bit and then I'll take him."

I was glad to escape. Bad enough that Nui was on my case about Channon. Why is everyone so against my relationship with him? It's not like we're dating. *Yet?* I grinned at the prospect.

I texted Channon about the dinner invite, which he accepted immediately, and said he would see me at breakfast too. That stupid grin widened.

Nui was probably at dinner in Bali, but I texted to say we needed to talk. And finally, I turned on my laptop to work on the report. It was ironic that Nui and I had created our problem through meditation, when the opposite was the goal. But like Channon said, logically we should also be able to reverse it. Mom's favourite saying was, 'what goes around, comes around.'

NUI

I WAS ABOUT TO FIND OUT IF I WAS TRULY LOSING MY MIND. I followed Mr Taylor and Luke to the third floor of the hotel, not quite clear where this was heading, but for now they were my only known points of reference. We entered a huge suite and Luke disappeared into a bedroom on the far left. *Now what?*

"I'm gonna go and shower. Do you want to have dinner by the pool or just relax and order room service, Luna?" Mr Taylor asked.

"Erm, I think I'll just take a shower and order some food here if you don't mind. I'm pretty tired."

"Of course, honey, get some rest. I'm so relieved you're ok, you gave me quite the fright. I'll come and check on you later. The doctor said we need to make sure you don't have a concussion." He smiled and hugged me again.

Not waiting for a response, he followed Luke into the

other part of the suite. Closing the door behind me, I surveyed the room. I recognized Luna's things but there was still no sign of her.

My phone pinged again reminding me of the waiting text message. Only 'call me'. *Ok, here we go!* I held my breath and hit the call button.

"There you are!"

"Hello?" I probed tentatively.

"Hey Nui, I have so much to tell you!"

My own voice came back over the speaker. Positively spooky, but at least *she* called me Nui.

"Nui, are you there?" The voice repeated.

"Erm, yes, who is this?" I asked, cautiously, almost afraid to hear the answer.

"What do you mean, who's this? It's Luna! Why are you being so weird? What's wrong?" The voice turned suspicious.

"Erm, I'm not sure."

"What do you mean you're not sure? What's going on? Are Dad and Luke ok? Now she sounded worried.

"Yes, they are fine." I took a deep breath, "Ok, this may sound weird but can you explain something to me? Why does your caller ID say 'Nui' on my phone and why is everyone calling me Luna?" Ok, that wasn't very articulate, but I didn't know where to start.

There was a long pause at the other end.

"Say that again. What do you mean, why is everyone calling you Luna? Are you kidding me?" The voice sounded puzzled, but also slightly annoyed. "Don't start playing games with me. I'm stressed out enough as is."

"I'm sorry, but I really need to know. I'm not sure what's happening. There was this accident this afternoon and now everyone is calling me Luna and I know I look like her but I'm not her." I sounded lunatic even to myself.

Another long pause. "You mean you have forgotten?" This time she seemed incredulous.

"Forgotten what?"

"Oh dear God, can this get any more crazy? You better sit down and you better believe every word I'm telling you!"

I flopped onto the bed and grabbed a throw pillow to hug to my chest.

"You are Nui but in my, Luna's, body, and I'm Luna in your body! Does this ring any bells?"

"Uhm, not really, but go on." I was anxious for the full story and got way more than I bargained for. She told a crazy tale of a temple, monk, meditation, out-of-body experience, switching bodies and living each other's lives. *Does she honestly expect me to believe that?* I got up to look at myself in the full length mirror on the wardrobe door. Yes, these were definitely Luna's blue eyes staring back at me! And all that white skin. Could her story possibly be true? Little bells in my memory started ringing, and puzzle pieces were clicking into place. It began to make sense, even if I couldn't get my head around it and would need time to digest the idea.

"You got it now?" The voice (*Luna?*) demanded.

"Hmm, sort of. I need to think about it."

"Oh God, Nui. Please don't do this. We have enough complications as it is. I can't deal with you not knowing what's going on. You need to play your part. And by the way, what was the accident? You ok?" The last part sounded perfunctory.

"Yeah, I'm fine. I went overboard during white water rafting and it knocked me out, so your dad had to jump in and get me. I have a few bruises but nothing major." I assured her.

"Gee, Nui, I'm glad Dad was there to fish you out. No more water sports for you, ok?" She mockingly ordered. Luna making light of the accident annoyed me.

Yes, I downplayed it, but I had been unconscious long enough that I'd lost part of my memory. She could have shown a bit more concern, especially as she knew how I felt about being in the water. *Does she realize that if her story is true, her own body could have been killed?* She didn't wait for a comeback but resumed her lecture at full speed.

"Anyway, while you were taking your beauty sleep, a lot of things have happened here, so please pay attention." Luna ordered. "I talked to Ajaarn Anurak today, but he didn't have much time. He's still in that retreat until Friday but he'll be back on Wednesday and said we should go to see him then. I told him what happened but I don't think he believed me. He said it's impossible, but he wanted to ask the other monks about it. Looks like we got into some unchartered territory. Let's hope they have an idea how to reverse it. I also got my hospital ID and this week I have morning and afternoon shifts. Oh, and I met Dearn and Toey today. They want to meet you, I mean, me, next week. And Khun Yaa invited Channon for dinner tomorrow."

My mind was racing to catch up but the last point caught my attention, "Hang on, who's Channon?"

"Oh come on, Nui. You met Channon, Krit's friend. I've been hanging out with him and he's helping me with Chone's adoption. I already told you that and you were asking Dad about it. Remember?"

There was simply too much information to absorb in one go, so I simply mumbled 'yeah' and let her continue. But I was wondering why Khun Yaa would invite some random guy for dinner? I'd bet my weekly allowance there was more to the story than Luna was letting on.

"Did you show Dad the pictures of Chone? What did he say? I'm worried someone might try to adopt him before Dad agrees."

"Did you send them to me?"

"Come on, Nui, get with the programme. I sent them to you this afternoon. Can you check?"

"I will, but I gotta go now." While I was eager for more information, I just couldn't take any more of her condescending tone. I'd rather figure out the rest by myself.

"Ok, so we'll talk tomorrow evening, but text me if anything comes up, ok?"

"Sure, good night."

"Night, Nui. And don't forget Chone!"

My mind was reeling, but mainly I was irate about Luna's flippant attitude. She was so damn preoccupied with her own little bubble, she didn't give a hoot about anyone else. *Give it a rest for now. You're still too shaken by the accident to make sense of any of this.* I figured I'd feel better with a shower and some food. I managed half of my club sandwich but kept nodding off, so I finally admitted defeat.

———

MY HEART WAS PUMPING FURIOUSLY AND I COULDN'T breathe. It felt like I was drowning. Desperate for air, I shot straight up trying to force oxygen into my lungs. My sleepshirt was soaked with sweat. *You're ok, you're ok, you're ok. Come on Nui, you can do this. Breathe in and breathe out. You're safe.* While I slowly got my breathing under control, my thoughts were off and running. *Holy Cow! Nui, you could have been killed and no one would have known it was you except Luna.* This was even more bizarre than just trying to come to grips with the mind-swap. *And then what? Luna would have just lived my life as if nothing had happened? She probably doesn't even care, now that she has Channon and that dog.* Ok, that was probably not true, but once I got started on this track it was hard to see reason. *She's so damn selfish and only cares about herself. She just takes what she wants, and she's messing up my life, volunteering for this and that, and seeing my friends and cousins. Who does she think she is? Does she care at all how I feel? Not Ms High and Mighty. For her, it's all about Chone and Channon and Channon and Chone.* I was shaking with resentment and anger.

Woah, woah, Nui, where did all this come from? Stop it. You know that's not how things are. I tried to reason with myself. *Just because you were unlucky today doesn't make it her fault. Maybe, but she didn't even care. It's always about her, her, her. Did she show any concern? Heck, no! She only made fun of it. Beauty sleep? How dare she?* I got out of bed and stepped onto the balcony to calm down and get some air. The sound of the ocean surf across the road was soothing. Suddenly, I heard steps behind me.

"Ah honey, couldn't sleep?" Luna's dad stepped out to the balcony. "Are you feeling ok?"

"Oh sorry, I didn't mean to wake you."

"You didn't. I was just coming to check on you and saw you were up. Too much excitement today?" He sounded understanding.

"Yeah, I guess. Thanks again for rescuing me. That was really brave."

"You're my daughter. Of course, I got you. I always will, you know that." He wrapped an arm around my shoulder and this time I didn't shrug him off. I finally felt myself calming down. *At least someone cares.*

"Thanks, Dad, I think I'll go back to bed. I feel better now. Goodnight."

"Goodnight honey, and sleep well. We'll take it easy tomorrow, ok?"

"Oh, by the way, Dad? I have been thinking about what you said about going back to the US early and I think you're right. Family is more important, so I'm fine with moving back as soon as possible."

"That's great honey. I'm glad you feel that way. We don't have to decide right now, we'll talk more when Mom is back. Sleep tight."

I went back to bed and only then realized that my subconscious mind had reconnected all the dots. I was back on a level playing field with Luna.

If she can take what she wants, so can I.

LUNA

I SAT ON TUM'S BED, STUNNED, REPLAYING THE conversation with Nui. The enormity of her not remembering our switch was mind-boggling. I hadn't really thought about it during the call but she must have been completely freaked out. I would have been. One mind swap was bad enough, but a double twist?! How do you keep your head straight after that? I felt a stab of guilt that I had been so caught up with my own issues I didn't ask if she was ok, although she seemed calm enough about it.

A shiver ran down my back as it hit me: my body could have been killed. Would that have meant I'd be stuck in Nui's body forever? What about my parents and Luke? They wouldn't have had a clue, and they sure as hell wouldn't believe me if I were to go to them as Nui to reclaim my own life. And Nui's family wouldn't have believed me either, or let me go for that matter, certainly not if it meant their own

daughter was dead. What a mess. My head hurt just imagining the consequences. I was breathing too fast, feeling light-
headed. *Christ, what have we done?* Scenarios like this
definitely hadn't figured in our plan. It was high time we got
back into our own bodies, regardless of how much we
enjoyed experiencing each other's lifestyles. *But you won't
get to see Channon or Chone anymore.* The thought was
depressing, but perhaps Nui's accident was the wake-up call
we both needed. *I'll just need to find a way to see them as
Luna.*

I decided to try meditating again but despite my best
intentions, my thoughts kept bouncing back to worst case
scenarios and I couldn't settle.

I gave up and went back to the kitchen to see Khun Yaa. I
figured I owed her an apology for my earlier behaviour. She
was sitting at the kitchen table writing her market list for the
next day.

"Khun Yaa, I wanted to… I mean… I'm really sorry
about what I said earlier." She looked up, waved my apology
aside and patted the seat next to her. "Come sit with me, Nui.
What has been bothering you? You have not been yourself
this last week. Are you sure I can't help you? You just have to
tell me."

*Gosh, she could probably coax a confession out of a
professional criminal with her sympathetic smile.* I was so
tempted to tell her the whole story but knew it was
impossible.

"It's ok, Khun Yaa, I just feel a bit out of sorts, but
nothing I can't handle. I'll tell you if I need your help, I
promise." I dodged.

"Well, I trust you, Nui. But, you know I'm here for you if
you want to talk. Maybe you should to come with me to the

temple tomorrow, and then we can go and see your cousins? It'll be good to pray and see the family."

"Sure, I'd love that. What time do we leave? I have to work in the morning."

"Just come back here when you're done and we'll go after lunch."

It wasn't quite what I'd had in mind, but it was time to earn some brownie points for Nui, even if she wouldn't know it.

NUI

AFTER MY DISRUPTED SLEEP, I WAS TIRED BUT HUGELY relieved to have my full memory again. Remembering was like having my balance pole back for the tightrope I was walking, not fool proof but definitely helpful.

"So, what do you guys want to do today?" Khun Mark asked, over breakfast.

"I have to work on my essay; it's due next week. Maybe you and Luke can go and I'll meet you later?"

"Luke?"

"Can we go to Seminyak and jet ski, Dad? Luna doesn't want to do it anyway."

"I guess we could go for a little while. Luna, do you want to meet us for lunch or do you want to stay here?"

"Depends how fast I get through this. Can you text me?" I didn't really feel like doing much, but I knew I'd regret not seeing other parts of the island.

"By the way, Nui sent me some pictures of that dog she was talking about. Isn't he beautiful?" I pulled up the shots on my phone. Chone looked adorable with his bandit mask and I thought she'd named him perfectly.

"Oh, let me see," Luke craned his neck. "Cool. He looks like a wolf. I really think we should get him. Can we go and see him when we're back, Dad?"

"Speaking of, how would you guys feel if we go back on Friday instead of Saturday? I know this trip has been a bit messed up, so I thought maybe we could spend a day together in Bangkok and do some things there? We never have much time for that."

"Oh, can we go to the tiger temple? Mom promised to take us." Luke immediately suggested.

"Luna? What do you think?"

"I'm fine with Friday. Maybe we could go to the pet hospital on Saturday?"

"Oh yes, let's do that." Luke instantly changed his mind.

"Ok, let me see if I can get the flights confirmed. Khun Bo won't be back until Saturday, but we'll manage. Luke let's go. I'll text you later, Luna."

After they left, I finished the report and emailed it to Luna for her comments and then took a short nap. Luna's dad messaged a few hours later to ask if I wanted to join them in Seminyak. I walked to the lobby, got a cab and automatically asked the driver to switch on the metre. He simply stated; "Flat fee, seventy-five thousand rupiah."

Knowing how cab drivers in Bangkok tried to play that game, I was annoyed, but figured it wasn't worth the hassle. We were only talking about $5 or so. *Nui, you're turning into a whitey. Ha! I AM a whitey.*

Khun Mark and Luke were waiting at a table on the

beach, munching on some appetizers. I joined them under the umbrella and inhaled the fresh ocean breeze.

"How was the jet ski?"

"Awesome! Dad let me drive and I did some wicked turns. Almost threw Dad off." Luke was pumped up.

"Hardly!" his father laughed. "But good driving Luke! Did you get your essay done, Luna?"

"Yep, all set. Any news on the flights?"

"Yes, we are leaving at five tomorrow afternoon."

"Great, and what time are we going to the shelter on Saturday? I need to let Nui know. She'll be there in the morning."

"Hey, I thought we were going to the tiger temple first?" Luke complained.

"We can't do both in one day. It takes over three hours to get there. And you said you wanted to see Chone too. That's more urgent."

Khun Mark jumped in, "Luke, how about we make the Tiger Temple a daytrip when Mom's back?" Luke shrugged and gave in.

We stopped in Legian on the way back as Luna's dad wanted to look at some of the newer resorts in Bali. The rest of the afternoon we relaxed by the pool. *Ah, now this is more my idea of fun.* I'd happily forgo any kind of water sports in future. I was sorry to leave Bali early but Luna and I had a giant mess to tidy up.

LUNA

THURSDAY WAS AN ODD DAY. I HAD NEVER BEEN MUCH OF A morning person, but now I was excited to get up early and have breakfast with Channon at Pi' Ohm's. This had become my favourite part of the day. Thank God I could use Joey as my excuse for our meeting.

My shift at the shelter didn't start until nine, but I wanted to spend some extra time with Chone. Deep down I already thought of him as my dog. He had bounced back remarkably fast from his ordeal and his energy was way up.

The first surprise came when the supervisor informed me someone had submitted an application for Chone on their adoption site. The centre had used my own photos and now I wished I hadn't taken them. I sent a silent prayer; *Hurry up Nui.*

The applicant, Khun Nattawut, wanted to know if Chone would be safe for his ten-year-old daughter. They lived near the Chao Praya river and claimed to have a big back yard and Chone would get lots of workouts. Khun Pim, my trainer, was teaching me what to look for in an applicant.

"They sometimes exaggerate the space or time they have. We'll have to make a house visit and we'll need some references. Not everyone can handle a big dog like Chone who's still young and needs to be trained." I was somewhat relieved, but knew we would have a similar issue at home.

"I think he's already had some training and follows commands really well."

"Yes, I noticed he listens to you, but we need to make sure he'll do the same with other people. Or maybe you want to adopt him?" Pim winked.

"I'd love to, but we already have Joey at home and I'm not sure my parents would allow another."

"Well, let's see who this Khun Nattawut is and when he's available."

As we were cleaning the pens and running area, the dogs kept running back and forth, constantly getting in our way and just nudging us for a scratch behind the ears. *God, I love it here. Maybe I should get a job working with animals. Channon seems to have found his calling early. I'll have to talk to him about it.*

At noon I ran home to meet Khun Yaa for our excursion. I texted Channon on my way out to remind him I was coming back later, and I'd also see him at dinner with the family. It was just the grandparents, Duen and me for lunch. I would definitely miss Khun Yaa's cooking. The pad gra prow, fried rice and pak choy were delicious.

Khun Bpoo dropped us at the skytrain. While Aunt Varaporn and Khun Yaa chatted in the living room, I took the girls to their pool. Eve played Arielle and Jenny was Flounder, her sidekick. Both were totally at ease in the water but looking after them was like herding a shoal of herring. *How did Nui do this if she is so afraid of water?*

After a quick stop at Erawan shrine, grandma and I got back on the skytrain. She insisted on taking two moto-taxis from the station instead of walking. My dad called them Bangkok Helicopters, and I was terrified to sit on the back of a bike weaving in and out of traffic, but with Khun Yaa right there, I couldn't object.

Unfortunately, I was wearing a skirt and had to sit side saddle which was even worse. I closely watched Khun Yaa's moves and clumsily tried to copy her. I overcompensated and nearly tipped over backwards, grabbing the driver's arm just in time. He rolled his eyes, shook his head and mumbled into his helmet. I didn't care. At least I was sitting now and Nui's reflexes finally took over as we started down the road. *Oh this is cool. I can finally do something I never thought possible.* I grinned but still held tight to the bar behind the passenger seat.

My shift was only one hour long, to settle the dogs for the night. Khun Pim confirmed we would go to Khun Nattawut's house at ten the next morning. We were closing the last of the pens when Channon showed up, freshly showered and smelling delicious. I was scruffy in comparison but would freshen up at home. As we walked I told him about the potential adopter.

"No point worrying about it until he's approved. I'm sure everything will work out ok," Channon tried to reassure me.

"Yeah, but what if he's ok, and then it's too late for Luna to get him?"

"I'm sure it'll be fine Nui, don't stress about it. At least he'll have a good home either way."

I knew he was right but still couldn't stop worrying. I really hoped Nui had prodded Dad on the idea.

If Channon felt he was getting the third degree at dinner, he didn't let on. Instead, he good naturedly handled the interrogation. Mae and Khun Yaa felt sorry about his dad and asked him to invite his mom over for lunch soon. Channon joined me on my evening walk with Joey and then left for his friend's house. We planned our usual breakfast the next morning. *What happened to your resolution of not getting more involved?* I masterfully ignored my own question. Time to call Nui for an update.

NUI

"HEY NUI, HOW ARE YOU FEELING? DO YOU REMEMBER everything now?"

Yeah, I think I'm fully recovered! Thanks."

"You know, I'm sorry. I wasn't really paying attention yesterday but you threw me for a loop with your memory loss. The accident must have been terrifying for you!"

What in the ...? Luna, concerned? What is she up to?

"Erm, it's ok, it was a lot to take in for both of us I guess, but I'm back now so let's just move on."

I didn't tell her how angry I had been during the night, or that I had given her dad the go ahead for the move. After all, she had kept things from me too. I was glad we weren't on Facetime so she couldn't see me pull a face.

"Ok great. So, what did you guys do today?"

Well it was nice while it lasted—a full second! I was

cynical and also suspicious of some ulterior motive on Luna's part.

"We went to Seminyak and Legian and I finished the report, did you get it?"

"Haven't checked yet, just got back from walking Joey, and I was at Aunt Varaporn's house with the girls this afternoon." Luna replied.

"Oh ok, let me know what you think. And let me know when you're done."

"Almost there. What else is happening? Did you talk to Dad about Chone? I just found out today there's a guy who wants to adopt him. We're going to the house tomorrow to check it out. You gotta hurry. I don't know how to keep Chone here otherwise."

"Yeah, I showed him the pictures and he seemed open to it. Luke of course wanted to have him yesterday, but I think that's only because Chone looks like a wolf. The good news is your dad got earlier flights and we're coming back tomorrow, so we can come to the shelter on Saturday. Morning is probably better as I need to check on the bazaar thing with Khun Sonia too."

"See, I told you not to volunteer me for this kind of cause," Luna said.

"Yeah right, says the one who signed me up for regular work at a dog shelter," I fired back.

"Mai pen rai ja. Just text me tomorrow about the time. I'll be there from nine to noon. And I'll try to hold off this other guy. Our own application is ready to go but Dad needs to fill in some final details and sign it."

"Gosh Luna, when did you become such an activist? I thought you didn't want to get involved at all! Anyway, we're leaving on the afternoon flight and will be back in Bangkok by eight. Anything else? How was dinner with Channon?"

"Hahaha, the poor guy, he got interrogated by Grandma and Mae. But he was a good sport about it." Despite her joke, Luna sounded hesitant. Now I wished we'd been on Facetime after all so I could read her reaction more clearly.

"Uh oh, don't tell me they were checking him out as boyfriend material for you, I mean me, were they?"

"Oh, come on, I have no intention to get involved at this point. He's a really great guy but what if we are switching back?"

"At this point? And *if* we're switching back?"

"I mean *when*! Geez, give me a break. Speaking of, did you try to meditate?" She was trying to avoid my questions.

"Don't try to change the subject, Luna. Just because you have a crush on Channon, doesn't mean you can mess up my life. It'll be up to me to sort it out next week. Can't you just chill for a few days until we've seen Ajaarn?"

"Stop patronizing me Nui, I know what I'm doing."

"Oh yeah? Doesn't look that way from where I stand. You're being irresponsible and mean leading him on."

"You have no idea what it's like to have a friend like Channon. Someone who actually cares." Luna spat back at me.

"Oh, you think he cares? And who does he care for? Me or you? He doesn't even know you're Luna. Have you thought about that?" I was done playing nice with her.

Dead silence.

"Look who's being mean now." Luna's comeback was lame. I could tell from her wobbly voice she was on the verge of crying.

"Damn it, Luna, we're in this together and need each other. I don't want to fight with you but you gotta stop making things worse. Can't you just wait until next week?"

"Fine, whatever. I gotta go. Night."

I carefully placed the phone down and shook my head. A fight wasn't going to help either of us. But neither was it ok to involve other people in our problem. Best case scenario would be for us to switch back and have Luna out of my life for good. *But with that my own dream of moving will evaporate into thin air.* Damn, I had to make some tough decisions myself. According to Buddha, I just had to be patient. 'Everything comes to you at the right moment'. *Yeah, but when is that right moment?*

LUNA

I SAT ON THE BED, MY HEAD BURIED IN MY HANDS, BITING MY lip to keep myself from crying. Lately, every single conversation with Nui ended in an argument. *Why is she so mean? All I want is to have Channon as a friend and now she's trying to spoil that too. Maybe she's jealous?* The worst part was she was right; Channon thought of me as Nui. *So, tell him the truth.* The thought stopped me in my tracks. Should I, could I? *No way, he would never believe you. Well, you won't know until you try.* I mentally slapped myself. *Stop Luna, this is nuts. You promised Nui you'd lie low until Wednesday. But, what if?* These internal monologues were confusing and getting me nowhere. Thank God I hadn't told Nui about my argument with her parents and Grandma. Given the way she judged everything I did, she would have ripped my head off.

To distract myself, I haphazardly finished the essay and mailed it off to Nui before going to bed. I was emotionally drained but even during the night I couldn't completely switch off and disjointed images kept spinning through my head: Channon -boyfriend? Chone - adoption? The switch -.

My dark mood hadn't really improved when I dragged myself out of bed to take Joey for his walk. By now Pi' Ohm treated me as a regular. Without asking, she just prepared an omelette for me. I left half on my plate and Channon picked up on my misery.

"What's wrong, Nui?"

"I'm worried about Chone and this visit to Khun Nattawut."

"Why are you worrying about something that might not happen. You know what they say - if you think about it constantly, you'll make it happen, whether it's good or bad."

I glared at him. "Great, now I have to worry about that too!"

He laughed. "Come on, let's drop off Joey and then you need some puppy love. Chone can cheer you up."

I don't know how he did it but I had to grin, despite my anxiety. *See Nui, this is what you don't get. Channon understands me and it's not because I'm in your body.*

Chone was extra sweet this morning and stayed close while I rushed through my chores. His presence was soothing, as always.

At nine-thirty, Khun Pim and I left for the river. We took the skytrain to Saphan Taksin, and from there, motorbikes to the house which wasn't far from Asiatique, a combination mall and night bazaar. *Typical Thailand—always opportunistic*, I thought grumpily, though the mall had nothing to do with my sulk.

Khun Nattawut lived in an upscale area, his teak house facing the Chao Praya river, a premium spot. My heart sank. He was obviously a wealthy man.

Khun Pim seemed impressed as well. The doorman ushered us in. A young girl in shorts and a Disney t-shirt came sliding down the hall.

"Where is he? Did you bring him?" She didn't even bother to wai, which showed a distinct lack of respect.

"Hi, you must be Nong Ying. Nice to meet you." Pim was going to conduct the interview.

"Yes, but where is he? Paa promised me a wolf."

Uh oh, this is getting off to a great start.

Khun Nattawut joined his daughter. "Khon dii, they need to see the house first to make sure Wolf will be ok here. Why don't you show them where he'll stay?"

Ying pivoted and dashed off, expecting us to follow.

I hated to admit that I was impressed by the house. It could have been the centrefold of a design magazine, to be shown off rather than lived in. We stepped into a big yard with a pool to the left and a covered dining/lounge area to the right. Ying was standing in the far-right corner pointing at a small dirt patch surrounded by a chain-link fence.

You've got to be kidding me! I turned to Pim. She sensed how angry I was and put a restraining hand on my arm.

"Khun Nattawut, is this where you plan to keep the dog? Where will he run?"

"Oh, my driver will take him out to run along the river."

"Yes, but during the day you mean to keep him in there? Where will he rest during the day, out of the sun?" Pim insisted.

"There's no sun here in the garden during the afternoon. And it's quite cool in the morning with the trees."

"But there's not even a dog house for him. Where will he sleep?" I interrupted. Pim was far too polite to the guy for my taste.

Khun Nattawut frowned at me. "What do you mean? I

thought he was a street dog so he's used to sleeping in the open?"

Pim took one look at my face and could tell that I was about to explode, so she quickly took over again.

"Thank you, Khun Nattawut, but all our dogs require some kind of shelter, especially during the rainy season. Would you be prepared to arrange this before we proceed?"

She added. "You also know there will be a number of follow-up visits to make sure the dog has settled in well?"

"Sure, sure, no problem." We waved us off like bugs.

Ying came running back. "Can we get him now? I need to train him."

"Train him for what?" I asked suspiciously.

Ying rolled her eyes. "For my birthday party tomorrow. Paa is building a real jungle in the garden. Everyone has to dress like an animal in the movie." She pointed at her t-shirt. "See, I'm Mowgli and I need a real wolf," Ying explained, like it was the most natural thing in the world.

Pim grabbed my arm. "Thank you Khun Nattawut, I think we have seen enough. We'll let you know about the adoption as soon as possible, ok?"

I was fuming and needed to walk off some steam on the way back to the station. Pim tried to keep pace.

"Nui, relax, I know this doesn't look too good, initially."

"Initially? Chone in some kid's party! Can you imagine? And that cage! There's not even enough room for him to move properly. They are totally unqualified to have Chone. I'd rather kidnap him."

"I know Nui, but just think for a moment. If Khun Nattawut opens up the cage and gets a doghouse, it's actually not a bad place, and you know we can't keep all dogs at the shelter. If we cannot adopt them out, we have to put them down."

I glared at her. I knew she was right but there was no way I would let that idiot have Chone for his even more annoying daughter.

I relayed the conditions to Channon at lunch. While he was not happy with the description, he tried to be pragmatic like Pim.

"I know, Nui, it's not ideal but you do know that we can't keep all dogs forever. So, let's just make sure that if Khun Nattawut adopts Chone, we keep a close eye on him, ok?"

"He'll adopt him over my dead body."

"Well, I sure hope it doesn't come to that." Channon tried to lighten the mood, without much effect. *Why does Chone mean so much to me? Was it foolish to think that I could have someone who belonged only to me?*

I didn't have anything to do in the afternoon before my late shift so I went home to research animal rights in Thailand. I signed up for news from the Soi Dog Rescue organization; it seemed to be the most active campaigning group in that regard. Maybe I could join them. *Hmm, Nui is right; somehow my entire outlook has changed. How did that happen?* I finally felt interested in something worthwhile. I didn't want to think too deeply about whether the reason was Chone or Channon.

NUI

W<small>E HADN'T MADE ANY PLANS FOR THE MORNING GIVEN WE</small> were going to the airport after lunch. Luke and his dad went to the pool. I read Luna's part of the essay and sent it back to her with a few comments. Her mum had also texted from Chicago saying she wanted to talk.

"Hello sweetheart. How is Bali?" Mum asked, as we FaceTimed. "Are you having a good time? Dad said you're flying back early. I'm sorry I haven't called you before. It's been pretty hectic here."

"Hi, Mom, yeah Bali's been great, but I think we're all ready to go home and have an extra day before school starts. We're going to the animal shelter tomorrow. Did Dad tell you?"

"Shelter? Tell me what?"

"Oh, I guess he forgot. You know Nui has been volunteering at a pet hospital? There's this dog that needs a home."

I told her as much as I knew about Chone. "Dad said we can go and see them on Saturday since we'll be back early."

"Sweetheart, I hear you, but I don't think having a dog is a good idea right now. Aunt Jane is getting out of the hospital tomorrow, but she'll have to start chemo next week. I will stay here for another week and come back next Saturday. Dad and I need to talk to you and Luke about what we're going to do. It's too complicated to get a dog now, Luna."

"Is it the same thing Dad mentioned, about moving back to the States? I told him I would be ok with it. It doesn't matter anymore if there's one more move, and maybe it's even better if I spend some time there before I go to college."

Mom looked stunned.

"Oh, what changed your mind? I thought you didn't want to move again so soon? And you like Bangkok and having Nui as a friend, no? Everything ok? What happened?"

"No, nothing happened, but like Dad said, family comes first."

"Wow, to be honest I didn't expect that." I could see her tearing up and reaching for a tissue. "That is very supportive of you Luna, thank you. Well, we don't have to decide right this minute, we'll talk when I'm back next week, ok?"

"Sure, Mom. Please say hi to Aunt Jane and the family. I gotta pack and meet Dad. Talk soon."

"Love you, Luna. See you next week."

I felt a bit guilty for going behind Luna's back but given the way she had been mooning over Channon lately, I doubted her full commitment to switching back. All I was doing was laying the groundwork in case our meeting with Ajaarn Anurak next week didn't go according to plan and she refused to switch. At least then I would get the opportunity to go on my first trip to US for Songkran.

At least be honest with yourself, Nui. How committed are

YOU to switching back? I quickly dismissed the thought. It was too complicated to consider, especially as I had to get ready.

Nice excuse, Nui. Can you really live with either outcome next week? Shut up!

LUNA

By six I was back at the hospital to help prepare for the night. Pim wasn't there but I knew what I had to do and worked with two other volunteers to settle the dogs. As I was leaving, the supervisor called me over.

"Nong Nui, thank you so much for all your help. We really appreciate it. We need more people like you." She smiled.

"Oh, you're very welcome. I love working here and I think everyone is doing such a fantastic job."

"Thank you. I noticed that you have become quite attached to Chone over the past few days, so I wanted to talk to you. I know that you and Khun Pim went to see a…" She flipped through some pages, "Nattawut Pimikol this morning."

I held my breath and clenched my fists. *Oh no, here it comes.*

"Khun Pim filed her report and I believe you agreed with her it wasn't the right environment for Chone, so I wanted to let you know we turned down that application."

"Oh, I am so glad to hear that. Thank you. Thank you." I slumped in relief! *Yes!* I almost missed her next sentence.

"But this afternoon we received another application for Chone, from someone we know quite well, and we've agreed to go ahead."

"You what?" I burst out. "You can't do that. My friend is going to come over tomorrow to meet Chone. Her family wants to adopt him. Can you please wait at least until they've seen him? Please!" I begged. I hadn't seen that one coming.

"Well, you know we have to do what is best for the animals. I personally know these people and I'm confident Chone will be in good hands. I'm sorry."

"How could you?" I was shaking and, to my embarrassment, I started crying. "He's my dog, you can't just give him away. Who are these people? I need to talk to them."

"Nong Nui, I'm sorry but didn't we tell you not to get attached to a dog when you started here, as we were afraid this would happen?" She looked taken aback by my accusatory words. I didn't care.

"Yeah, but he's the reason I started here in the first place, and I found him a family. They are coming tomorrow."

"I don't know anything about that. I haven't received an application and the other family is ready to take him now. I'm really sorry."

"Who are they? Can I talk to them?"

"We don't give out information about our supporters."

I tried another tack. "When are they picking him up?" *Maybe I could wait around and talk to them.*

"I don't think it's a good idea for you to be here; you're so upset."

"But I want to talk to them. Please let me wait here and speak with them."

She sighed. "Oh alright, just wait here for a few minutes."

I sat on one of the benches in the waiting area wiping my eyes. I couldn't believe it. This would have never happened if Nui had been faster in getting Dad to agree. *That's not fair Luna, she couldn't have known this was coming and neither could you.*

Does this mean I have to say goodbye to Chone now? And I will never see him again? The thought brought a fresh round of tears. *My life sucks! This wouldn't have happened if we hadn't tried this stupid switch.*

Just then, the door to the pens opened and Channon walked out with Chone at his feet. I ran to them.

"Channon, did you hear what happened? I can't believe they let someone else adopt him. Oh Chone!" I knelt down and hugged him. "I'm so sorry, I thought I had it all figured out and now they got someone else for you." He licked my face.

"Hey, Nui." Channon said.

"Have you met them? Who are they?"

"Actually, it's me."

"I know it's you. I meant have you met the adopters?"

"That's what I mean. I adopted Chone. I wanted to get a dog anyway and I knew you were so worried about him going to someone else, so I just went ahead. And because I work here I jumped the formalities and they let me have him!"

My mouth dropped wide open.

"You what?"

"He'll stay with me but he's really your dog as we know, and you can see him anytime. I may have to ask you to check on him when I'm at work or in Uni. Deal?" Channon grinned.

"OH MY GOD! You really did this?" I squeaked, and

before I could think about it, I jumped up and hugged him tight.

"I don't believe it. No one has ever done anything like this for me." I burst into tears again.

Chone pressed close.

"Hey, I thought you'd be happy!" Channon looked concerned and a bit embarrassed. I didn't care.

"Of course, I'm happy you idiot. I'm so happy I'm crying." I couldn't quite figure out myself if I was laughing or crying or both.

"Come on, let's get out of here and celebrate. I'm going to take him home to my friend's tonight and then he'll be at my mom's for a while—she has a big back yard. But you can go to see him anytime, ok? I'll be staying with her again when I start Uni."

"Oh wow, how did you organize all that in such a short time? We only talked about the adoption at lunch."

"You know I'd been planning to get a dog all along, so I'd already talked to Mom about it and said it was ok. Chone will keep her company and we have a helper and a driver at home who can look after him when she or I are not there, so that's easy."

We reached the Blooming Gallery and they allowed us to take Chone on their little deck in the back.

I felt hyper and didn't even give Channon a chance to settle in. How often would I be able to see Chone? Would his mom be ok with me just dropping by, or would we need to arrange a schedule? Did he have all the equipment he needed? Would Channon keep Chone's name? Had Chone been registered?

Channon patiently answered all my questions. I was so awestruck, I almost forgot to pet Chone. *He really is the nicest person I know. I could fall in love with him.* My mouth went dry. *Remember, he doesn't know you as Luna. I know we have chemistry but maybe he's not even interested in farangs. Yeah, but look what he did for me.*

If Channon knew only half the thoughts running through my mind, he would have called me crazy.

"Are you ok, Nui?"

"I'm better than ok, I'm just overwhelmed, that's all." *Understatement of the year.*

Another thought occurred to me. "Oh Channon, what do we do about Luna? I more or less promised that she would get Chone. They are coming over tomorrow to meet him."

"I suppose you'll have to tell her he found a home already. There are plenty of other dogs they could adopt if they want. They live in a condo building, don't they? Do they even have space for him? Maybe they should get a smaller dog."

All good points but they didn't touch the issue that concerned me. And what if we're moving back to the States? Then I won't have Chone or Channon anymore. *Shit, shit, shit. Can't something be easy for once?* For now, I had no choice but to play along.

"You're right, he's probably better off with you, but could you bring him back tomorrow morning, so they can meet him? And then take him back to your mom's place in the afternoon. Will that work?"

"Sure. I can't leave him at my friend's during the day anyway. And you should come with me to meet my mom."

Did he really just suggest for me to meet his family? It's for Chone, Luna. Still, I found myself grinning.

"Sure, that'll be great."

We spent the next hour making plans. There were just too many things piling up for next week—school, volunteering, visiting Chone, and most importantly, meeting Ajaarn Anurak on Wednesday. If we were going to manage the switch, how would I be able to justify seeing Chone? *One thing at a time.* Maybe Nui has some ideas. She was due to land shortly, so I told Channon I had to get Joey for his walk and I was expected home by eight thirty. He offered to come with me. It would be a good opportunity to introduce the dogs.

Khun Yaa was pleased to see Channon and fussed over Chone who soaked up the attention. Joey and he sniffed each other carefully, but seemed to get along. We took both dogs for a walk through the streets. Joey was off his leash, but we didn't know enough about Chone yet to see how he would react to Soi dogs. Given he had lived on the streets, it was likely he'd had some altercations with them. *This is so nice. Don't get used to it. But I can at least enjoy it while it lasts, can't I?* I thought, and again felt a jolt in my belly, reminding me that by Wednesday, everything would change.

Thankfully, Khun Yaa was watching television when I got home so I didn't have to answer any loaded questions about Channon getting a dog for me.

71

NUI

I TOOK A LAST WALK AROUND THE ROOM TO MAKE SURE I HAD packed all of Luna's things. Sadly, my first international trip had only lasted four days, but even with the accident and short term amnesia, I had really enjoyed the luxury experience. I knew it was time to get back and sort things out with Luna, but now I'd had a glimpse of what it was like to travel, I was more determined than ever to make it happen for me too in future.

"I talked to Mom," I said to Luna's dad as we rolled our bags to the elevator.

"What did she say?" Luke asked. "Why didn't I get to talk to her?"

"You were at the pool. She said she'll call you later, ok?" I assured him. "She said she hopes to be back by next weekend."

We went to the main restaurant for a quick buffet lunch

before heading to the airport. I now felt like a pro going through the check-in and security process. It occurred to me I was probably breaking international laws travelling on Luna's passport. The thought made me laugh out loud. Luke and his dad looked at me wondering what was so funny. I shrugged sheepishly.

"You're weird, you know that?" Luke was again annoyed that we had to check my bag and would have to wait for it again on the other side. Spoiled brat.

This time the flight was really bumpy, like a rollercoaster, and I was happy to leave Luna's pre-ordered bland food untouched.

We were back in the condo by nine o'clock. I offered to start the laundry but Khun Mark said to leave it for Khun Bo to deal with. I really could get used to this life of leisure.

With nothing else to do I made a quick check-list for things to do the next days.

Saturday—meet Luna at the pet hospital

Sunday—volunteer at the bazaar at the hotel; call Khun Sonia re: schedule

Monday— first day of school

Wednesday—3 p.m. Ajaarn Anurak at the temple.

Ok, let's see what else Luna has managed to mess up. I texted her to say I was back and ready to talk.

72

LUNA

THIS WAS THE FIRST CALL SINCE OUR FIGHT ABOUT CHANNON. I was determined to not let Nui rattle me this time.

"Hey Nui, welcome back. What a day—I have so much to tell you."

"Thanks, it's good to be back. Tell me. Oh, before I forget, I talked to your mom today."

"What did she say?"

"She's coming back end of next week. She wants to wait for Aunt Jane to start chemo. But get this, she also brought up the move. I tried to convince her it wouldn't be a good idea, but she said we'll talk next week."

"Oh shoot. Damn, this really couldn't have come at a worse time." I paused for a second, knowing Nui wouldn't like what I had to say next.

"You know Nui, we have another problem. I, or rather *you*, now own a dog." I told Nui about my visit to Khun

Nattawut and how Channon had jumped in to save the day, except that he had unwittingly complicated things.

"For crying out loud, Luna. Are you actively looking for trouble? So, now you expect me to visit a dog, pretending to be you, I mean me, or whatever? Damn it!"

I tried to interrupt, but Nui wasn't done with her tirade. "And don't tell me Channon did it just for himself. He clearly has a soft spot for you. What guy would adopt a dog just to help a friend? Seriously. Could you make it any more complicated?"

Yup, here we go again. The cease fire didn't last long. I ignored the jibe and focused on the 'soft spot' comment instead, feeling a warm tingle in my stomach.

"You think?" I asked.

"Think what? That he likes you I mean me? Duh! Isn't that obvious?" Nui pulled a face.

"Oh Nui, I know it's messed up, but my head is all over the place."

"Clearly! So should we still bother to come over tomorrow to look at Chone? You think Channon will agree for us to take him? At least that way you would have him when we switch back."

Except I won't get to see Channon again. Better not bring that up.

"Yes, come tomorrow morning around ten, ok?"

"And will you come to the bazaar on Sunday?"

"Oh, yikes, I completely forgot. Channon wants me to meet his mom tomorrow. She's keeping Chone for the time being. I was thinking of going again on Sunday but I'll work around it."

Nui exploded. "Luna, you're still doing it. You're digging yourself deeper, aren't you? Remember, I'm involved too!"

"I know, I haven't forgotten, but what do you suggest I do? It's not like I came up with this idea in the first place."

"Oh, here we go again, so it's all my fault? Looks like you're quite enjoying yourself and have completely taken over my life. Why are you getting involved in all these issues that I have to deal with later? It's so selfish of you." She threw up her hands, and for a second I thought she was going to hang up.

"Oh yeah, and what about you? Giving Dad ideas about me going into the hotel business, volunteering at the bazaar and going on holiday to Bali? Seems like you have adjusted quite well too, so stop blaming me for trying to make the best of the situation."

Despite my best intentions, I had let myself get drawn into an argument again. "And adopting a dog is anything but selfish, as you should well know. I have been taking care of Joey for you. All I'm asking is that you do the same."

"Oh yeah? I've been laying low, but you are actively instigating trouble. And I didn't give your Dad ideas; I only asked out of curiosity, as any daughter would do. And I've been smoothing the way for the dog, too. What else do you want me to do?"

Nui was so darn self-righteous it made me sick, but I knew the argument wasn't getting us anywhere, "Argh! Time out. We already agreed that fighting is not helping. I'm sorry, Nui, I know things have gotten out of hand. Just come over tomorrow and we'll talk, ok?"

"Fine! See you at ten. Bye." Nui didn't bother to wait for my reply but hung up.

Ouch! If this constant bickering continued, our temple session was doomed.

73

NUI

I was still annoyed after hanging up on Luna. Why was she stirring up so much unnecessary trouble? All she had to do was lie low for the week but no, she had to get her nose into all sorts of things. *Typical farang! Taking over my life like that. So arrogant.*

Luke and his father were watching some kind of science fiction movie in the living room. I told them we had to be at the hospital at ten the next morning. I didn't mention Chone's adoption, figuring they needed to meet him first anyway. *I hope that dog is worth all the trouble he's causing.*

By the time I got to the kitchen the next morning, Khun Bo was already bustling around, stowing away groceries from the market.

"Good morning, Nong Luna. What would you like for breakfast? I have some nice papaya here for you. How was holiday?" Though she now knew I spoke Thai, she preferred to practice English.

"Sawasdee ka Pi' Bo. The holiday was nice. Thank you. Do you by any chance have some noodles or congee?" I was tired of eating the same fruit and cereal every morning. Time to get ready to be me again and if Luna could do what she wanted, so could I.

Bo smiled at me. "Ah, you like Thai breakfast? Go take shower, I'll make breakfast."

"That's great. Thank you. Are Dad and Luke still sleeping?"

"Khun Mark had to go to hotel for little time. He said he meet you at shelter. You know?" She shrugged.

"Oh ok, that's fine. I'll be right back."

Breakfast was delicious, a spicy broth with noodles. I only missed the meat balls.

I woke Luke and rushed him out the door at nine thirty. He barely had time to grab a pop-tart. I wasn't feeling charitable and deep down I suspected that this had more to do with mentally prepping myself for another argument with Luna.

74

LUNA

MAE CORNERED ME AS I WAS SETTING OUT WITH JOEY.

"Nui, come to the kitchen please. You can take Joey out later."

Uh oh, that sounded ominous. Something was up.

"Erm, sure. Let me just let Channon know I'll meet him at the hospital."

There was a foreboding atmosphere around the breakfast table. Khun Yaa was bustling about, avoiding my questioning look.

"That's exactly what I want to talk about, Nui. We have hardly seen you this week; you spend all your time with Channon. You're starting school again on Monday, and we think it is time you concentrate on that. We're paying a lot of money for BIS and you need to study and keep your grades up, and not run around with Channon."

"What do you mean, run around with Channon? We only

see each other at the hospital and you were ok with me working there. You signed the form and now you're saying it's not ok?"

"You know we like Channon, he's a very sweet boy but your grandma told me he got a dog for you! Nui, you cannot accept that. First of all, you already have a dog, and secondly what does Channon want in exchange?"

I knew Mae was only concerned for me but I was fed-up with everyone getting into my business. "What do you mean? He doesn't want anything. He did it as a favour so Chone wouldn't be adopted by someone else. It was the nicest thing anyone has ever done for me." I felt trapped in a pressure cooker. First Nui, now Mae. Why did everyone think they knew what was best for me?

Mae looked hurt. "Your dad and I have given you the entire week off so you could have some time for yourself, and what have you done?"

"Done? I helped with Tum's ordination, I looked after Jenny and Eve twice and I've been volunteering at an animal shelter. What have I done wrong?" My voice was shaking with hurt and anger.

"Nui, watch your tone. You do not speak to your mother like this," Paa interjected sharply.

Oh great, now two against one.

"I don't know why you make such a fuss about this. There's nothing between Channon and myself. And don't worry, Chone will be at Channon's mom's house anyway. We're dropping him there this afternoon. And Channon will start vet school soon so he won't be at the hospital anymore."

"Nui, you know we have nothing against Channon or the hospital. All I'm saying is school has to be your priority, ok?" Mae tried to defuse the tension.

I bit my tongue. *Just think Wednesday, just think Wednes-*

day, then you don't have to deal with this shit anymore. Yeah, right, just a whole new set of problems. My day couldn't have started off worse. I was doomed if we switched back and doomed if we didn't.

Breakfast was a silent affair, which was pretty much unheard of in this family. Even Duen picked up on the tensions and kept quiet. I escaped as soon as I could to take Joey out. He seemed confused as to why we didn't stop at Pi' Ohm's this morning. Channon must have already left for the hospital. *Is nothing going right today?* I felt like screaming.

75

NUI

WE MET LUNA IN THE RECEPTION AREA AT TEN. HER FATHER hadn't arrived yet. Luna and I hugged. It was good to see her, despite our fights. Her dad walked in ten minutes later and I could tell Luna would have loved to hug him instead of extending a simple wai.

Entering the dog run, Chone came up immediately and sat down next to Luna as if to wait for official introductions.

"Isn't he beautiful?" She scratched his ears.

"He sure is," we all agreed.

"He really looks like a wolf. I bet he would scare off any burglars." As usual, Luke's mind ventured off into action game territory.

"Well, he isn't called Bandit for nothing," Luna laughed.

"That's right, Nui here named him right on the first day." Channon had snuck up while we were all watching Chone. He looked very official in his short white smock.

"Hi, Mr Taylor? I'm Channon, I work here with Nui. Hi Luna, nice to see you again." Channon spoke English to accommodate father and son.

Khun Mark shook Channon's hand. "This is a great facility and the dogs look very well taken care of."

"Yes, they are, thanks to volunteers like Nui here. I understand that you came to meet Chone. I'm not sure if Nui told you already, but we were afraid he would be adopted from under our noses yesterday, so I went ahead and adopted him myself. I'm really sorry if this disrupts your plans. But as you can see, there are a lot of other dogs here that need a home. So perhaps we can help you pick an alternative?"

"Well as a matter of fact, it was really Luna who was so keen on helping Nui, but it might be better this way. We have a new situation at home now and we're not sure how long we will be here. So maybe it's best to shelve that decision, for now anyway." He shrugged apologetically.

"Oh, but Mr Taylor you only just got to Thailand. It would be a real shame if you moved again so soon, right Luna?" Luna jumped in trying to discourage the idea.

"Yeah, right." My own support sounded lukewarm even to my own ears.

Luke started laughing, "Man, Luna, you're really nuts. I heard you tell Dad that you were ok with the move. And now you want to stay? Just make up your mind already, ok?" He shook his head and moved off to play with the dogs.

Luna looked at me with narrow eyes, clearly taken aback. I kept my head down scuffing at the dirt with her flip flops, feeling slightly guilty.

Channon continued his conversation with Khun Mark as if nothing had happened.

"I see. Well, as you can see, there are a lot of other dogs who need a home, so if you change your mind, we'd be grateful for your help." He got ready to leave. "I need to get back to work. Nice meeting you all."

Khun Mark shook Channon's hand. "Nice to meet you too and I'm glad Chone found a good home with you." He went to join Luke with the dogs.

Channon turned to Luna, "Nui, I'll see you at noon. You're coming with me to see my mom, right?"

"Yeah sure. See you," Luna nodded distractedly.

LUNA

I FELT LIKE I WAS STUCK IN QUICKSAND, SLOWLY SINKING, AS I looked at Nui in shock. *Had she been lying to me all this time? And only pretending to be keen to switch back? How dare she? Does that mean she is trying to move to the States with MY family.* Just the idea of that was too big to get my head around.

My thoughts were interrupted as Nui hissed; "Are you still telling me there's nothing going on between Channon and you?" She probably thought she could distract me from Luke's comment by attacking first.

"Oh no. Stop right there. Care to explain why you told Dad you were ok with the move, when you said the exact opposite to me?" I wasn't going to let her get away with that.

"It's not like it'll make any difference what I say." Nui casually brushed off the accusation. "I figured it would be easier to just go along with what he wanted."

"Oh, so you lied to me the entire time, and now you expect me to accept you didn't do it for some ulterior motive? I can't believe you'd be that calculating." I was disgusted.

Nui seemed slightly chagrined but then she shrugged it off.

"Whatever happens, happens. And we're switching on Wednesday anyway, so there. And meanwhile, you are the one leading on Channon, huh? Guess, you're not so innocent yourself. What's this about you visiting his mother?"

"I told you yesterday we're dropping off Chone this afternoon and he wants me to meet his mom so I can visit by myself later."

Nui had regained her combative attitude, "So, after we switch, you expect me to take over? Forget it. I'm not doing it. And don't expect me to sort it all out once we're back. You started it, so you figure it out."

I was ready to fire back but then stopped myself deliberately. I knew this wasn't getting us anywhere. "Shit. We've only been here half an hour and we're already fighting again. What's wrong with us, Nui?"

"Other than messing up our lives and walking in each other's bodies, nothing really." Nui tried to suppress a grin but couldn't help herself. It was either that or cry.

We were both way too tightly strung and even the tiniest bit of comic relief was welcome. Seeing Dad and Luke coming back we quickly snapped back to our game faces.

Dad seemed in a hurry. "Luna, we have to go. I just got a call from Mom Luang Teerawat. They heard we came back early and invited us for a barbeque at their house."

He turned to me. "Thanks again, Nui. I'm glad Chone is being taken care of. Maybe we'll see you next week."

As Dad and Luke walked out, Nui hung back to deliver a

last warning shot. "Just remember, we're changing back on Wednesday, so don't do anything stupid today, ok?"

I'd had enough of people telling me what I could or couldn't do, and didn't bother responding. *Mind your own business*!

NUI

K<small>HUN</small> P<small>AK</small> <small>WAS WAITING IN FRONT OF THE HOSPITAL.</small> O<small>N THE</small>
drive home, Luke worked hard to convince his father what we
absolutely had to rescue a dog—the bigger the better. I let his
chatter wash over me. I felt embarrassed and annoyed that
Luke had blurted out my conversation with Luna's dad. My
relationship with Luna had definitely shifted, not only
because of my own transgression but also because of what
she had set in motion with Channon. How did she think this
was going to work after Wednesday? I would end up looking
like a complete bitch if I refused to see Channon after the
switch, especially now that my own family knew him as well,
and he had adopted a dog for 'me'. And I definitely didn't
intend to trek God-knows-where to see Chone, just to keep up
appearances. I had my own life to live. This was so damn
selfish of her.

"What do you think, Luna?" Khun Mark nudged me.

"About what?"

"We'll have a quick lunch at home, you can talk to Sonia about the bazaar and then we'll leave for ML's house at four. It'll take us an hour to get there with all this traffic."

"Sure, that's fine, Dad. Where do they live?"

"Somewhere in Ekkamai. It's a big family compound."

Though Luna's dad had said it would be a casual family affair, I decided a dress and sandals were more appropriate for meeting ML and his family, rather than shorts and flip-flops.

We reached Ekkamai shortly before five. The house was on Soi twenty-two and as we drove through the narrow streets, I could only guess what lay hidden behind those big gates. This part of town was known to be very affluent.

The guard at the gate waved us through into a driveway connecting three separate houses in a semi-circle. I glanced around, speechless at the size of the place. We stopped in the centre and got out. A maid opened the door with ML Teer-awat waiting behind in the entry hall.

"Welcome. No need to take your shoes off if you feel more comfortable otherwise." ML ushered us in.

"Oh, I think we've all become used to it by now. Thank you for having us Mom Luang Teerawat!" The men shook hands, I wai'ed and Luke just waved his hand.

What a stunning house! Even if I didn't know the last thing about decorating, I could tell there was serious money behind the furnishings and artwork. Thanpuying Wassana joined her husband.

"It's so lovely to see you all again. How was your time in Bali? I'm sorry you had to cut it short, but that's our good luck. Come in and I'll show you around. Oh, and Mark, thank you so much for the flowers and goodies from the hotel. Kind of you to remember that I have a sweet tooth for that cheese-cake." She smiled.

I was again struck by how kind and warm the family was. Luke's friends dragged him into the garden for more football talk.

Khun Mark and I joined ML and Thanpuying on a short tour of the house before we made our way to the back. If the front and interior were impressive, my mouth literally dropped open when I saw the back. A huge lawn, half the size of a football field, was surrounded by mature trees with a junior Olympic sized pool off to the side. The trees offered complete privacy on all sides and you would never have guessed you were still in the middle of Bangkok.

"Wow, I had no idea there were such big properties here." That was probably too forthright, but I couldn't help myself.

"Well, it's actually three plots that we bought over the years and connected. The kids loved the neighbourhood and as everyone has their own home it works well," ML explained.

The rest of the family had assembled on the patio around casually arranged tables. After greeting everyone, Khun Mark accepted a beer and I sipped a lime soda. A big BBQ was set off to the side.

"I may need your help with the grill, Mark. As an American, you're probably much better at this than I," ML joked.

I was pretty sure he had some chefs around who could handle the grill just fine, but Luna's dad played along, "I'd love to. Haven't had much of a chance to do that lately."

We chatted about Bali and that Khun Susan would be coming back next week. Khun Mark didn't mention the potential move, so I kept my mouth shut too.

"So, Luna, what's new on the travel writing? Have you started your career yet with your trip to Bali?" ML teased.

"You know, maybe I should, but we only got back last night and this morning we were at the pet hospital on Thong Lo to look at a dog."

"Oh, you're getting a dog? That's nice. Our grandchildren are very keen too and I think maybe they are old enough now. We didn't want them to think a dog is a toy that can be discarded at any time."

"I can get you some information about adoption if you like. My friend Nui works there and I'm sure she'd love to help you and show you around. " *See Luna, don't say I'm not supporting your mission.*

The men retreated to the grill and I stayed with Thanpuying and her daughter and daughter-in-law. Luke and his buddies were getting ready to jump into the pool to cool off.

I seriously could get used to this, mingling with the hi-so. Luna doesn't know how lucky she is. I wish there was some way I could use the connection while I have it. Or find a way for Luna to introduce me as Nui. She owes me anyway.

"Are you alright, Luna?" Thanpuying interrupted my thoughts. I had spaced out trying to come up with an idea how to keep the connection active after our switch.

"Oh yes, I'm so sorry, I was just thinking of something I have to do next week."

After that, I paid more attention and the conversation flowed easily as we seamlessly switched between Thai and English. I would have killed for one of the burgers that were being dished up, but knew I had to stick with salads for appearance's sake.

"Oh, I almost forgot," ML spoke to one of his staff and she brought out an extra dish—a vegetable burger just for me.

I was embarrassed but touched. "I can't believe you thought of that. That is so very kind of you, Mom Luang."

"Well, you can't have a barbeque without a burger, even if it's the vegetarian version." He grinned at me, chuffed to have surprised me.

And there I thought that all hi-so were arrogant. Duh! Do you actually know any hi-so, Nui? I gritted my teeth, not too pleased to admit my own prejudice.

As the sun went gone down, solar flares lit the garden and mosquito coils kept the bugs away. At nine we said our good-byes. Since Luna's dad had send Khun Pak home after dropping us, ML insisted one of his drivers would take us. Thanpuying promised to come to the hotel for the bazaar, though it was obvious she didn't really need to buy anything; she would probably just donate.

I hope I'm this gracious when I'm their age. Yeah, and ideally with just as much money. I cringed at my own snobbery.

I hadn't heard from Luna but couldn't be bothered to text her. We both needed a time out anyway, judging by the tension building between us.

LUNA

CHANNON PICKED ME UP AT NOON. "I TOLD MOM WE'D BE home for lunch. My car's out front."

Chone jumped into the backseat without hesitation, but put his head on my shoulder to look out front. I had been brooding over Nui's words all morning and was glad to focus on something more pleasant.

I laughed and scratched Chone's face. "Hey buddy, I think you better lie down in back. It's not safe like this." I pushed him onto the backseat and thankfully he cooperated.

"Wow, Nui, how do you do that? Chone must weigh almost as much as you do but he listens to you like you've been training him for ages." Channon said, approvingly.

I felt a warm rush of pride but modestly waved it off. Saturday traffic was in full force and creeping along, slowly. It took us almost an hour to get to Channon's mom's house. She lived on a side street on Soi Pradiphat, a stone's throw from Chatuchak market. Channon used a remote clicker for the electric gate. Chone wedged himself between the front seats again as we pulled into the driveway.

"Welcome to your new home, Chone!" Channon announced. "Let's get you settled and give you some water."

The front door opened and a beautiful Thai lady in blue capris and tie-die blouse stood waiting. She was tiny, even compared to Nui's size. I had been nervous about meeting Channon's mom for the first time but she had a big welcoming smile on her face.

"Nui, meet my mom, Khun Kannika. Mae, this is Nui, and this beautiful boy is Chone." Channon bent to kiss his mom on the cheek. I wai'ed, probably too high.

"Hello son, hello Nui. Oh, look at this handsome fellow." Khun Kannika fussed over Chone, and with her grey pixie cut, matched him perfectly in colour. I hid my grin behind my hand and any remaining anxiety drained away.

"Come in, come in. It's too warm out here."

We took off our sandals and stepped into a cool entry hall.

"Mom is a bit of a hippie," Channon whispered. "You'll see."

Walking through to the living room I understood what he meant. The house was filled with jewel colours and an eclectic mix of Thai artefacts, from bright umbrella lamp-shades to bird cages to multi-coloured throw pillows, all mixed beautifully with antique teak and modern Thai furni-ture. The room felt at once comfortable, classy and avant-garde. If she had done it herself, she clearly had an eye for interior design.

I mentioned as much to her, but she laughed it off. "There are some benefits to living close to JJ market. Or maybe not. I tend to accumulate too many things. Come, Chone, I'll show you your new home."

We walked through a formal living area to a smaller family room. She opened the patio doors to a spacious, grassy backyard secured with a high wooden fence. Several coconut and palm trees provided lots of shade. A covered deck held a few chairs and loungers. It looked like a place where I could quite comfortably spend an entire afternoon.

"I don't have a dog house yet, but I think as a husky, he might prefer to sleep inside anyway. I found a nice dog bed at JJ yesterday and I think we'll put him here in the family room, what do you think?"

"Perfect as usual, Mae," Channon said, affectionally patting his mother's shoulder.

"Khun Kannika, this is fantastic. I'm sure Chone will be very happy here. Thank you so much."

"Don't mention it. It'll be nice to have a dog in the house again. Come, let Chone explore his home while we eat."

Lunch was a variety of noodles, rice and mixed vegetables and steamed fish. Channon must have mentioned that I didn't eat meat. I finally brought the conversation around to how often I would be able to visit Chone.

"You're always welcome here, Nui. I'll give you my number and you can just text me or Channon when you want to come over. If I'm not here, Khun Sai can let you in. Channon said you're back in school next week, so I assume it'll be mostly afternoons, correct?"

"Yes, we start on Monday and I also promised to continue with my volunteering, so I won't have too much time, but I hope to see him maybe once every other day if that's ok? I'll miss him."

"Like I said, you're welcome anytime. See how you manage. I'm sure Chone will be happy to see you." I made a mental note to bring her a gift next time.

We spent the rest of the afternoon sitting on the patio

taking turns to throw balls for Chone while we chatted in the shade.

I finally figured it was time to get home, especially after Mae had given me such a hard time this morning. Channon walked me to the skytrain. He was going to spend the night at his mom's house as he had Sunday off work.

"I don't have to work tomorrow, either. Can I come back sometime late morning? I have to meet Luna at the bazaar later." I wasn't really looking forward to that, but the meditation afterwards was too important to miss.

"You heard Mom, you can come back anytime."

I knelt to say goodbye to Chone. Though I knew he was lucky to have found such a perfect home, I still felt emotional. I had become used to seeing him every day and he had definitely grounded me during this crazy week and given me something else to think about.

"I'll see you tomorrow, Chone. Be nice to Khun Kannika and don't mess around with Channon either, you hear?"

"I really think he understands every word you're saying, but let's see if he takes it to heart too," Channon laughed.

I stood up and hugged him. "Thank you so much for everything you've done. You've been amazing." I looked up at him and for a second my heart stopped. *He does have the most beautiful eyes in the world.* We didn't move. Chone finally got bored and nudged me.

Channon cleared his throat. "I'm glad I was able to help. You better get going. I'll see you tomorrow."

I walked up the stairs to the station but when I turned he was still standing there watching me with Chone at his feet. I waved and entered the station.

A kaleidoscope of butterflies launched in my stomach. *Ground control to Luna. Just because he got Chone for you, doesn't mean he likes you that way.* Maybe all this talk by Nui and Mae had me imagining things. *But wouldn't it be nice?* A tiny voice in my head whispered. *And how are you going to explain to him that you won't see him again after Wednesday? Oh God, Nui was right. I WAS making a mess of this.* My head was hurting from trying to sort everything out.

The family had already eaten when I walked into the kitchen. Mae and Paa had left for some birthday party and Duen was again sleeping over at a friend's house since it was the last free night before school. I decided to watch a bit of TV with Khun Yaa and Grandpa, but by nine I was nodding off in front of the TV. I still had to drag myself out for Joey's walk, which ended up being super short.

"Joey, I'm really sorry, it's not that I don't like you, I just have so many things going on that I haven't had much time for you. Next week, you'll have Nui back and things will go back to normal, I promise."

I was in bed by ten and fell asleep right away but had some weird disjointed dreams involving wolves and spider threads and flying and laughing brown eyes.

NUI

Luna's dad and I went to the hotel early for a quick breakfast before I had to report to duty.

"So honey, did you think any more about doing an internship at a hotel?"

I was biting into a croissant and got some powdery sugar up my nose. After sneezing five times into my napkin, I finally managed to breathe normally again.

"Sorry about that. Hmm, no I haven't really thought about it, but yeah, I still think it's a good idea. Where do you need interns?"

"I'd have to check with Human Resources, but to be honest I don't think it's a good idea to do this in my hotel here. I don't think the staff would feel comfortable with it and you probably wouldn't get the full experience either."

"So, where do you think I should do it?"

"I can ask some of my colleagues at the hotels in

Bangkok if they'd be willing to take you." Khun Mark sipped his coffee.

"You know, Dad, I had an idea. You remember how Nui took me around town when we first moved here, to show me all the local places that tourists normally don't see?"

"Sure, I remember, and I also remember how much you hated it at first. Guess that has changed?" Luna's dad winked.

"Yeah, yeah, I know I wasn't happy about it then, but the good part is I now do know all the places that visitors never even hear about. I'm sure you have a lot of teenage guests with their parents who'd love to see a bit more than the usual touristy places. How about I put some itineraries together for them, or better yet, I could take them on a tour?"

"You mean like a teen concierge?" Khun Mark asked. "That's actually a brilliant idea, Luna. Why didn't I think of this?" He smiled.

"Guess you need to be a teen to think like a teen, Dad. And you're too old for that." I teased him.

Khun Mark chuckled. "Don't let it go to your head, Luna! But seriously, I think it's a great idea. Let me talk to HR about it and see what we can do. Maybe you could work here at the hotel after all."

I was pleased with myself. I'd get to do what was natural and easy for me, and at the same time get a glimpse into a potential career.

At eight thirty I went to the ballroom to help with the bazaar. Khun Sonia asked me to help unpack boxes, set up the registration desk and just pitch in wherever needed. The ballroom was big and crammed with at least a hundred tables piled high with shoes, sweaters, purses, suitcases and other items. Clothing racks displayed formal long gowns next to short casual dresses, hats, jackets, scarves, and who knows what. I wondered where all of it came from.

The doors opened at ten and the first wave of bargain hunters poured in. They were professional second-hand shoppers and they expertly scoured the goods. Everyone had to pay one hundred Baht entry fee. For that they could snap up designer wear below half price. Not a bad deal given that most of the clothes had barely been worn. I suppose hi-so couldn't be seen in the same outfits more than once.

I ended up selling raffle tickets at fifty Baht each, for anything from luxury trips—Khun Mark's colleagues had donated generously—to paintings to tailoring of dresses to expensive dinners. I wouldn't have minded winning a trip but figured people would think I had rigged the raffle so I just ended up donating fifty Baht.

LUNA

I WOKE UP FEELING GROGGY. THE ENTIRE WEEK, I HAD BEEN getting up earlier than normal. With that, and having to pretend to be someone else and constantly on guard was wearing me down. *Three more days and life will return to normal. But is that what you really want Luna?* So much had happened that I couldn't tell if I was coming or going.

Last night I had promised Khun Yaa I would join her and Khun Bpoo at Erawan shrine for prayers, collecting more brownie points for Nui. The shrine was technically Hindu, but it was highly revered by Buddhists as well. I had passed it many times on the way to Dad's hotel and it was always packed with traditional Thai dancers, worshippers and tourists, but I had never gone inside. Part of the reason I wanted to go was the shrine was close to Chidlom station and I would be able to go from there to see Chone.

The shrine was busy, even early on a Sunday morning.

Khun Yaa bought flowers and incense from one of the vendors lined up outside. Space was tight, but everyone found their own little niche in which to say a prayer. The air was heavy and cloudy with incense smoke. At least it wasn't too hot yet, otherwise I would have fainted. I half-heartedly offered my own prayers to whatever deity would listen.

Khun Yaa and Grandpa continued on to meet Aunt Varaporn and the family for lunch. I decided to get a coffee at the station but by ten I was standing in front of Khun Kannika's gate. I texted Channon.

The gate rolled back and there he was with Chone beside him.

"Morning Nui, come on in." Channon smiled.

Chone danced around me and his tail wagged so hard it almost dragged him around. He was too well behaved to jump, but I could tell he was about to forget his manners.

"Hello handsome! I missed you. Have you been a good boy?" *Yikes—baby talk.* But frankly I didn't care, and figured Channon didn't either.

His mom appeared in the doorway.

"Good morning, Nui. Come on in and have some tea with me while you visit my boys." I blushed. *Please don't let her start on me too.*

It was a beautiful morning to sit on the patio with Chone at my feet.

"Has he behaved himself?"

"He didn't make a peep during the night. He is so gorgeous and I'm glad to have him here. Right, Chone?"

I could tell he liked her and I hoped he wouldn't forget me, though I felt we had a special link.

"Thank you again for letting him stay here. I'm so grateful he has a safe home now."

"Stop thanking me Nui. He's doing me a favour by being

here. He got me out of the house this morning already for a walk, and I forgot how nice it can be to just wander around the neighbourhood."

"That's great. I can't stay long as I promised my friend I'd go to the bazaar at her dad's hotel. A group of women have organized a fundraiser."

"What are they selling and where is it?" Khun Kannika asked.

"On Rajadamri. They are mainly designer items that were donated by local hi-so and expats. I haven't seen it yet, but I understand it's been a huge success in the last few years."

"Maybe I'll come with you to have a look around."

"Yes, please come. I'm sure you'll find it interesting."

"I have to go to Central Embassy later anyway, so this is on the way. Why don't we take my car?"

"Sure, that would be great."

"Ok, let me get organized and we can leave in thirty minutes. Is that good?"

"Perfect."

She left, and Channon and I sat in somewhat awkward silence. That had never happened before, and I didn't like it, but thought it best to let sleeping dogs lie. *Ewww! Bad metaphor.*

"What are you up to today, Channon?"

"Nothing much really. It's just nice to have some free time. I'll meet some friends later for a beer and maybe try that meditation you were talking about."

"Yeah, Luna and I will meditate later too. Do you want the recording from Ajaarn Anurak? He's got an amazing voice. I can send you the first few sessions."

"Sure, that would be great. Maybe we'll connect in the ether some time."

Don't go there! Or maybe, do? I stared at him and didn't know what to say.

"Erm, right."

"That was a joke, Nui! I'm sure it's not that easy," Channon cringed, slightly embarrassed.

"No, it's not, but I can tell you it's worth it." *Do not, repeat, do not open that door. You've messed up enough as is.*

Instead, I reverted back to safe ground. "Are you back at the hospital tomorrow? It's our first day at school so I won't be able to come until later. I need to figure out my new schedule and see when I can come back here again."

"Actually, I've asked if I can bring Chone to work during the day. I think it will be good for him to socialize a bit more with other dogs. As long as I get him out by six or seven every night and pay for the food, they are ok with it."

"Oh, that's fantastic. That means I don't have to make the trip over here? Not that I mind, but it would make life so much easier. Channon, you are indeed a life saver. How can I ever repay you?"

"How about you go out with me one evening?"

My mouth dropped open.

"You mean like on a date?" I stammered.

"Yes, like on a date." He waited.

Go for it Luna. What have you got to lose? Want me to count the ways? Shut up.

"Erm, I'd like that." I grinned.

"Ok great. How about Tuesday evening? I'm sure tomorrow will be hectic with the new term starting but is Tuesday ok?"

"Yeah, sure." I couldn't believe we were sitting on his mom's patio and he was asking me out! *Life is good Luna. But what about Wednesday? Forget Wednesday. Enjoy Tuesday and we'll see.*

"Why do you always look like there's a major discussion going on in your head?" Channon smiled.

"Hahaha, that's because there is," I had to grin too.

Just then his mom came back to the patio.

"Ready to go, Nui?"

"Sure. Bye, Chone. Be good. Bye, Channon, see you tomorrow." I didn't hug him his time, but he touched my arm in farewell raising goosebumps along my arm.

"Bye Nui, see you tomorrow. Have fun, Mae."

As usual there was heavy traffic heading into central Bangkok. We listened to some music but Khun Kannika kept glancing at me as if she was making up her mind about something. I was too distracted replaying the scene on the patio and couldn't stop smiling. *Better not tell Nui or she'll have a fit.*

As we left the parking garage, Khun Kannika finally spoke up, "Nui, I know Channon likes you a lot, but please take it slow. I don't want him to get hurt; he's been through so much."

My happy bubble popped. *Why does everyone expect me to mess things up? This is so unfair.*

"No, of course not. I like him too. He is a great guy and you must be very proud of him."

"I am. He's got a bright future ahead and I don't want him to get side-tracked."

"I will do my best not to side-track him," I said, formally, trying not to cringe.

"Thank you, Nui. Now let's go and shop." Khun Kannika linked arms with me and we walked through the lobby into the ballroom. I felt like crying.

NUI

L<small>UNA SHOWED UP AFTER NOON WITH A</small> T<small>HAI LADY WHOM SHE</small> introduced as Khun Kannika, Channon's mom, and now the host for Chone. *What game is that girl playing?* I'd have to have a more serious chat with her later. They browsed through the aisles, but by one Luna was back and ready to go. I signed off with Khun Sonia and handed over the raffle desk.

We decided to go straight home. Pi' Bo prepared a quick lunch of fried rice and vegetables. Neither of us wanted dessert and we went straight to Luna's room.

"What's the deal with you bringing Channon's mom?" This came out a bit more aggressively than I had intended.

"What do you mean? I told you I was going over there this morning. She decided to come along as she's meeting a friend at Central Embassy later. Is everything my fault now?" Luna was pissed off, but she avoided eye contact and sounded a bit guilty. I was sure there was more going on but decided to drop it.

"Ok, so we now have both parts of the essay. I think it's pretty much good to go. Should you or I put it together?" I asked.

"Either. I can do it later or you can. I think the printer here is better, so why don't you do it and make two copies? There are some folders here in my desk you can use."

"No problem. So, what about school tomorrow? How are we going to handle that?"

"Well, I think tomorrow will be fairly easy since it's our first day back. If it's anything like the other schools, there'll be lots of admin stuff to go through so we should be ok. I'm more worried about Tuesday or Wednesday. What do we do?"

She was right. I was especially nervous about English Literature, kind of ironic for someone who wanted to become a writer. Luna for that matter would have to deal with Social Studies, especially the political and historical aspects which was my favourite class. Given how much she'd travelled, she should have been an expert, but she obviously preferred to live in her little expat bubble.

"I guess we'll just have to lie low for two days." I suggested. "What else can we do?"

"But what if they decide to do a test?"

"Gosh Luna, I don't have all the answers. Depends on what it is I suppose, we could do the tests for each other. Just write my name on top and I write yours. No one needs to know. At least we're together in most classes, so it'll be easy to switch papers, ok?"

Luna started laughing, "You know what's really funny? Even if we got caught, we wouldn't have cheated. Not that they would know that, but we can have a clear conscience. Oh, before I forget, I need to text Toey and Dearn. We were supposed to meet them on Wednesday afternoon, but we'll be at the temple."

"Just ask them if they have time on Friday. Give us a day in between to get back to normal," I suggested.

"Ok fine. Now, shall we see how it goes?"

As I locked the door I made a suggestion. "You know, I thought maybe it would help if we stayed in meditation a bit longer. I've combined the last two sessions we did with Ajaarn into one, but we only have to do the breathing exercise once. You good with that?"

"Sure, let's give it a try." Luna agreed.

I hit start.

LUNA

Maybe it was the extended time or simply the fact we were meditating together again for the first time, but I was a lot more relaxed and in 'whatever happens, happens' mode. I felt on the verge of lifting but couldn't quite achieve 'take-off'. I did feel the connecting threads to other people starting to appear again, including Nui's. At the end we both looked at each other with a smile.

"That felt a lot better Luna, didn't it? I think we're getting there. I'm so relieved." Nui exhaled loudly.

"Yeah me too. Let's not jinx it, but hopefully Ajaarn has some ideas on what actually happened. I wonder if you can practice it to such a level that you can switch at will?"

"Oh no, don't get any ideas!" Nui sounded horrified. "I don't even want to think about that. You would end up living two lives permanently. Talk about a basket case. It's hard enough as it is."

"Hmm, maybe that has happened to some people but no-one believed them. Do you think?" The thought hadn't occurred to me before, but it kind of made sense now.

"Luna, stop. Why do you even say that?"

"Well, can't you imagine that other people also might want to see what it's like to live someone else's life."

"Yeah, but did you seriously think it was possible?"

"Not really, but at least I didn't disregard it completely, otherwise we wouldn't be here, would we?" I shrugged.

"Fair enough," Nui acknowledged and added; "To be honest, I thought it was pretty cool to live in your world for a while, but I'm ready to go back to mine, aren't you?"

"Yeah, of course." I didn't sound entirely convincing, even to my own ears. *Remember you won't see Channon again.*

Nui unfortunately picked up on my thoughts.

"What is going on, Luna? You don't sound like you mean it. Is there something I should know?" Nui squinted at me.

I figured I owed it to her to come clean, sort of.

"Well, Channon asked me on a real date."

"He what? You're kidding me. I hope you said no."

"Well..."

"Luna. What the ...? When?"

"Tuesday evening. But we're only having dinner."

"You have to cancel. You can't go on a date and then the next day be a completely different person. How would you explain that? Don't expect me to act like I fancy him. You're crazy. And all of that because of a dog? You're practically throwing yourself at him. Would you behave like that if you were in your own body? Or do you think you get a free ride because you're in mine?" Nui asked in a nasty tone.

"I'm not, and you don't have to be so mean about it. It's not because of Chone, well not entirely. Channon is a really nice guy. He's so considerate and kind, and yeah, he's hand-some too."

"Oh God, Luna, you have a total crush on the guy so you definitely don't want *me* to go out with him. And if you want to see him as Luna, how are you going to explain that?"

"I know, I know. Maybe I need to tell him before?"

"Don't you dare!" Nui jumped up. "He wouldn't believe you anyway. How would you even prove it was you when you show up as Luna?"

"Well, it's not like you know everything we talked about, is it?" I was annoyed with her and myself. "I know that logi-cally it doesn't make sense, but still."

"No 'still'. Promise me you won't say anything, and after Tuesday you can pretend the date didn't work out and no-one will be any the wiser." Nui was so full of herself for coming up with a solution. Well, her solution not mine.

"But what about Chone? I still want to see him."

"That's easy! I can say you are taking over for me as it would be too awkward to see Chone and Channon at the same time after the date. Ha! Actually, that's brilliant. That kills two birds! You get to see Chone and I don't have to date Channon. And maybe you can convince Channon that he should date a farang, since you know him so well now!" Nui looked smug.

"Ouch, why are you being so nasty? Fine, I won't say anything." I got up too. "I'm going home."

"Come on, Luna, don't be like that. Imagine yourself in my shoes."

"Ha, that's rich. I don't have to imagine that now, do I?" I knew I wasn't being fair to Nui, but she hadn't played entirely straight either as I had found out yesterday. *Don't think about it now. Let's see what happens on Tuesday and Wednesday.*

"Gotta go. See you at school."

I got home just in time for dinner. I looked around the table and realized how much I had come to like the family. Mae asked a few things about the bazaar but didn't bring up Channon again. I texted Toey to postpone our Wednesday meeting to Friday.

That night I was restless again. *Could I have done anything differently? What happens now? What do I do about Channon and Chone?* Unfortunately, no miraculous answers were forthcoming.

NUI

LUNA'S DAD WAS STILL AT BREAKFAST WHEN I WALKED INTO the kitchen on Monday morning.

"Morning, Dad. How did the rest of the day go?" I asked Pi' Bo to prepare a Thai breakfast for me again. She was only too happy to oblige.

Khun Mark looked incredulous as I heaped on the chillies.

"Are you sure this is not too hot for you Luna?"

"Nong Luna likes my cooking," Khun Bo laughed, and went back to the stove.

"You get used to them after a while, Dad, you should try it."

He grimaced. "I think I'll take a pass. So, yesterday went well. They closed up at six and from what I heard it was a huge success. They don't have the final numbers yet but they think they exceeded last year's result. Thanks for helping out Luna."

"No problem. It was fun."

He got up from his chair. "I have to get going but can you make sure your brother is up and ready in half an hour?"

"Sure, Dad. I'll get him. You go ahead."

"Thanks, sweetheart. I'll see you later. I won't be late tonight, so we can have dinner together, ok?"

"That would be great. Bye, Dad."

I knocked on Luke's door, "We're leaving in thirty. You want breakfast?"

"Yeah, yeah, coming. I'll just get a muesli bar."

"Khun Bo made pancakes for you."

"Oh cool. I'm coming," Knowing Luke's appetite, I predicted he'd be out in ten.

Sure, enough we left on time to catch the school van.

WALKING INTO BIS WAS LIKE STEPPING INTO A BEEHIVE. Everyone was running around and shouting at volume as if they hadn't seen each other in years. I said hello to a few girls in my class and eventually found Luna in front of our classroom door.

First class was social studies with Mr Campbell. We stayed for a few extra minutes to hand over the meditation essay. It would have been a whole lot more interesting to make it about our experience, but that of course had to remain our secret. The rest of the day, as Luna had predicted, included a lot of new admin rules and regulations. The teachers knew the students were too restless to get any real work done and were fairly relaxed. They told us we'd be assigned college counsellors soon to help us decide which universities to apply for and they wanted us to start thinking about it.

"You know, Mom already said that we're going to look at some colleges over Songkran. What are you thinking? Will you go abroad or stay here?" Luna asked.

"Ha! It's not a matter of what I want. I can't afford a US college, so I'll have to look at a Uni here, which sucks."

"It can't be that bad. At least you won't have to pay for it."

"Yeah, but if I want to study politics, what do you think I'll actually learn here with a military government in place?"

"Fair point, I guess that could be an issue. You think they'll censor the history?"

"Call me cynical, but doesn't everyone? Besides, my parents want me to become a doctor or lawyer anyway. I need to figure out how to get out of that. There's Luke. I better go. See you tomorrow or text me later!"

"Bye."

We didn't have any assigned homework, so I decided to use some of Luna's money to go shopping. *Might as well get something nice for myself to remember my stint in fantasy land.*

My emotions were constantly see-sawing. One minute I was feeling great for having managed the swap, but the next minute I felt sorry for myself that my dream of flying high would come crashing down once we switched back with Ajaarn's help. Now that I'd had a glimpse of the opportunities I would be missing out on, it would be even harder to resume my old boring life.

LUNA

I TOOK THE SKYTRAIN HOME AND DETOURED TO THE HOSPITAL to see Chone. This was definitely easier than making the trek to Khun Kannika's home. I was just getting ready to leave when Channon stopped by.

"Hey Nui. How was your first day?"

"Pretty good and easy today. I just came to say hi to Chone and see if the front desk has my new schedule."

"I'll walk out with you."

The shifts would be pretty flexible as it all depended on how I could work it around my classes. They wanted me for about four hours a week and I thought I'd be able to manage that, if only on the weekend if needed. During the week it would have to be late afternoons, but I figured I could squeeze in at least one hour here or there to get the dogs ready for the night.

"How long are they allowing Chone to stay here?"

"They said at least until next week, unless we get a huge surge of rescues. After that, we'll see," Channon shrugged. "It's great right now, but we're ok either way."

"Sounds good. Did your mom enjoy the bazaar yesterday?"

"I haven't talked to her yet. I left early this morning to drive back here."

"Ah, ok. Please tell her I said hi."

"Will do. Have a good night. I'll see you tomorrow."

My stomach somersaulted. Tomorrow—date night!

NUI

TUESDAY WAS A MUCH QUIETER DAY IN SCHOOL AS EVERYONE settled in. Luna and I barely spoke to each other. Judging by the way she was fidgeting and blushing, she clearly was pre-occupied with her upcoming date and I wasn't sure I had the nerve for another argument about that.

"Toey and Dearn confirmed for Friday, so we're all set," Luna said as we walked out.

A thought occurred to me. "You know, I realized your mom is coming home Friday but I'm not sure if that means she's leaving Chicago on Friday. If so, she won't get here until Saturday or Sunday. I'll have to check with your dad and let you know later."

"Sure." Luna said, barely acknowledging my comment. She was off again in La-La land. It was time to snap her out of it and remind her that I was affected too.

"You have your date night tonight, don't you?" I thought I

managed to sound pretty neutral but even if I had shouted, it would have gone straight over her head.

"Yes. What do you think I should wear?"

Yup, La-La land. "Luna! You are supposed to downplay this, so it won't come as a total surprise when I ditch him."

"Why do you have to be so mean? He's a nice guy and doesn't deserve to be treated like this." For the first time that day, Luna actually focused.

"Well, either you down-play it, or I'll ditch him for sure after tomorrow. Your choice." *Why doesn't she get that there's no other option?*

"In which case, he'll say you are a bitch, and remember, he's Krit's friend too. Are you sure you want to explain that to your brother?"

The gloves were off. "Now who's the bitch? You got us in this mess, so you better figure out how to get us out."

"Whatever. I'll think of something," Luna said, brushing me off.

"You better. I'll see you tomorrow. Remember, we need to leave right after school for the temple."

"Trust me, I haven't forgotten. Bye." Luna had a bounce in her step as she moved away, which almost set me off again.

Our friendship had become brittle, and huge cracks were starting to show. I wasn't sure if we would recover from that after the switch back.

LUNA

THANKFULLY, SCHOOL WAS EASY AS I COULDN'T concentrate to save my life. I hadn't slept and my dreams had been a jumble of images like an old movie rail skipping frames. *Yup, that's my life now. Nothing fits together.*

I wasn't ignoring Nui intentionally, but every time I thought about my upcoming date, my heart started racing. *Get a grip, Luna. It's just another dinner with Channon. No, it's not. He asked you on a date. So what?* I couldn't remember ever having had such full-on arguments with myself before.

Instead of stopping by the hospital after school, I went straight home to take a shower and get changed. I decided to play it safe, a ruffled above-the-knee black skirt and pink sleeveless blouse, but not a dress. Nice, but not too obvious.

Khun Yaa didn't think so. "Where are you going Nui? You look nice all dressed up."

"Dressed up? This? I'm having dinner with Channon and

Chone." I hoped she wouldn't give me any grief about it, even though it was a school night. Luckily, Nui's parents weren't home yet.

"Oh, so Chone is your chaperone?" Khun Yaa winked. "Have fun but don't be late. You have school tomorrow."

"I won't. See you later." *Wow, that was easier than I thought. Grandma really is the best.*

Channon had texted to say he'd made a reservation for seven at Moon Glass, a European Bistro on Sukhumvit fifty-three that allowed dogs on their terrace. He'd wanted to pick me up, but I preferred to meet him at the hospital. I didn't want to risk more scrutiny or comments from the family.

I walked into the adoption area to say hello to some of my colleagues. The dogs were already in their pens, except Chone who sat in the corridor between the stalls.

I had to laugh. "Don't look so smug, my friend. Just because you were lucky to get adopted doesn't mean you can lord it over the other dogs, ok?" He wagged his tail and pretended to look humbled. I was willing to put money on it that he understood every word I said.

"Nice try, Chone!" Channon's hair was still wet from the shower. "Hello Nui. You look very nice. Ready to go?"

"Hi Channon, yes let's get this show-off out of here." My nerves had vanished the moment I saw Chone. He was anchoring me as usual.

Channon held the door for me, guiding me outside. "How was school today?"

"Pretty normal but they want us to start looking at Uni's for next year. All the foreign kids have to start their application process this summer."

"Aren't you?" Channon asked. "I thought you wanted to study journalism in the States."

"Well, want and can are two different things. I'm not sure

I can afford it to be honest. And now, I'm not even sure anymore if I want to do journalism or something to do with animals."

"Ah ha! Chone, you hear that? We have a convert!" Channon laughed. "But jokes aside, you still have a bit of time to decide what you want to do, so don't stress about it. And I'd be very glad if you stayed," he added.

Puff! My calm attitude evaporated. *Does this mean what I think it means?* I blushed.

"You're right but I have to consider the family too, don't I? They sent me to BIS so that I could become a doctor or lawyer or something like that. Anyway, let's not talk about that right now."

Moon Glass had valet parking but the attendant took one look at the big dog in the car and allowed Channon to park right up front.

The sun had gone down, and the temperature was pleasant. They gave us a big table on the terrace to accommodate Chone underneath.

We both ordered lime sodas. Channon still had to drive home. We decided to share a few dishes; roasted vegetable salad, grilled squid and scallops, and Channon got some grilled chicken for himself. Chone was content to take a nap under the table.

"When is Krit coming home?" Channon asked. "He must almost be done with his service."

"As far as I know, end of Feb, so it'll be another few weeks. By the way, did I tell you I ran into Sri the other day? He totally dismissed what he did on New Year's Eve."

Channon immediately became irritated. "That jerk! I still think you should tell Krit, or I will."

It was stupid of me to have brought him up.

"Let's just forget about him, he's really not worth our

time." Desperate for another subject I asked; "So, did you try the meditation yet?"

Channon smiled. "Just because you're changing the subject doesn't mean I have forgotten about Sri! But yes, I tried your meditation and have to say, I have no idea why I ever stopped. You were right, it is very peaceful, though I'm nowhere near your level, of course."

"You do know it's not a competition, right? I'm pretty sure it can benefit anyone at different levels," I wagged my finger at him.

"Yes, oh wise one. I know. I'm just teasing you."

"Very funny! Luna and I are going back to see Ajaarn Anurak at the temple tomorrow. We had a few questions for him."

"What questions? I thought you're done with your class."

"Well, yes, but I told you that Luna and I had gotten to a stage where we had out-of-body experiences and we want to know more about that."

"Wish I could get to that point," Channon sounded almost envious.

"Ha! Careful what you wish for. It's not all sunshine and lollipops."

"How so?"

"Well let's just say, hypothetically, what would you do if you lifted out of your body and accidentally switched into someone else's?"

LUNA! Are you mad? I didn't know what had come over me.

Channon's eyes widened in surprise.

"What are you saying, Nui?"

"Nothing, but think about it. If you can get out of your body, couldn't that mean you can also get into someone else's body, if you're both in the right time, place, wavelength or whatever?" I was scrambling. *You idiot! Did you have to bring this up?*

"Well, yeah, I see what you mean. But wouldn't that be cool in some way? It would allow you to see the world through someone else's eyes." Channon toyed with the idea.

"Yeah? And what would you do about your own world? By default, it means someone else would be in your body. Would you really want that? I don't think it's like a switch you can flip back and forth."

"You're right, that would be odd. No, I don't think I would want that, although I think some people would definitely benefit from seeing the world from someone else's perspective."

"Oh, I agree. And so, Luna and I want to speak with Ajaarn about this some more. We did this essay for school, but it only really brought up more questions," I was back-pedalling very fast. Thankfully, the waiter interrupted to clear our plates and deliver more dishes.

Change the subject Luna, change the subject.

"You know your mom said she doesn't want me to distract you?"

Not THAT subject Luna. Gosh, you're a complete moron. What has gotten into you?

"She WHAT? You gotta be kidding me. What did she say?" Channon almost choked on his soda.

"Oh God, I don't know why I even brought it up. I'm so sorry, that was stupid. I think she's just concerned for you and doesn't want you to get hurt."

"Why in the world would she say something like that? Are you planning on hurting me?" Channon tried to make light of it, but I could tell he wasn't happy about his mom interfering.

"Of course not! But you know how moms are!"

"That doesn't give her the right to mess in my private life!" Channon was seriously annoyed now. I had never seen him this way.

Luna, what the hell? What else can you possibly mess up? Keep it up and there definitely won't be a second date.

"Please don't tell her I told you. Why did you ask me out anyway?" *Oh gosh, now you sound like a complete loser.*

"Nui, what's gotten into you today? You are all over the place. What happened? You know I like you, and I like hanging out with you, and I thought it would be great to get to know you better outside of the shelter. If you're having second thoughts, then just say so," he leaned back and crossed his arms.

Chone had sensed the tension between us and sat up looking from me to Channon and back again. I felt sweat trickling down my back, upset about my own stupidity.

"I'm so sorry, Channon. I really have no idea what's wrong with me." Then decided to forge ahead. "Ok, you're right." Deep breath.

"First of all, I was thrilled you asked me on a date as I really like you and I think you know that. But there's something I have to do tomorrow that may change what you think about me, and I'm nervous as hell. I'm so sorry. I really didn't mean to upset you, and maybe we should have waited a few days."

"What in the world is happening tomorrow, Nui?" Channon looked completely perplexed. Not that I could blame him. I really didn't make much sense. He connected the dots faster than I thought possible.

"Does this have anything to do with your meditation thing at the temple tomorrow?"

"You know, can we just drop this for now? I'm really

sorry to have ruined your evening. Maybe we should just call it a night? I have school tomorrow anyway."

"Nui, if you are afraid why don't you just tell me and maybe I can help?" Channon instantly switched into trouble-shooter mode.

"No, no, seriously there's nothing you can do and it's not that I'm afraid, I'm just nervous. But I promise I will tell you, ok?" This was probably the last promise I should make but I needed to get out of this conversation fast.

"If you say so. Ok, let's get the bill." He looked around for the waiter. "Are you coming to the hospital tomorrow?"

"I'm planning to. Not quite sure what time we'll finish at the temple, but I want to come over after and I'll talk to you then, ok?"

"I guess that has to be good enough for now. Let's go. I'll drive you home."

Channon paid the check, although I offered to split since I knew I had spoilt our date. Thankfully, I had asked for some extra cash from Nui out of my weekly allowance at home.

He dropped me off and touched my shoulder.

"Good night Nui, and good luck with whatever you're doing tomorrow. I'll see you after, but call me if you need anything, ok?" How he could be so understanding after I'd messed up the evening was beyond me.

"I will. Thanks Channon and sorry again for spoiling the evening. I'll make it up to you, ok? Bye Chone."

I didn't want to talk to anyone and just grabbed Joey for his walk. Even he realized that I was off and kept looking back at me as if to make sure I wasn't going to abandon him.

"Well Joey, tomorrow you get your Nui back and I'm sure she'll be a lot more attentive than I have been. I'm sorry." Gosh, I was apologizing to everyone this evening.

NUI

KHUN MARK WAS JUST LEAVING FOR WORK WHEN I WALKED
into the kitchen. This would be the last time I'd see him at
home.

"Morning, Dad. Busy day?"

"Pretty normal; we got some VIP arrivals and I may have
to attend their dinner, or at least the reception but I'll see if I
can delegate it and come home early tonight. What's your
plan today?"

"Remember, Nui and I are going back to the temple this
afternoon right after school. So, I won't be home before
six, ok?"

"Sure, just let Khun Bo know and she can have dinner
ready for you and Luke then."

"Dad, did Mom say if she was arriving here on Friday or
leaving Chicago on Friday? I can't remember."

"Actually, she's leaving just past midnight Friday

morning but with the time difference and layover, she won't get here until Saturday late morning. That reminds me, she won't want to go to the shelter that day, so you better tell Nui that we'll go another time, ok?"

"Sure, Dad. I'll see you later."

I felt a bit emotional saying good bye. He had saved my life after all, even if he didn't know it.

I had to wake Luke again and we just barely caught the van.

"Why is it so difficult for you to get up just ten minutes earlier? I always have to rush because of you." I felt cranky.

"Stop bugging me. You're usually the one who's late, and Mom basically has to kick you out."

"So not true!"

"Oh yeah? Shall we ask her?"

Maybe that subject was better left alone.

LUNA DIDN'T LOOK VERY EXCITED EITHER.

"How was your date?"

"I screwed up and he probably won't want to see me again! Happy now?" Luna spit out.

"What happened?"

"Just forget it, ok? I don't want to talk about it." She stalked off.

We both had a lot riding on the afternoon, and I didn't want to risk another fight. Secretly, I was glad that at least that problem seemed to have resolved itself, even if I felt sorry for Luna. I knew she hadn't purposely tried to create an issue for us, but she should have thought about that before falling for Channon.

School was pretty uneventful. We had some test dates

coming up, but I wasn't concerned about that since everything would be back to normal by then.

I told Luna we wouldn't be able to visit the shelter on Saturday, but our meeting with Toey and Dearn could go ahead on Friday. Otherwise, we barely spoke that day. I felt myself getting more tense as the day progressed and I was eager to put an end to this mess.

LUNA

WALKING INTO WAT PATHUM WITH NUI, I FELT I COULD finally breathe again for the first time that day. My morning had started off awfully and only gone downhill from there. Waking up to the humiliating memory of the botched date and then having to say my own private goodbye to Khun Yaa as her 'granddaughter' had left me in a fragile mood. It didn't help that I knew I had no-one to blame but myself. I had snapped at Nui when she'd cautiously asked about the date, and then felt guilty about it afterward. *Why do I even have to choose between Channon and my family? Why can't I have it all?* It was time to stop the emotional see-saw or I'd go mad.

More tension drained away after a brief prayer at the spirit house. I had no idea what the outcome of our session would be, but I'd resigned myself to letting our spirits figure it out.

"Ok Nui, are we ready for this?" I offered her an olive branch.

"Absolutely!" She smiled back, clearly relieved that my mood was lifting.

The temple grounds were quiet and the sala empty. We walked to the office building where I had seen one of the helpers previously. They knew Ajaarn Anurak was expecting us and directed us to the open pavilion. We silently arranged two bamboo floormats on the floor to wait, both lost in our thoughts.

Ajaarn Anurak didn't say anything when he arrived shortly afterwards. He sank into a Lotus position in front of the Buddha, closed his eyes and chanted a short prayer under his breath. Nui and I waited quietly.

Finally, he looked at me and asked in a neutral tone; "Yohm Nui, do you want to tell me again what you said on the phone? I want to make sure I fully understand the situation."

I wai'ed. "Thank you Ajaarn for seeing us today, kha. I know our story sounds bizarre but let me try and explain. As you know, Nui and I have both been able to achieve out-of-body experiences during your class. We continued meditating, as you suggested, and we were getting very good at maintaining that state but at some point Nui and I ended up switching our bodies. We don't know why it happened or how we can reverse it. We tried, but it's not working and we need your help please."

He looked at us sceptically. "And you expect me to believe that?"

Nui jumped in. "I know it sounds crazy and I don't know how to convince you, so we just have to ask you to trust us, kha."

Ajaarn Anurak kept glancing back and forth between us

with a slight frown. He wasn't fully convinced, but eventually offered some insights.

"As I mentioned, I spoke to some brothers about the likelihood of a mind switch and asked if any of them were aware of the possibility. They are all keen to hear more about it, but the closest we came to an explanation is this…".

I sensed Nui tensing beside me and reflexively held my breath, scared of what would come next.

Ajaarn continued. "I had mentioned to you before that we believe all life forms are connected through vibrations, and essentially we all come from the same life giving force or energy. We all have maintained that connection, whether we feel it or not," he paused to collect his thoughts.

"So, if for some reason you were able to achieve a direct link through the source energy between you, while not bound in your bodies, then there does indeed hypothetically exist the potential for crossing over into each other's body. Again, this is somewhat theoretical but not so dissimilar to reincarnation in nature."

Ajaarn paused to give us time to catch up. What he said made sense to me but I was afraid that was only half the equation.

"However," Ajaarn resumed, "we also believe this could only happen if both parties have agreed to the cross-over of their own free will. No one will ever be able to force a soul into another body, no matter what the movies may tell you. So my question is, is this what you had set out to do?"

He looked at us somewhat reproachfully.

Out of the corner of my eye, I saw Nui immediately shaking her head. It didn't feel right lying to a monk but we couldn't really admit to being so reckless, especially given his earlier warning about experimenting with the out-of-body state. We couldn't risk him refusing to help us.

I'm not sure if Ajaarn Anurak fully believed Nui's denial but he continued, "Let me repeat that, this could have only happened if both of you were fully aware, open and willing. That means your intention and belief that it is possible is what matters the most." He paused, building up to the conclusion. "So, equally you both must have a very strong desire, without any doubt or reservation, to reverse this. Then, in theory, you would be able to return to your own bodies. Think carefully. There is no room for uncertainty."

Nui raised her arm as if we were in a classroom. "Ajaarn kha, so what you're saying is that because Luna and I were not resistant to the idea, it became possible?" Thank God, she was already up to speed with the explanation while I was still trying to digest it.

Ajaarn nodded. "That's exactly right. Our mind is very powerful, and humans only use a fraction of its capabilities. It allows us to achieve certain feats that cannot be rationalized by science alone."

"So, all it would take is for us to have the intention and no resistance, is that correct?" I finally understood where he was going with this.

Ajaarn agreed. "Yes, that is correct. But it may sound easier said than done. Often, we tell ourselves there is an experience we want but in the back of our minds we doubt that the outcome is possible. The good news is, you both say you are very clear you want to return to your own bodies, and you already know it's possible to switch, so that should make it easier." He paused again, almost as if he had to make up his mind whether to believe our story or not.

My fingers hurt from crossing them tightly until he finally said; "Are you ready to try now?"

Nui and I exhaled deeply with relief and looked at each other. I think we replayed in our heads things that had happened these past weeks—positive and negative. Which side would tip the balance?

Suddenly, I had to smile. "You know Nui, it's been an amazing experience, I have to say."

"Yes, I agree Luna, and I'm really happy that I got to walk in your shoes for a while."

Ajaarn Anurak asked us to sit in our usual positions.

"We are going to start this off with our regular breathing exercise, but I may change some of the mantras to help you ease into the out-of-body state."

Maybe it was hearing Ajaarn's actual voice, maybe it was having made peace with Nui, maybe it was because I was tired of having to make so many decisions, but I found myself drifting off more quickly and deeply than I thought possible after our last few tries.

Ajaarn Anurak's voice deepened and fell to the background while I felt the familiar surge of energy as a part of me lifted out of my body. The sensation felt much more intense than before, and my connection with Nui clicked in more quickly and soundly than before. A continuous flow of vibration began streaming between us as if we were communicating telepathically. There were no recriminations, no justifications, no excuses, just thoughts that we both absorbed without judgement. There was no hidden agenda or misplaced ideas on what we thought the other wanted to hear, just an exquisite sense of wellbeing and feeling that everything was alright. I simply had to trust her and she me.

I don't know how long we stayed in this state until finally Ajaarn Anurak's voice penetrated again.

"We are now coming out of this meditation. I will count from one to five and at the count of five you will open your eyes and feel refreshed and calm. One, two, three, four, five. Take a deep breath in and release. Open your eyes."

I turned to look at Nui, relieved to see the real Nui this time. We smiled, more relaxed than ever.

Ajaarn Anurak was waiting. "And?"

Maintaining eye contact, Nui and I responded simultaneously. "We need more time!"

Ignoring Ajaarn's gasp, we deliberately closed our eyes again. This time we didn't need any mantras or commands. The reversal was easy, with both of us knowing we had made the right decision: to finish what we had started.

GLOSSARY

Ajaarn - *Teacher*
Arai wah! - *What the ...? (swearing)*
Chai - *Yes*
Chai laew (khrup/kha) - *Yes*
Chai-mai kha? - *Right? Isn't that so? Isn't that true?*
Chai-mai ja? - *More casual/familiar than 'kha'*
Farang - *Foreigner*
Green mango with nam pla wan - *Sweet/sour sticky dipping sauce*
Ja - *Casual version of kha/khrup*
Ja bah ror - *Don't be ridiculous*
Jai yen - *Calm down*
Kha (female) Khrup (male) - *commonly added to a sentence to make the sentence more polite and formal*
Khob khun maak (kha/khrup) - *Thank you very much*
Khon Dii - *Sweetheart*
Khun + First name - *Form of address i.e. Khun Susan, Khun Mark, Khun Bo etc*
Khun Bpoo - *Grandpa (paternal grandfather)*
Khun Yaa - *Grandma (paternal grandmother)*

Khun Yaai - *Grandma (maternal grandmother)*

Klong - *Canal*

Koh - *Island in Thai*

Kuate arai khuen? - *What happened?*

Loy Krathong - *Festival in November to give thanks to the goddess of water*

Nong - *Form or address for a younger person*

Pi' - *Form of address for an older person*

Sabai di - *I'm well*

Sabai di mai (kha/khrup)? - *How are you?*

Saswadee dee mai - *Happy New Year*

Sawasdee khrup/kha - *Hello/goodbye*

Soi - *Side street*

Soi dog - *Feral street dogs*

Tuk-tuks - *Three-wheeled open-sided motor taxis*

Wai - *Hand gesture (hands together in prayer form in front of the body) as a greeting or show of respect*

Wat - *Temple*

Yohm - *A monk addressing a non-monk (i.e. Yohm Luna/Nui)*

TO MY READERS

Thank you so much for choosing to read Plyan. If you enjoyed it and want to keep up to date with my next release, please go to https://mariakuhnbooks.com. Your email address will never be shared and you can unsubscribe at any time.

I love hearing from readers. You can get in touch with me through my website and Goodreads page. Also, if you are up for it, I'd really appreciate it if you'd leave a review and hopefully recommend Plyan to other readers. Reviews and word-of-mouth recommendations go a long way in helping others to discover my books for the first time. Thank you so much for your support. I hope to see you next time!

Maria Kuhn

P.S. If you're interested in any of the places that are mentioned in Plyan please have a look at my website www.-mariakuhnbooks.com

STAY IN TOUCH

A City in Turmoil – A Chance Encounter – Lasting Consequences

FREE DOWNLOAD: SHORT STORY

Get your copy of *CHANNON* for free. Simply sign up here:

https://www.subscribepage.com/mariakuhnbooks

About once a year or so, I send an email telling readers when a new Krung Thep book is launched, or when I have something else that I think you will really want to know. To get these messages, just sign up for my Reader's Club. You'll also get an exclusive free CHANNON companion story to read.

ACKNOWLEDGMENTS

My very first impression of Bangkok was that of utter chaos. Hot, pungent, illegible signs and incomprehensible language, street stalls and people everywhere. Little did I know that ten years later I would actually move to the City of Angels and come to love it. I hope that in some small way I conveyed my affection for this city and country.

Much, of course, had to do with the people I met along the way. Mary and Peter who were partially responsible for my move and helped to make the first few months of transition easier. A special thank you to Liam and Dominik for inspiring the idea for Plyan. I am so proud of the fine young men you have become.

Meeting my 'Friday night gang' was a stroke of good fortune and they'll be my Thai family forever. Through them I experienced the Thai (and Indian) way of living that most visitors can only get a glimpse of. Thank you to the Bajaj's for 'adopting' me and to Zenya and Nayal for letting me graduate with them and for answering endless questions about the international school system.

Thank you also to my diverse group of beta readers for the early feedback and of course my amazing writing group led by Neil Arksey who challenged, prodded and encouraged me constantly. Specifically for the invaluable support, friendship and lifeline during the virus lockdowns. And thank you to Mrs and Mr O' for being there every step of the way.

Many people helped in so many ways with background information, but in particular I would like to thank Alex for sharing her knowledge about soi dogs, Nickie for correcting my admittedly poor Thai language skills and pointing out cultural idiosyncrasies, and Laura and Manuel for translating my vague ideas into a beautiful cover design.

Of course, I've changed huge chunks of the story over time, so any mistakes that have crept in are entirely of my own making.

ABOUT THE AUTHOR

Maria grew up in a tiny village in the German countryside. She now lives in London after thirty years of criss-crossing the world working in five-star hotels. Along the way she made wonderful friends, met quirky characters, tasted delicous cuisines, experienced diverse cultures, enjoyed bustling cities and awe-inspiring nature. All of these deserve to have their own stories told – eventually. Plyan is her debut novel.